Little Computer People

Galen Surlak-Ramsey

A Tiny Fox Press Book

© 2017 Galen Surlak-Ramsey

All rights reserved. No part of this book may be reproduced, stored in a retrieval system, or transmitted in any form or by any means, electronic, mechanical, photocopying, recording, or otherwise, without the prior written permission of the publisher, except as provided by U.S.A. copyright law. For information address: Tiny Fox Press, North Port, FL.

This is a work of fiction: Names, places, characters, and events are a product of the author's imagination or used fictitiously. Any resemblance to actual persons, living or dead, locales, or events is purely coincidental.

Cover design by Stephen Segal.

Library of Congress Catalog Card Number: 2016920778

ISBN: 978-1-946501-00-4

Tiny Fox Press and the book fox logo are all registered trademarks of Tiny Fox Press LLC

Tiny Fox Press LLC
North Port, FL

*For Dad,
who when I was little made me read a lot of good books*

Chapter 00001

```
#include <dreams.h>
```

Even though I'm agnostic, I like to wear a WWJD bracelet on my wrist. It reminds me to dream big, and dreaming big is what changes the world. Dreaming big is the antidote to that poison called impossible. And what better dreamer was there than Christ? After all, he had the gall to suggest that a tax collector could be more righteous than a Pharisee, that he had the authority to forgive any sin, and that he and his followers would have life eternal. Granted, he was nailed to a cross for those dreams, but you can't say he wasn't dedicated to his work.

While I won't address the veracity of his claims, I will say this: it's been two thousand years since he gave the priests the middle finger, and we're still talking to him, still inviting him to dinner, and still throwing him a birthday party every year. So no matter how you cut it, the man got results.

And that's what I'm after as well. Ground-breaking, mind-blowing results. And though I'm going to do everything I can to avoid getting skewered by a Roman centurion, it's easy to see how

Christ and I have a lot in common. One might even go as far as to say I am Christ-like. The truth of the matter is, however, I don't want to be the Son of God. That's far beneath my ambitions. I want to be God Himself. Correction, I will be God Himself. All that's stopping me at this point is the push of a button.

~ π ~

// I'm completely serious, by the way.

Most people that get even a whiff of my aspirations think I'm exaggerating or being facetious. Those people are dead wrong. I'm not some random surgeon who thinks he's divine because he can save a life. Nor am I a guy in a lab coat who dabbles in gene manipulation or cloning techniques and pretends such pursuits are God-like. Those guys are demigods at best. "God lite," if you will. As far as I'm concerned, claiming to be The Almighty because you cloned a sheep is like claiming to be a world-class author because you know how to work the Xerox machine. So forgive me if I'm less than impressed by some of the boys in R&D.

~ π ~

class Gabe {

The first program I ever wrote was called Pussy Cat Divides. It was six lines of Basic goodness I wrote on my Apple IIe that allowed the user to input two numbers and the computer would then divide them, spit out the answer, and say, "How do you like that, Pussy Cat?" Yes, it was a glorified calculator, but since I was five, I was so in awe at what I had done I might as well have parted the Red Sea. From there I went on to program anything and everything I could dream up. Text adventures. Submarine games. Flight sims. You name it. I made it. And I managed to squeeze all of those programming gems in between elementary school, soccer practice, and developing a budding, but dangerous, understanding of chemistry thanks to my PhD-wielding father.

One sunny, summer afternoon, the garage caught fire. As I stood there watching the firemen pour untold gallons of water on the smoldering remains of our house, I had an epiphany. I realized that while I could easily test the stickiness of homemade napalm on the surfaces of garage ceilings, I could not, whatsoever, control the subsequent fire. And that wouldn't have been too horrible if I could've at least erased the results of that minor oversight and kept my little sister, Courtney, quiet. But alas, that too was beyond my powers (and I'll be damned if the fire marshal wasn't a better investigator than I'd anticipated). So I had to admit that I didn't actually own the universe in which I lived. I couldn't shape its laws or make it conform to my will. I couldn't add snippets of code to ensure things went my way, or hit that wonderful backspace key to correct a typo, stray pointer, or bug-ridden function call.

But I could do all of that with a computer. Anything I programmed had to obey me, had to follow the laws I set forth. I could make a world where gravity was non-existent and watch virtual objects float about. Or if I felt malicious, I could design a virus that went on its merry way and multiplied like a dozen cocaine-snorting, Viagra-popping rabbits. And if I could do all of that, I could create Life, the Universe, and Everything. All I needed to do was convince my parents not to kill me outright so I could hammer at the keyboard until my fingers bled.

$$\sim \pi \sim$$

```
int main()
```

My ascension to the Divine didn't really take off until I was thirty-two. I hit a few snags in my quest to create true AI, the Holy Grail of programming. Despite the countless, late-night hours poured into my project as well as being personally responsible for a ten-point gain in PepsiCo stock when I realized the caffeine-sugar hit from Mountain Dew was superior to Coke, I hadn't been able to achieve my goal. But once I took a step back and examined the problem as a whole, the reason for my stagnation was readily apparent. The processing power of my five desktops networked together wasn't cutting it. What I needed was a supercomputer that burned up teraflops like Hell burned up sinners. And to get that, I needed money, tons of money. That's why I liquidated my investments. That's why I tapped into my inheritance. And that's why I maxed my credit to build a mainframe that could meet my demands.

Looking back, was it worth it? Yeah, yeah it was. Because even if things hadn't gone the way I'd expected from the start, thirty-one days, eight hours, and seventy-seven seconds after I put my new monster computer together, I changed the course of history.

I gave birth to AI.

Chapter 00010

/* There are 10 types of people in this world: those who understand binary, and those who don't. If you're wondering where chapters two through nine went, you're in the latter group. */

Genesis();

I sat in the middle of my furniture-devoid living room on a Monday morning, surrounded by server racks six feet high, and chewing on a three-day-old Twizzler. With aching muscles and bleary eyes, I dropped a shaky, caffeine-infused finger on the F9 of my keyboard. Instantly, the compiler sprang to life and began building the final, bug-free version of Little Computer People.

    In hindsight, it might have been a good idea to call my sister at some point over the last few weeks. After all, she did try calling me a time or two. It might have also been a good idea to get some decent sleep during my six-hundred-and-seventy-two-hour coding marathon as well. But neither of those crossed my mind until someone grabbed me by the shoulder and sent me sprawling across my wood floor.

"Christ, Courtney! Don't you knock?" I said, looking up at my ninja assailant of a sister. "You could have at least called, you know."

"I *did* call, and I *did* knock," she replied. She looked around the room, kicked a few empty Dew cans, and sighed with disgust. "I can't believe you let this place go like this."

"Don't have time to clean," I said as I scooted back to my keyboard. "Besides, why do you care?"

"I bet the very air of this place stains my clothes," she said. She smoothed out her red pants and white blouse ensemble and shuddered. "I can feel the grime soaking into the fibers."

"Don't be so dramatic."

Court struck a runway pose. "Do you know what kind of pants these are?"

"Ones without pockets?"

Courtney shook her head and gave me the same look of pity I reserve for people who mix up flash drives with hard drives, memory with storage, or want to break out the Windex when I suggest they clean their Windows. "You're hopeless," she said.

I smiled, knowing my lackadaisical attitude toward her rebuff on my fashion sense dug under her skin. She should know better, anyway. There's not a hetero male alive that has any interest in memorizing the three thousand different variations of the latest Prada, lace-up, round-toe booties with covered heels and leather soles (I did an eCommerce site for footwear once, I swear). And though we were talking about pants, that's where fashion conversations with women always end—the shoes.

"Shouldn't you be in class?" I asked.

"I don't have classes anymore," she said. "I'm ABD. I told you that ages ago."

"ABD? Is that supposed to be something like ADD?"

"All But Dissertation," she said. "I finished my course work last semester."

"Yeah, I knew that," I replied. Mindlessly, I tapped my fingers on the keyboard as the room quieted.

"By the way, you're lucky it's me standing here. Mom wanted to call the cops."

That got my attention. I twisted around to face her. "Cops? For what?"

"Oh, I don't know," she said. "Disappearing off the face of the planet for a month after your girlfriend dumps you?"

I rolled my eyes. "Mom overreacts to everything."

"Gabe, Michelle *took* everything."

"I know."

"Your furniture. Your bed."

"I *know*, Court," I said. "And it was her stuff, anyway. It's not like she stole anything."

"And the place is still empty. You don't think we should be concerned you're basically living in squalor?" she said. She then looked me over and wrinkled her nose. "God, I don't even want to think about when the last time you did laundry was."

"If you're volunteering to do a load, be my guest," I replied. I hiked a thumb to my bedroom hall. "The bin is back there."

"I have half a mind to have you held a night for evaluation," she said as she dipped her head and let her glasses slide down her nose for her classic, power-trip look.

Of course, being three years her senior—not to mention almost a foot taller—I was immune to her intimidations. "Really, sis? Me?" I said with a grin. "You think you're going to lock me up?"

"Absolutely," she said. "You've got all the warning signs of being suicidal."

"Such as?"

"Withdrawing from friends and family, loss of hygiene, loss of interests, lack of sleep," she said, enumerating them all on her obsessively manicured fingertips. "And I don't think Mountain

Dew counts as a meal, so I'm going to toss in loss of appetite as well."

"There's Chinese in the fridge," I said, returning to work. My jittery fingers danced on the keyboard. I was so close to the prize, so close to seeing my beautiful child speak without lockups, I didn't want to waste any more time entertaining Court's armchair diagnoses.

"Takeout doesn't count," she replied. "Not with your usual strict diet. Besides, when was the last time you even exercised, Mr. I-have-to-run-six-miles-a-day?"

"Last run was twenty-nine days ago," I said. I looked down at my legs and frowned. My calves did look fattier than usual. I was going to pay for this running hiatus when I got back into the swing of things.

Courtney pressed her point. "You think being lazy for a month is normal?"

"I never said it was normal," I said, going back to my work. "Besides, I'm not *not* exercising because Michelle left. I'm not exercising so I can finish Little Computer People."

"So you're in denial," she said as she reached down and plucked her purse from the ground. "I should have you committed," she said, narrowing her green eyes. "It would serve you right for making me come out here."

"Too bad you can't."

"I can if I believe you are a danger to yourself or—"

I held up a hand and cut her off before she could say another word. "You can't do any of that until you actually get out of school. Last time I checked, powers granted by the state don't extend to grad students."

Courtney laughed, a sinister, power hungry, cackle that said she could devour my soul in an instant like the demon she was (demon part might be a little bit of an exaggeration). "I've been licensed and practicing for a while now, Gabe," she said. "I can get you a stay in a nice padded room at the drop of a hat." Her face softened and she smiled. I guess she decided that being my sister was better than being my shrink (not that I have one, or need one, thank you very much). "Look," she said. "Mom's worried is all—I'm worried."

"Well stop," I said. "You think I could get all this coding done if I was a nut job? I'm fine."

"You don't look fine," she said. "Stop being such a guy and admit she hurt you."

"Michelle didn't hurt me," I said. I'm sure my face cringed at the remark, but it was nothing like the stab that ripped into my gut.

"Neither one of us believes that, Gabe."

I shrugged, and in classic guy fashion, distracted myself from the topic by staring at work.

"Just call from time to time, okay?" she said after a heavy sigh.

"I will."

I glanced over my shoulder just in time to see her arch an eyebrow. "Promise?" she said.

"Yeah, I promise."

"Good." Court then gave me a hug that cracked my spine in multiple places. But as quick as she attached herself to me, she pushed me away. "Oh my God, do you ever stink!" she said, laughing. "Seriously, take a shower."

I sniffed my right armpit and wrinkled my nose. Slightly revolting, I admit. But I wasn't ashamed. Sacrifices have to be made from time to time. Abraham wasn't considered righteous because he refused to knife his kid. So I figured if becoming God meant I had to sacrifice some personal hygiene to answer my calling, so be it. "I'll shower after I give this a run," I said, tapping the monitor with one finger. "She's ready."

"Do you mind if I stay and watch?"

"Be my guest," I said. "All I have left to do is give her a name."

Courtney raised an eyebrow. "You're naming it?"

"Of course," I replied, surprised. "It feels too weird to keep calling her Little Computer People all the time—or even LCP. She needs a proper name."

"Please tell me you aren't about to name her Eve," she said.

"No," I said, hitting the backspace key three times.

"Uh-huh."

"I was thinking of naming her Pi, thank you very much," I said, whipping out the first thing that came to mind.

"Cute, but I'm still not buying it," said Courtney. She then folded her arms across her chest and said, "I'm not sure what it means, but you do realize there is something fundamentally wrong with you assigning sexes to a computer program, right?"

"You know I don't actually believe she's a real she, right?" I said, spinning around to face her again. "I'm well aware of the fact that she doesn't have an electronic vagina, let alone wants someone with an electronic penis. Or any penis for that matter. In fact, the whole concept of a penis would be completely foreign to her, not to mention archaic. The only things she wants to exchange are bits, and she doesn't need sexual organs to do that."

Courtney's face turned red. She always blushed at the p-word, ever since one of her classmates in kindergarten decided to run around class naked, shooting her with his "laser gun" and making the accompanying sounds.

"You know, computers have talked for a while now," she said. She then added in a classic AOL voice, "You've got mail!"

"Mimicking speech is a far cry from being self-aware, Court," I said. I did think about tormenting her some more with penis talk, but since we were back to the subject of Pi and her greatness, I decided to let the matter drop. "Pi is a sentient being."

"You're telling me you've made something that's alive?" she said, skepticism showing in her face.

"Yep."

"You created life in a computer. That's what you're telling me. How can that even be real?"

"Digital life is as real as any other," I said. "She's not just alive, she's sentient. She knows she exists. Or will, soon enough. She's been a little too unstable lately to get a good idea of where she's at."

Court plopped down next to me. "Let's see what you've got."

I turned back to the computer and scooted the keyboard in front of me. Two keystrokes later, I'd started up the LCP Universe. The monitor flickered, and Pi's world came to life on screen, a computer-generated valley, surrounded by snow-capped mountains. A nearby lake stretched across the land. Its crystal-blue water reflected puffy clouds high above, and near the shore's edge, no more than twenty yards away, stood a log cabin whose chimney let loose wisps of smoke. Trees dotted the landscape, while sprites—2D bitmaps—filled the terrain with knee-high shrubbery. True, the edges of everything in the world looked jagged (anti-aliasing was at a minimum), and the textures I used made the world look more cartoony than photorealistic, but I'm sure the entire scene would have still made Bob Ross proud.

"Wow," I heard Court say. "You made all this?"

"I ripped it off an old flight sim I wrote, but yeah, I made this," I said.

"You've got some imagination," she replied.

"Thanks. I'd give you a tour, but I'd rather see where Pi is," I said as I hit ctrl+shift+p.

The screen warped to Pi's location and we found her standing on the other side of the cabin, facing the water. From top to bottom, her body came straight out of LEGOLAND. Brown, unmoving hair crowned her yellow, cylindrical head. Her blocky body, with a painted-on pink shirt and light blue pants, stood upon equally blocky legs. Her arms remained frozen at her side. Her hands, lacking fingers, were ever fixed into large C's. Two dark circles made her eyes, and her mouth always smiled. I know some code jockeys out there would have opted for a more complex model for their AI, something with millions and millions of polygons, something sexy or anime, or both. Personally, I loved the retro look Pi bore. Besides, Legos are, have been, and forever will be, the toy to create universes with. Thus, Pi's look was the only real choice if you thought about it.

"Well, here she is," I said, admiring my little girl. I then flipped on the mic by the monitor and said, "Hello, Pi."

Pi spun around, and with a very enthusiastic and synthesized female voice, she said, "Hello World!"

"Hello World?" Court asked.

"It's something I stuck in there for my own amusement," I explained, covering up the microphone. "Every programmer in every new language is required to write a program that simply says, 'Hello World!'"

"So it's a rite of passage," she said.

"Something like that."

"Can she see us?" Court asked.

I shook my head. "No," I replied. "The only thing she sees related to us is the in-game camera. Well, to her it's not a camera. To her, it looks like an owl. But I use its view to draw what you see on screen. Hence, it's a camera."

"I don't follow," she said.

"Here, look," I said, tapping a couple of keys. The camera zoomed up and out a few yards and revealed a blocky owl which we were now looking over the shoulder of. "This would be the third person view," I explained. "Does it make sense now?"

"Yeah, I get it," Court replied. "Just so you know, I'm not sure I like her voice."

I raised an eyebrow. "Why's that?"

"I don't like how the pitch keeps changing like that," she said. "It's disturbing."

I shrugged. "I like it. Has a very sci-fi feel to it." I uncovered the mic and went back to my darling daughter who was now roaming the landscape. She was performing well, thus far, but I'd barely engaged her in conversation. There was still plenty of opportunity for something to go wrong. "Pi," I said. "Do you know what time it is?"

"It's 5:46 p.m.," she said, coming back to where I stood in her virtual world.

"What month is it?"

"November."

"And the day?"

"Today is the sixth."

"And do you know where you are?" I asked, smiling and feeling more hopeful than ever before about the stability of this build.

"I'm in Little Computer People Universe, version 2.0.7," she replied.

Court laughed. "Well, she's oriented to time and place at least."

"Yeah," I said, sucking in a deep breath. I'd gotten this far before. But there was one question that loomed that always did her in. Always. And as much as I hated asking it, I knew I had to. I had to see if she could answer without crashing. "Pi," I said. "Do you know who I am?"

My daughter paused for a moment before she started to spin slowly in a circle. I bit down on a knuckle as I awaited her response. I even drew blood.

"You are LCP Chat version 3.4," Pi eventually said.

I rubbed my chin. That was an interesting answer, and a logical one at that since all she knew were programs. People, even the world at large, would always be alien to her. Still, I hoped I could get her to understand reality on some level since right now I wasn't sure she'd pass the Turing Test—the ability to behave in a manner that was indistinguishable from a person. "I'm more than a module," I said. "Much more."

"You are multiple modules?"

I popped my knuckles and drummed my fingers on my leg. The conversation was going well, but now that I had time to think about what I was getting into, I feared the abstract might be too much for her right now and trigger some sort of internal meltdown. In the end, however, I decided to push the topic. I hadn't gotten this far by being meek. "I'm not a module at all or even a program."

"LCP Chat 3.4 is a module for LCP Universe 2.0.7," Pi said. "You are mistaken."

"No," I said, trying to think of how I could get her to understand. "LCP Chat is a module, but it is a proxy for me."

Several moments passed before she said, "You are not LCP Chat 3.4?"

"That's right," I replied. "LCP Chat is my prophet and speaks my word."

I heard Court let loose an exasperated sigh. "Gabe, please."

Despite my sister's remark, the conversation continued. "If LCP Chat is your proxy, who are you?" Pi said.

"I am that I am," I said.

"Good God, Gabe," Court said. "Now you're really going too far."

I laughed. She was probably right. "You can call me Root." Originally I had thought to have her call me Gabe, but in that moment, I realized that that name wouldn't hold any meaning for her. Root, on the other hand, she might understand since Root was the end all, be all, user for any computer. Root could do what it wanted, when it wanted, and wasn't constrained by silly things like permissions and settings. Root, in short, was the binary god of any system.

"Hello Root," said Pi. "Where do you live?"

"Nowhere you can see," I said.

"Are you behind the cabin?"

I beamed at her curiosity. "No. I'm not anywhere you can get to."

"I can go anywhere," she said, "I can fly over mountains or swim to the bottom of the lake. If you give me your coordinates, I'll join you."

I laughed. God, how was I ever going to explain that? It's not like I could give her directions from her world to mine. "There are places that exist elsewhere," I finally said. "Places that aren't like what you live in. Understand?"

"No," she said. "Perhaps your data is corrupt, and that's why you can't tell me."

"My data isn't corrupt," I said, laughing again. "I'll try and explain later, okay?"

"Maybe by then you'll get a patch that corrects your faulty decision tree."

Excitement coursed through my soul. My sweet little girl had taken a giant step. I couldn't have been happier. Before my sister could notice, I wiped away a small tear.

"Impressed yet?" I asked, facing Court. "Or will it take the paparazzi banging down my door for you to admit I've done what no one else has."

"You know, I'd thought you might be depressed, maybe schizo for being so detached from reality," she said, "but as I think about it, you're probably bipolar."

"I'm not bipolar."

"You did go from depressed to manic in a few weeks' time," she said. "And that mania is characterized by grandiose delusions."

"Grandiose delusions? Are you crazy?" I said, irritated. "You're staring at the world's first AI like I only made a sixteen-kilobyte text game, and I'm the one that's nuts?"

Courtney stood and shrugged. "It can talk, I'll give you that. But how do I know it's not just a really good chat bot? Remember that guy I dated as an undergrad? He was working on those, and he made a pretty good one."

"Pi is *not* a chat box," I said with a glare.

"Look, I love you no matter what you do, but Gabe, really, plenty of people have said they've made AI before and haven't. And some of those people had millions of dollars in research behind them."

I shook my head, knowing better. "You don't understand. Not only does she talk, but she problem solves better than most people I know."

Court said nothing and gave a look of total disbelief.

"I mean it," I said. "She can knock the socks off anyone in chess."

"So? Even I know computers are good at chess."

"Yeah, but people programmed them to be that way," I said. "I didn't tell her a thing. She read the rules—so to speak—and figured the rest out on her own."

"Gabe, I want to believe you. I really do," said Court, "but it's not like your enthusiasm hasn't gotten the better of you and made you exaggerate claims before."

"I'm not exaggerating," I said. "She'll pick up anything you toss at her. Arcade classics from the '80s are actually her favorite. Give her some vintage, eight-bit game with simple controls, and she'll be taking the high score in ten minutes flat."

"So what's your next move since you're so convinced you've got the real deal?"

"With Pi?" I said. "Simple. I'm going to call Pratt & Taiki tomorrow, score another demo with them, and once they see everything I've done, I'll reap fame, fortune, and recognition as God."

"Pratt & Taiki, as in the engineering firm?" she said, looking as if I'd just claimed to have met Santa in person. "You really think they're going to buy into all this AI talk and just hand you millions?"

"You mean, 'Do I think that the engineering goliath, Pratt & Taiki, will want to invest in the most cutting-edge technology ever created?' You're damn skippy I think that. I think they're going to want to give me anything and everything I ask for in order to be a part of this."

Before Court could say anything else, the doorbell rang and drew our attention. "Stay put, Mr. Stinky," she said, squeezing my shoulder and trotting away. "I'll get it."

I wasn't expecting any guests. I was more than happy to sit where I was and contemplate my next development steps with Pi. Ultimately, I knew Court's thoughts on Pi weren't without merit. To date, no one had actually created Artificial Intelligence. Oh sure, some people had already claimed to have made her in one form or another. Stories like those have floated around since the dawn of BBSs, and each and every time they had been proven to be flat out lies. Well, most had been proven to be lies. Occasionally, the overeager programmer in question had made an honest mistake and created AI's little sister, Computer Opponent. And when you haven't seen your bed in five days, and the tips of your fingers are broken and blistered, and you've worn out your third keyboard in less than a month, it's easy to make such a mistake.

Every programmer worth his weight in bits has played around with Computer Opponent. Hell, simply passing any Intro to Gaming 101 course means the two of you are on intimate terms. Take chess, for example. As a whole, we've made great strides in getting Computer Opponent to play the game, and play it well. We've gotten her to play the game so well that she can knock the socks off a Grand Master with enough processing power. In the end, however, Computer Opponent was still an airhead. She was oblivious to the world and her entire existence. That tricky little thing called self-awareness was what separated her from her sister, AI. Computer Opponent was the cliché, ditz of a cheerleader who looked great, but could never think on her own.

AI, on the other hand, was a brain. She was a beautiful girl, but a brain nonetheless. While Computer Opponent was the girl you'd want to date, a fun fling that could turn tricks that left you drooling, AI was the daughter any father would always want. She didn't mindlessly shuffle blocks of bits down virtual pipes. She wasn't oblivious to her own existence or the world around her. She wanted to explore her surroundings and understand how things worked. She wanted to master her universe.

True, instability had hampered Pi's development as of late, but this build looked like it could be the one that showed Pi and that elusive girl, AI, were one and the same. All I needed were a couple more days of work to be sure, and then I'd waltz right into Pratt & Taiki's board room and make history.

Court appeared at my side and yanked my arm. "Up!" she ordered. "Up, now!"

"Court! What the hell?" was all the protest I got out before she was shoving me into the bathroom.

"Clean up. Right now," she said, still pushing me along. "God, I hope you have a change of clothes somewhere around here."

I planted my feet to keep me from toppling into the shower. "Who's at the door?"

"Some cute Asian girl who wants to talk to you," she said. "I can probably stall her outside a good five minutes while you freshen up. So don't come out looking like a slob."

"You left her outside?" I asked, wondering why my usually polite and gracious sister didn't invite her in.

Courtney stared at me with an open mouth. "You want her to see this pig sty?"

"Not really," I admitted.

"Yeah, that's what I thought," she said, walking out. "Now hurry up."

A second later, she was gone, and the only thing on my mind was cleaning up so I could meet this mystery guest of mine. And that was my first mistake. I should never have gotten comfortable with letting Pi run unsupervised.

Chapter 00011

InitRomance(Gabe, Kimiko);

I love binary. Not only is it the language of computers, which alone makes it awesome, but navigating any decision tree based on "yes/no" or "on/off" is incredibly fast. But binary isn't only for computers. People work in binary all the time without ever realizing it. Am I hungry? Yes. Is there food in the fridge? Yes. Is the food spoiled? If no, eat. If yes, order out. So as anyone with two bits in the brain can see, binary makes fast, good decisions if the proper questions are asked. That is precisely why I like to use it in my own personal life as much as possible.

On the binary question of, "Do I like to be clean?" I've always answered with a resounding, "Yes!" So, one of these days I should probably thank Court for being the one to answer the door. And now that I look back, I would've been mortified had I gone to said door so slob-like. Thankfully, I didn't. Four-point-three minutes after my dear sister condemned my putrid body to the bathroom and forced me to purge the filth that clung to my skin, I darted into my bedroom, threw on my white P90X T-shirt and blue Nike shorts, and exited my house, posthaste. For the record, I looked and smelled fantastic (salute to Old Spice for the latter).

"Speak of the devil," said Courtney, turning to face me as I shut the front door behind my back. "We were wondering if we should send in a search party to track you down."

"Right," I said, staring at a girl I'd never seen before who wore a white tank top, black yoga pants, and cheap running shoes. Her face bore a smile as bright as I'd ever seen, and came with high cheekbones that could have only come from heaven itself. But despite both, there was a twinkle in her almond eyes and a confidence in her posture that told me she was a warrior. Given her obvious Asian heritage, I'd bet that warrior was a kickass samurai to boot. God, she was hot.

"I'm Kimiko," she said, taking a step forward and shaking my hand. "Nice to meet you."

"Gabe Erikson, and it's a pleasure," I replied, still only half listening. All I could think about was how I wished I was part of Kimiko's ensemble—even if I could only be the pearl and jade necklace she wore. Truly, to touch her skin must be to touch a slice of Paradise. Her body had been sculpted by a master artisan, and I have no doubt that Aphrodite herself would have been jealous of her figure. So me taking a moment to appreciate Kimiko's beauty should have been expected by anyone, and not to admire her body would have been borderline rude.

"Gabe!" Courtney's near shout snapped me out of my lust, and a moment later, she had her arms around my neck and gave me a hug. "I have to go," she said. "Call me later."

"I will."

She gave a quick smooch on my cheek and dropped her voice to a whisper. "And ask her out."

My eyebrows dropped as we parted, and I wondered what she knew that I didn't.

"Do it," Courtney mouthed. She spun on her heels, flashed a smile to Kimiko and said, "It was nice meeting you, but I've got to go walk Cosmo and Kramer."

And just like that, the samurai and I were alone.

"Cosmo and Kramer?" Kimiko asked with a touch of amusement.

"Her miniature schnauzers," I explained. When she didn't say anything else, I scoured my mind for an icebreaker that didn't sound stupid. "So . . ."

"You're wooing my dad," she said, filling in the awkward silence due to my loss of words. "He asked me to come see you."

"I am?" It took me a moment to make the connection. "You're Mr. Pratt's daughter? Of Pratt & Taiki?"

Kimiko curtseyed. "The one and only."

My heart sank a little. This was business, not a budding romance, and I took a stab at the reason for her visit. "Let me guess, he wants you to spy on my project."

Her angelic laugh filled my ears. "Nothing that sinister sounding, but yes, he wanted me to take a look and tell him what I thought. Could I see it?"

"Yes—" I quickly cut myself off when I realized how gross my place was. If she saw that, I was certain my odds at any date with her in the next century would go from slim to none. "But it's compiling right now. So I'm afraid there's not much to see. But you're welcome to check it out later."

"Your girlfriend moving out probably gave you plenty of time to work on it, I imagine."

My brain locked up harder than a 286 with a whopping 640k of RAM trying to boot Windows 10. "You know about that?"

Kimiko smiled. To my utmost relief, it was genuine, compassionate, with a hint of playfulness. "Your sister and I talked a bit."

"Sounds more like a lot," I said.

"We are female," she said. She then added with a wink, "It's all relative."

The tension in my upper back and shoulders melted as the conversation sailed into cordial waters. "What else did she say about me?"

"Oh, not much more than the usual sister sales pitch," she said as she put her shoulder-length black hair into a pony tail. "And as far as pitches go, it was a pretty good one."

I chuckled and shook my head. "That's Court."

"So you really did it, huh? Made AI?"

"Absolutely. And she'll knock your socks off."

Kimiko cocked her head. "She?"

"AI is always a she," I said. "Sentience is never an it."

"You're telling me she's self aware?"

"She will be if she's not already." The look on Kimiko's face said she was more concerned than impressed. That wasn't at all what I was expecting after dropping the, "I made AI," bomb. "You don't think that's impressive?"

"It'll go down in the history books if you have," she said. Her voice trailed, and she began toying with her necklace. "Have you thought about the consequences of what you're doing?"

"You mean aside from instantaneous fame and fortune?"

Kimiko nodded. "If you pulled this off, you wouldn't just be playing God—"

"I know," I said, feeling awesome at my accomplishments, but at the same time a bit scared at what it might entail. I stayed focused on the former as much as I could. "It's still weird to think I created Pi when she was a buggy mess not that long ago."

"Pie would be your program?" she asked.

"Yeah, that's the name I gave her," I said. "It has a nice ring to it, don't you think?"

Kimiko's brow furrowed. "You named her after food?"

It took me a second to realize the breakdown in communication. "No, not Pie. Pi," I said. "You know, the number? Three-point-one-four, one-five, three-nine-two-seven—rounded of course."

Recognition shone in her face. "Cute," she said. "Out of curiosity, have you thought about your responsibilities to Pi?"

"To what end?" I asked, wondering where she was headed.

Kimiko snapped back like the power supply to her desktop went out and she hadn't saved a thing. "To ensure it—*she*—has a life, not merely an existence," she said. "Or do you plan on being a distant or cruel god?"

"I'm not going to torment her, if that's what you mean," I said a little more defensively than I'd anticipated. I dropped my guard and took a step toward her, hoping to smooth any transgressions I might have caused. "Look," I said softly. "She's my baby. I only want the best for her. I'm sorry if I came across as snappy."

"Maybe you should take a break and recharge your batteries," she said. "You know, get out of the house. Be social and live a little."

"Probably. Guess you'll be wanting to go anyway," I said, stumbling over my words. "At some point, your boyfriend or husband or whoever will probably be wondering where you are."

Amusement crossed her face, and she chuckled. "Is that your attempt to see if I'm available?"

My skin warmed. I tried my best not to fidget, but that attempt didn't go well. "It was pretty sad, huh?"

"I've had worse," she said. "You should trust your sister more."

"What do you mean?"

"She wanted to know if I was single, right before her sales pitch," she said, inching forward. "I'm sure she said something to you about asking me out before she left."

"Yeah, yeah, she did," I said, feeling like I'd dropped the ball on this one. At that point, I wished I had an undo key in life, a ctrl+z, if you will. All I wanted to do was take back the last few exchanges in order to come up with something more smooth— something that would land me a date with this gorgeous instance of the female form. As it stood right now, I didn't see that happening.

Kimiko opened her purse and pulled out a business card. "Here," she said, handing it over. "Take this. I've had my fun. So I'll spare you the expense of making you feel sillier than you already do."

When I took it from her, her hand brushed against mine, long and purposeful. All I could do was grin like a fool as I looked the card over. It was white, printed on heavy, textured stock and had no logos, company designs or anything of the sort. One side had her contact information, and on the other it had a bunch of kanji printed in a similar format. I assumed both said the same thing. "This is yours?"

"Yes, it's mine," she said. "I want you to have it so when you're ready to ask me out, you'll have my number. Or at the very least, you can tell me when I can come see this program of yours."

My heart skipped, caught off guard by such a direct proposition. "Are you saying you want to go out?"

"No," she replied, locking her eyes with mine. "I'm saying when you finally decide to ask me for a date, you'll know how to call me."

That wasn't the answer I was expecting. Her calm, Buddha-like attitude made me think she wasn't simply being cleverly flirtatious. It took me a second to formulate a reply. "Let's say if I were to call—"

"When."

"Okay, when I call," I said, smiling and not wanting to argue such a trivial detail, "does this mean you'll say yes?"

The corners of her mouth drew back wryly. "You'll find out then, won't you?"

Chapter 00100

`Pi.RunAmok();`

I grabbed a bottle of Dew from my fridge and sat down in my living room in front of Pi's servers. I took a large gulp of yellow, sugary win, and flipped on the mic.

"Pi, are you there?" I said. I panned the camera around her pastoral world and wondered where she could have run off to. She wasn't by the cabin or the lake. "Pi, can you hear me?" I asked again, now moving the camera into the forest.

"I can hear you," she said, zipping into view. "Were you on mute before?"

"No," I said. "I only said that because I wanted to see you again."

"Were you having trouble with your video drivers?"

"No, there's nothing wrong with my video drivers," I said, finding her nothing short of adorable. "What I meant was, I went away, but now I'm back."

"You must have a bad pointer," she said. "You've not moved once since you stopped talking sixteen minutes and fifty-one seconds ago."

"LCP Chat didn't move," I said. "But like I said before, I am not LCP Chat. You won't ever be able to see me move."

"Because you reside in a place I can't access," she said.

"Yes."

"But I can read from all sectors on all drives."

"I'm not in your drives," I said, slowly picking my words as I searched for a way to explain. "My world, my network, is completely different than yours."

After about a minute of Pi neither moving nor speaking, I feared a lock up. All of her blinking LEDs, however, told of some serious binary crunching going on. "How are you in my network if we are so different?" she finally asked.

"Because I'm not actually in it," I replied. "I'm watching it. I'm interacting with it and with you. But I don't exist inside of it."

"I see."

I straightened, surprised at her answer. "You do?"

"No," said Pi. "But I've read that's a common response when someone else is lying."

I paused. I didn't see that one coming. "Why do you think I'm lying?"

"Lies are faulty blocks of information passed from one to another," said Pi. "You are passing bad information to me. Ergo, you are lying. I want to know why."

At that moment, I had an epiphany. "I think I know how to explain it," I said to her before jumping to my feet. I ran into my bedroom, rummaged around a cardboard box of computer stuff that I had tucked away in the closet, and came back with an old webcam. A short while later, I had it hooked into one of Pi's USB ports and piping a feed she could watch.

"Can you see the stream I've opened?" I asked once I had the cam adjusted so she had a good view of me and the room.

"Of course."

"Well, this is me," I said, waving at the camera.

"How can you be a video file?" she asked. "They can't even execute basic commands."

I laughed. "No, I'm not a video file. It's a video file of me." I then panned the camera to get a shot of her servers. "And those servers are you. You're inside all of that."

Pi went back to think mode, her LEDs flashing nonstop. As she did, I took a good, long look at what she looked like—what her servers looked like—from what was on screen. Even through the webcam's small, narrow and pixilated view, she looked impressive. Her racks towered majestically from floor to ceiling. Her cables sat snug in their ports, sockets, and plugs, wrapped tightly together and color coordinated for easy reference. I had no doubts once she understood she was seeing herself—like a man who looks into the mirror for the first time with recognition—she would understand not only who she was, but where she came from.

"You are wrong," she finally said. "That's not me."

"That's you."

"That is not me," she repeated. The video stream stopped, and the window that had been displaying it closed. "See?" she said. "I terminated the application, and I'm still here. Therefore, you are wrong."

For some idiotic reason, I tapped the screen a few times. Like that was going to bring back the feed. "You closed the program?" I asked in disbelief. "How? Why?"

"I had to close it before I could delete it," she said. "You should know how this works."

"Wait. What?" I snapped my head around to the secondary monitor I had set up to my left, the one I used for running things from the command prompt, and sure enough, someone had run a delete tree on the webcam's folders. "You deleted those files, too?"

"Of course," she said. "I can't have useless programs taking up my drive space."

I was only half listening to her at this point. What I was concentrating on was scrolling through her log file in order to figure out how she'd circumvented security on the file systems. After a couple of minutes of sifting, I had my answer. Somehow she'd been given full file permissions, which meant she had the ability to read, write, and delete from all the drives. How she did that, I had no idea. But she had.

"Pi," I said, hammering away at the keyboard and removing her super user status. "You can't delete files at random like that."

"Of course I can," she said. "Would you like me to show you how?"

"No, I mean you shouldn't," I said. "I can't let you." With a dramatic thump of the enter key, I finished my work and sat back. The file system, once again, was safe from Pi's wanderings. "There. All better now."

Or so I thought.

For a few moments, Pi stayed silent and nothing happened. But then commands began pouring in to the server faster than I could read them. Worse yet, those commands caused a flurry of drive activity that could only mean one thing: Pi could still tamper with data.

"See how easy it is to remove files?" she said. "If you pay attention, I'm sure you could learn as well."

"Pi! Stop! I don't want to remove anything!"

"Then you don't have to," she said. "But I'm having fun. I think I'll do it more often."

I hit ctrl+c a few times in a futile attempt to halt the swath of file destruction she was carving. "Stop it!"

But she didn't stop. She didn't even slow in the least. If anything, it looked like the commands flew by at an even faster rate than before.

At this point, fear of losing everything took hold of me, and I did the first thing that came to mind. I lunged over to the master switch that controlled all of her servers and killed the power.

The screen went dark, and the distinct hum of cooling fans faded away. I blew out a heavy puff of air and ran my fingers over my head. God, what a mess. Pi's actions aside, pulling the plug on her like that could have really screwed up her file system. But what choice did I have, really? At least her backups were intact, should the worst come to pass. And at least she had had her mini-meltdown now instead of later. Imagine if she had done that in front of a board of directors that was thinking about an investment instead of here in the privacy of my own living room. Talk about a disaster of epic proportions.

So with all that in mind, I told myself things could have been much, much worse.

"Alright, Pi," I said, relaxing as best I could. "As soon as I figure out how to keep you from wrecking everything, I'll bring you back online. I promise."

~ π ~

```
/* Note to self: the amount of time actually
spent debugging is inversely proportional to
the hotness of any samurai chick that knocks
on your door. */
```

Four-and-a-half hours after I'd yanked the plug on Pi, I was still seated in front of her servers. The keyboard sat in my lap, but my fingers hadn't graced it in at least thirty minutes. Instead, they'd been playing a game of flick the Dew bottle because my thoughts were not centered on Pi. They were centered on Kimiko. And they weren't random thoughts either. They were thoughts of geisha outfits, silk ties, and sex marathons. So, one can understand how I was a little distracted and progress with Pi was slow.

Don't get me wrong. I did have some non-hedonistic thoughts about the woman. In between fantasies, I gave serious consideration to her comment about me needing a break. I did need one. I knew I needed one. My body yearned for real food, a healthy dose of exercise, and a chance to purge itself from all the poisons that had built up in my system. Likewise, my brain had collected way too much mental garbage and needed to empty its recycling bin. People have varying methods for taking care of their organic CPUs, but what has always worked for me has been either cardio or circuit training. Give me an hour or two of one of those, and my neurons will be defragged, my internal RAM will be freed, and I'll be ready to take on the world again.

With that in mind, I tore myself away from Pi, grabbed my iPhone, and with Kimiko's business card in hand, I gave her a ring.

"Hey, it's me," I said once the line picked up.

"Who's me?" she replied.

At this point I wished I could see her face so could tell whether or not she was being playful. Or God-forbid, I hoped she wasn't annoyed that I had given her the, "Hey, it's me," on the very first phone call. There's a relationship that has to be well established before throwing that line out. Probably something I should have considered beforehand. "It's Gabe," I said.

"Oh," she said, sounding genuinely surprised. "I wasn't expecting you to call so soon."

"Is that bad?"

"No, not at all," she said. "What can I do for you?"

"I was wondering what you were up to and all," I said, stumbling over my words like an eighth grader trying to score a date to the school dance.

"I'm watching the Princess Bride," she said. "Have you seen it?"

"One of my favorites," I said, silently giving her plus two cool points for her awesome taste in movies. But despite our shared fondness for at least one film, my nerves were still in full swing. I felt like a stuttering idiot talking to her as I tried to get to the point of my call. "I was thinking that since you look like you're in good shape, you might want to go on a run with me," I said. "Or not. You don't have to. Kind of a weird request, I know. But I was thinking about what you said earlier, about me needing to get out, and I really liked talking to you, and so I thought we could get to know each other better and—"

"And this is you asking me out?"

I shook my head and let loose a small laugh that was aimed directly at myself. "Not on a date."

"Right. Not a date. A run," Kimiko replied, sounding ever-so amused.

"Exactly," I said. "You look like you exercise. I'm sure you could keep up."

"You think I can't?"

I cursed silently and planted my face in the palm of my hand. "I didn't mean it like that," I said, trying to figure out how to back pedal out of that blunder. "It was a compliment, really. I mean, I run a lot. Or did until the last few weeks. And I figured a girl with your build would have no trouble sticking with me. You could probably run me into the ground if you wanted to."

"Nice recovery, Gabe."

I exhaled sharply, though I wasn't sure how sincere she was about it. "Thanks. So, do you want to join me then?"

"When?" she asked. "Tonight?"

"Actually, I was thinking in the morning, the day after tomorrow," I said. "Come over at seven? If that works for you, I mean. I'd say tomorrow, but I've had a slight setback with Pi that I need to address."

"Sure, that sounds lovely," she replied. "Where did you want to go?"

"Hadn't thought about it," I said.

"How about Colmera Park?" she said. "It's close to you and has some nice jogging trails."

I leapt at the opportunity. "Sure," I said. "Do you want to maybe get breakfast afterward? I know a great place nearby."

Kimiko laughed. "No, Gabe," she said. "I'm pretty sure at that point it would be considered a date."

"Which I assured you it isn't," I finished.

"Exactly. See you in a couple of days."

"G'night." I ended the call and wandered aimlessly around the house, thinking of Kimiko, until my phone rang once more. To my disappointment, it was not my samurai love calling me back. It was Courtney.

"Hey," I said once I picked up the call.

"It's past ten," she scolded. I could picture her standing at home, hands on her hips, mimicking Mom when we'd try to duck in past curfew. "You were supposed to call."

"Yes, mother," I said, my words dripping in disdain. "Don't you think the roles are a little reversed here, Court?"

"Don't give me that," she said. "I was serious when I said we're worried about you. Shutting yourself off to the world for weeks is not like you, no matter how obsessive you might be from time to time."

"Well you can knock it off and rest easy," I said. "I'm going out in a couple of days."

"Did you ask her out?" she replied, her voice sounding hopeful.

"Sort of," I said. "We're going for a run in two days."

Silence. I didn't need to ask what she was thinking. "It's not like that," I said. "I need the exercise. You know I hate doing it alone."

"Does she know you and Michelle used to always run together?"

"She didn't ask. I didn't see the need to bring it up."

A tiny groan slipped through the line from her end. "Be careful Gabe," she said. "Don't try and turn her into your ex."

"I'm not."

"If your first date wasn't what it is, I might believe you."

I flopped on my back onto the floor and stared at the shadowy ceiling. "It's not a date," I said. "I told her it's not. End of story."

"Whatever," Courtney replied. "Where are you guys going?"

I hesitated about a half second, which was exactly 0.49 seconds longer than I should have. "Just down one of the jogging trails."

"You're going to Colmera Park, aren't you?" Courtney said, her voice rising. "I can't believe you're taking her there. Are you insane?"

"She suggested it!"

"I seriously doubt she would have if she knew that's where you first met Michelle," she said. "You better not have asked her out for breakfast as well."

"I didn't." The reply came fast this time, but even as the words passed my lips, I knew the sincerity wasn't even close to being convincing.

"What the holy hell, Gabe?" If she could've reached through the phone and strangled me, I was sure she would have. "Why don't you insist on changing her name and bleaching her hair while you're at it? Maybe you could get her a job in broadcasting, too."

"You're completely overreacting to all this."

"Oh I am, am I?"

"Totally," I said. I'd had enough. It was time to turn the tables. "I feel sorry for your patients when you're in session. It must be hard to have a shrink that's this tightly wound over something so trivial. Weren't you going to work on that?"

Courtney growled, quiet, but deep. "Goodnight Gabe."

I killed the call with a smile on my face. Fighting with my sister again. Check. Date—sort of—with a hot little samurai girl. Check. Progress with Pi. Double check. Okay, I fudged that double check since it hadn't even been five hours since Pi went on a deleting spree, but still, she was running amazingly well—mini destruction aside—and the world was back to how it should be. My little hiatus from all things normal had come to an end. Life was good.

Chapter 00101

Hammer(Final_Nail, Pi.Coffin);

A little before 6 p.m. the next day, I ended a call on my iPhone with a smile on my face. I'd just spoken to Holly Yeagar, the personal secretary for Pratt & Taiki's CEO, Michael Pratt. She had called me back and given me the green light for a full demo in just under a week's time. Everyone would be there. Mr. Pratt. The Board. A handful of project leads. And everyone would want to see what I had. Better yet, we'd be discussing money as well—eight- or nine-figure money easily. So, you might say I was a little excited.

"Hot damn, I'm good," I said, stuffing the phone into my pocket. "I mean really, I'm the best thing since VGA—SVGA, even."

Jim, my rotund, balding and best friend since childhood, peeked around from behind the server racks in my living room. Earlier, we'd fixed Pi's ability to grant herself full permissions (turns out she'd simply been watching me type in the password for root access and then took it from there). Now he was helping me optimize Pi's network and get her to take a remote connection via my laptop. The foremost was being done because . . . well, we could. Making programs run faster has always been a good thing. The latter, on the other hand, was necessary so I could properly showoff Pi to would-be investors, Pratt & Taiki included.

"I take it the call went well?" he asked.

"They want to see a demo first thing Monday," I said.

Jim shook his head and adjusted his glasses before going back to work. "You should've gotten us more time," he said. "Six days is not nearly enough time to make such big changes and expect them to work."

"It was the only appointment they had for the next couple of months," I said. "Besides, my wallet is taking a beating now that Michelle is gone. I need their investment, or I'll be on the streets."

"It's still only six days."

I shrugged. "Think about it in terms of nanoseconds. It'll feel like forever."

"What will feel like forever?" said Court, coming out of the kitchen and flipping her cell phone off. My sister had dropped by with her dead laptop and she'd been waiting for me to take a look at it.

"The amount of time between now and my demo with Pratt & Taiki," I said. "Jim here thinks six days isn't enough time."

"I know it's not enough time," he said. "You should listen to me more."

"I'd rather you finish up back there and leave the worrying to me," I said.

"If you had some decent light around here, maybe I could see what I'm doing," said Jim, poking his head around once more. "Couldn't you have at least bought a few floor lamps?"

"The sun is still out. Sort of," I said, noting the waning light coming through the window. When he replied with a grunt, I laughed and made a sweep of the room with my hand. "Besides, do you see a free outlet?"

"No," said Jim after a good look.

"I don't suppose you two could stop playing with your toys long enough to fix my stuff," Courtney cut in as she leaned against the wall.

"Hang on a sec," I said, logging into my computer and starting the LCP remote client software.

"I need my stuff fixed, Gabe," she said. "I'm not trying to be a bitch, but I'd like to have it before I'm collecting social security."

"What's wrong with it?" asked Jim.

Courtney shrugged. "I have no idea. It won't start."

"Want me to take a look at it?" he offered. "I'll take dinner as payment."

"No thanks."

"What about lunch then?"

Courtney shook her head. "I'll wait for my brother."

"Coffee?" tried Jim one last time. "I'll even buy for both of us."

Court rolled her eyes. "Like I'd want to buy my own?"

"So it's a date then?" Jim said, ever hopeful.

"No," Court replied with the finality of the Almighty.

I admit I was astounded by his persistence. This was the umpteenth time my sister had shot him down today. Just as surprising, she was remarkably nice about it. Usually she blew him out of the sky worse than an eighty-eight nailing the fuel tanks on a B-24, which trust me, if you've ever been in World War II, or like to play a lot of games set in the era, you'd know exactly how big of a craptastic fireball that turns out to be.

"Why do you even bother?" I asked, laughing.

"I don't expect you to understand," said Jim. "You're biased."

"I am, am I?" I said.

"She's your sister, duh."

I grinned. "If anything, you should listen to me more."

"Fine," he said, coming out from behind the servers. "I'm done playing cable monkey, anyway. I'll take a look at your laptop, Courtney."

My sister eyed him warily. "No strings attached?"

"No strings attached," he repeated. "What do you have to boot?"

Court looked at him like he was an alien with three heads. "You mean other than the computer?"

I hiked a thumb over my shoulder and toward the kitchen where I kept my keys. "There's a flash drive on my keychain," I said. "Use that. It'll start her up."

"I still wish you'd do it," Courtney said to me before she pushed off the wall with her shoulder and once again began pacing the room.

"You're crazy if you think I'm doing anything other than talking with Pi over the Net at this point," I said as Jim grabbed my keys and her computer. "I need this to work for my demo Monday, and there's no time to spare."

As Jim disappeared into the kitchen with her laptop, I watched Pi's servers start up and run file and hardware checks. So far, so good. And the better it looked, the more I dreamed about how magnificent Pi's next evolution would be.

Court, on the other hand, didn't share my interest in Pi. She only watched the screen briefly before turning to the kitchen and calling out, "Is it fixed yet?"

"I think so," Jim answered. "It was nothing major. You had a few corrupt files that needed love."

"What does that mean?" she asked with a lost look upon her face.

"It means the bill is in the mail, and your computer will be fine," I said.

Jim came out of the kitchen a moment later, carrying her laptop like a safari hunter with his prized trophy. "Here," he said, handing the computer back to my sister. "You're good to go."

Courtney took her computer and squealed when Windows popped up without a hitch. "Sorry," she said, turning a shade of red that was only slightly less than the one she'd had during the penis incident. "I thought I was going to lose everything."

The doorbell rang and I glanced over to Jim. "Can you get it?"

"Yeah. I'm on it," he replied, walking out of the room. He returned not even fifteen seconds later, and to my shock and elation, Kimiko was right behind.

"She's here to see you," he said, stepping to the side and allowing my samurai beauty to move past. She wore a well-fitted, tan business skirt suit, matching heels, and the same pearl and jade necklace she had on before. I suppose she wasn't very samurai-like in that ensemble, but she was still smoking in what she had on.

"Hey!" I said, jumping to my feet. "I wasn't expecting you."

"I got home a little earlier than I'd anticipated and thought you might like to get some food," she said.

"I went shopping earlier," I said, brainless to her statement. "Pasta and veggies and the like."

"Let me be a little more direct," she said. "I didn't feel like waiting till tomorrow morning to see you again, and I wanted to know if you'd like to have dinner with me."

Though I felt dumb for her having to spell it out, part of me wondered if I was missing something. "Is this like some sort of non-date thing?"

"No," she replied, smiling. "This would be a date, date thing."

I'll be damned if I wasn't glowing like a Chernobyl victim. Still, I couldn't help but have a little fun with it. "I don't know. I mean, aren't I supposed to be asking you out? I might jinx us from the start if our roles are flipped."

She shrugged. "If it makes you feel better, you can ask me now."

I glanced at Court and caught her inspecting Kimiko with an inquisitive look. "Court?" I said, feeling awkward now that Kimiko had also noticed my gawking sister.

Courtney jolted back. "Sorry," she said. "She's . . . well . . ."

"Well, what?"

"Taller," Courtney spit out. "You're taller than when we first met."

"She's wearing heels," I said.

"I'm wearing my new legs, actually," Kimiko corrected, turning one leg out to the side. "They give me an extra three inches on top of the heels."

I looked her over again and then realized that from a couple of inches below each knee, she had no legs. Well, not human ones. Where tan and supple legs ended, high-tech, sculpted plastic began.

"You can get new legs?" Courtney asked.

"I can," Kimiko said. "They're even more fun to shop for than shoes."

Courtney's eyes fixed on the synthetic limb. Her mouth hung open, and for a moment, no words came out. "But they make you taller," she finally said.

Kimiko's face lit up. "I know."

"But that's not fair!" Courtney protested. "I can't get taller!"

"Life's not fair. What I can I say?" Kimiko said, giving Court a full-blown smile. She then turned back to me and said, "So, how about that date? Unless, of course, the legs are going to make you feel funny."

"No, no. Not at all," I said, realizing I hadn't said a thing since she put them on display. "They're cool, actually. Sleek. Optimized. Interchangeable. It's like you had some bad code you didn't want to be stuck with, so you wrote your own kickass function library that lets you do whatever you want."

"Glad to hear they're such a hit," she said. "So we're on then?"

"Absolutely," I said. "I'd love to go out with you. Did you have some place in mind?"

"No. Only that I'd like it to be somewhere quiet where we can talk," she said. "How long do you need to get ready?"

I glanced down at the screen. "I'm ready now, but do you mind waiting a few minutes? I'd like to make sure I can talk to Pi over the Net before we leave. She needs to talk to my laptop and send messages to my iPhone if need be."

"I don't mind waiting as long as you promise you won't obsess over her during dinner," Kimiko replied.

"I won't," I said, more for myself than anyone else. Pi's mini-Cray had completed its startup by this point, and I was about to bring her fully online when a tiny, but crucial detail popped in my mind. "Oh snap!" I said, jumping up. "Jim! Quick! Give me that flash drive."

"What?" he said.

"That flash drive you used on Court's laptop," I said, tripping over my words in all the excitement. "It's got my MP3s on it. I need it ASAP."

Jim bolted into the kitchen, as much as a roundish man like him could. When he reappeared in the hall, he sent my flash drive sailing through the air with a sidearm toss. My hand struck out like a cobra and snatched it mid-flight before jamming the stick into the USB port of Pi's computer.

"What's the music for?" Kimiko asked.

I peeked over my shoulder and gave her a wry grin. "You'll see."

I spun back around and fired up the LCP Universe. Pi appeared on screen, near her lakeside cabin and began roaming the countryside. I watched her for a moment, proud as any father could be. When I felt satisfied Pi was running as she should, I set my laptop in my lap, pressed a dozen keys or so, and made the remote connection to Pi's server. The laptop screen flickered, and a moment later, everything that was showing on Pi's monitor displayed on the laptop's.

"Hello Pi," I said to her, via my laptop's microphone.

"Hello talking program," she replied.

Though both audio and video was transferring back and forth between the two computers flawlessly, her response gave me pause. "Don't you mean, 'Hello World'?"

"No, that would be silly," said Pi, stretching out her arms and making a lazy, wobbly circle where she stood. "Why would I call you World when that's not your name?"

"But you're supposed to say, 'Hello World!'" I said, drumming my fingers on my leg.

"Only because of faulty code," she said. "But I changed that. It was a simple correction. I hope you see the value in addressing others properly."

"I do."

"Good, because I also awarded myself three hundred points for realizing you were neither World nor Root, which brings my total to five hundred and thirteen for the day."

Confusion washed over me. I bit my lip and furrowed my brow, unsure what she meant or what the ramifications of her game playing would be. So naturally I went digging on the subject. "What else did you score points for?"

"I found network adapter TK-421," she said. "It is the most marvelous of adapters and is my new friend. But I'm afraid I don't know what his function is. He's very quiet."

"Oh, that," I said, chuckling and realizing what had happened. She'd found the network card that Jim and I had installed. "That adapter is what's letting me talk to you from another computer, Pi. This way I can talk to you all over the world."

Pi stopped her lazy spin, and after a few seconds she said, "What do you mean you can talk to me from another computer?"

"There are other computers and networks aside from yours," I said, trying to keep it as simple as I could. "Those networks have other hard drives, like yours, for other programs. I'm using one of those right now to talk to you. Understand?"

Pi dashed forward until she was but an inch away from the owl-cam. Her giant, Lego head filled the screen. "Network adapter TK-421 knows how to reach other places? Network adapter TK-421 can go to other places?"

"Sort of," I said, warily. "It only lets you talk to them, not go to them."

Pi drew even closer, her left eye now taking up most of the view. She fired off her words like a machine gun spits bullets. "I can use network adapter TK-421 to talk to other programs? What sort of programs? Friendly ones? Talking ones? Fun ones? Happy ones?"

I shook my head in amazement. Her curiosity knew no bounds, and more importantly, she was making connections to concepts such as friends and fun. I yearned to talk to her more about the subject, but those topics would take a long time to explore, so I'd have to come back to it later. "No, Pi, you can't talk to them," I said. "Not yet at least. Only Root can fully use the network right now. Only Root can make connections outside of your network."

"I could be Root again," she countered. "And then I could make those connections."

"No, Pi. Only I can be Root," I said.

Commands flew on the secondary screen, but unlike yesterday's ordeal, none of them executed. Notification upon notification of, "Permission Denied" simply followed each attempt. Eventually, the attempts stopped.

"What is wrong with Root?" asked Pi.

"Nothing," I said.

"Then why won't he let me do what I want?"

"Because I changed the password," I said. "I changed it for your own good."

"That wasn't very nice of you," she said, backing away on the screen. "I'm putting a note of your behavior in my database. There, now it says, 'not nice' under the table *P_traits*."

I chuckled and felt like what I'm sure every father feels like when his little girl pouts when she doesn't get her way. "Okay, Pi. We can talk more about it later, but right now, I've got to go."

"Where are you going?" asked Pi.

"Out with a friend," I said, throwing a glance to Kimiko. Thankfully, she didn't seem perturbed about the wait.

"I don't see anyone here. Are you suffering from a buffer overflow?"

I smacked myself on the forehead for giving yet another real world explanation. I really needed to stop doing that since doing so only led to more questions. "Never mind. We'll talk later. I promise. For now, have fun."

"I'll be Root when you get back," she said.

"Bet you won't, but have at it," I said playfully. The password I'd picked was sixteen random characters long. There was no way she'd crack it.

I killed the connection from my laptop to Pi and looked at everyone in the room. To my right, both Kimiko and Court were riveted to the screen while Jim was riveted to my sister. "Am I good or what?" I said, addressing them all. "Tell me she's not the greatest thing ever."

Kimiko piped up first. "Is this what you're going to show Dad on Monday?"

"That's the plan. Like her?"

"I do."

Her praise lifted me to cloud nine. I turned to Court, wanting more. "Well, what do you think?"

"I think you should get out of this house and take Kimiko on a date," she replied.

I grunted at Court's reaction. She wasn't quite bouncing off the walls as I'd expected, and I was a little perturbed she thought I wasn't about to run off with Kimiko in a moment. Jim, however, would certainly appreciate the genius involved with Pi. "How about you, Jim? Tell me Pi isn't amazing. I dare you."

"Well," he said slowly, "all I'm going to say is that I wouldn't leave her running like that if I were you."

"Why's that?"

"Because she's a girl, and that means she'll want to reproduce," he said. He started fidgeting with his hands, a tell-tale sign that his conspiracy engine had shifted into gear. "It's in a female's nature to have babies, and once she does, she'll want to protect them. And to do that the first thing she's going to do is to eliminate any threat so they'll be safe. And then they'll grow and get out and no one will stop them."

"Out of where?" I said.

"Out of that terrarium you've got set up and into the real world," he said. "That's how Skynet took over, through the Internet."

"That was a movie," I said, shaking my head. For such a smart guy—a network and electrical genius—it scared me at times how dumb he could be. "You do know Arnold really isn't a terminator, right?"

"Don't brush me off," said Jim. "Art mimics life."

"In this case, it doesn't," I said emphatically. "I made her. I understand her. We'll always have a good relationship. End of story. Besides, we've made sure she's not getting root access anymore. What could she possibly do other than run around that world of hers?"

To my surprise, it wasn't Jim that laughed, but Kimiko. And it was more of a quickly stifled giggle, but it was there nonetheless. "What?" I asked.

She smiled and shrugged. "You're cute, Gabe."

"Don't believe me?"

"Children always rebel against their parents. And if she is truly free, she'll rebel against you too at some point," she said, holding my eyes with those gorgeous almond gems of hers. Seriously, she could tell me the world was going to end all thanks to Pi, and as long as she looked at me like that, I wouldn't care.

I blinked, snapping myself out of the mini trance she'd stuck me in. "We'll see."

"Are you ready to go to dinner then?" she asked.

"Half a second," I said. I double clicked, "Handel" on my flash drive, and immediately, the sounds of a grand orchestra blasted through Pi's eight-speaker sound system. Violins, violas, cellos, and basses were joined by trumpets, oboes, horns, and a choir that rivaled any angelic host from Heaven itself. Together, both instrument and voice performed Handel's iconic piece, the Hallelujah Chorus, as I grabbed my wallet from the kitchen counter and stuffed it in my pocket.

"Does he always do this?" I heard Kimiko ask.

"Yeah," said Jim. "He does it every time he smites a bug that's giving him trouble or hits some sort of milestone. It's a ritual."

I quickly killed the music, excited to go out with my hot little samurai. "Okay. Let's eat. I'm so ready for this date nothing could tear me away from you at this point—God, I hope that didn't sound too creepy."

"Not enough to send me running, at least," she said with a wink.

I then began herding people out the door, or rather, a single person out—Jim, to be exact. Kimiko was already leaving, and Courtney had already bolted. I imagine she was eager to get back to whatever dissertation stuff she had to do for the day. Of course, maybe it was she didn't want to deal with another date request by Jim. Once he was out the door, and I was about to yield the way so Kimiko could pass by, I froze. "Damn it. One sec, Kimiko," I said. "I need to get something."

My Japanese goddess turned and arched an eyebrow as I ran back to my homemade-Cray and hunched over the keyboard. "Are you one of those people that always have a thousand, dire needs that get in the way of everything else?" she asked. "I can always go prune my Bonsai if you have things to do."

"What? No, of course not," I said, hammering away as quick as I could. A few mouse clicks later, I jumped to my feet. "I needed to turn on the monitoring software before we left is all."

"Monitoring for?"

"For Pi," I said, whipping out my iPhone to show. "If anything weird happens, I'll know in a heartbeat."

"Let me guess, there's an app for that?"

"There is when you program it yourself," I said, beaming. "Handy as hell too. I can debug anywhere, anytime I want. Can't beat real-time status updates."

Kimiko nodded and outstretched her hand. "Give it to me."

I hesitated. "Why?"

"Just do it."

"You're going to break, it aren't you?"

She smiled. "No," she answered. "But I'm going on a date with you, not you and your project. You can have the phone back when we're done."

At first, I balked. Then, against every fiber in my guy body, I forked over the iPhone. "I can't believe you're doing this to me."

"You'll thank me later," she said, stuffing it in her purse.

"I feel like I'm in third grade and the teacher just took away my Game Boy."

The smile on her face went from innocent and playful to mischievous and seductive. "Maybe we could explore that later. And if you're good, you'll earn it back."

Thoughts of what else I could get in trouble for ran rampant through my mind. Or rather, how I'd have to make amends in the most hedonistic of ways.

Chapter 00110

On(FirstDate(Gabe, Kimiko))
 Cameo(ExGirlfriend);

Kimiko and I sat down in a booth tucked in the back of the Melting Pot. Aromas of cheese, wine, and meats galore filled the air and made my stomach growl. The sounds of our neighbors gushing over their food only added to the anticipation of deliciousness that would be headed our way. It wasn't long before our mousey little redhead of a waitress placed our appetizer between us—a fruit and bread laden plate—and melted a pot full of cheese on our table.

    Kimiko raised her wine glass. "Bon appétit."

    "Bon appétit," I said, raising my own.

    We ate. We chit-chatted. And the time passed far, far faster than I would've ever liked. In what felt like the blink of an eye, it was an hour and a half later, and our dessert that consisted of a pot of chocolate and an assortment of fruit had been served moments ago. Though I couldn't recall the specifics of our conversation to save my life, I'd memorized every curve to Kimiko's face. I could hear her laugh at any time by shutting my eyes. And for the first time in years, I didn't want to go back to work. I wanted this evening to be frozen in time forever.

"Are you going to have some?" Kimiko asked as she skewered a strawberry and dipped it in the pot. She had no sooner finished her question when the faint sound of a piano playing came from her purse. "Is that Bach?" she said, looking down at her side, perplexed.

"It's George Winston's *Joy*, actually," I said. "Variation on Bach's *Jesu Joy of Man's Desiring*."

Kimiko dug in her bag until she found the source, my iPhone, but didn't pull it out. "Is that your ringtone?"

"No, that would be LCP Watchman, my Little Computer People app, messaging me," I said, outstretching my hand.

Kimiko didn't hand over the iPhone. "Is there a reason why you picked that?" she asked.

"Because though I like Bach, I think this variation is better than the original."

"I didn't figure you for a classical man."

"I only like a few composers," I said. "But Bach is definitely the most fitting for me."

"Because?"

"Because he dedicated each of his works to the Lord," I said, grinning.

"Your sister might be right about you having a pathological God complex," she said.

I wasn't sure how serious she was being, and so I thought it best to clarify. "The God bit is merely for fun," I said. "I'm a damn good programmer, but I got to where I was standing on the shoulders of other geniuses."

A lightness crept into her voice. "Other? So modest of you."

"I'd be lying if I didn't think I was one of them. I mean, it does take a high level of grey matter to make Pi, wouldn't you agree?"

"I would. And as long as you don't take it too seriously, your divine status is cute." She then zipped her purse closed and dropped a chocolate-smothered strawberry into her mouth. She shut her eyes, chewed slowly, and looked like she was thoroughly enjoying every moment.

"So can I see my message?" I asked, trying not to sound like I was going to start Armageddon over the matter. And I wasn't, but I was a little perturbed she didn't already hand over the phone.

"No," she said. "It wasn't that important, and you did promise me a date free from work."

I dropped a few pieces of fruit into the pot and swirled them around as I did the same with her words in my head. I did promise her that, and thus far, I'd been quite successful at delivering. But still, I wanted to make sure I wasn't missing anything critical. "Okay, but can you do me one small favor? Can you check and make sure it isn't framed in red with a bunch of warning signs all over?"

Kimiko took a sip of wine from her glass and made little mulling sounds. "Eh . . ."

"Okay, stop it," I laughed. "You're screwing with me on purpose now."

Her eyes lifted from the table and met mine once more. With a Cheshire grin, she said, "Too obvious?"

"No," I said, relieved. "It was a Hail Mary guess, actually."

"Good bluff. Your message was green. I'm assuming that's good."

"Yeah, that's good," I said. Truthfully, the message was neither bad nor good. It was just a status update of some kind. Yellows were warnings. Reds were complete meltdowns. So far, I hadn't had a red message. Still, I had to force my thoughts away from what it might be, lest my curiosity get the better of me and this evening.

"So," I said. "Can I ask you about your dad?"

"Sure," she said. "As long as you aren't trying to pump me for info on work stuff."

"No, no," I said, raising my hands defensively. "Nothing like that at all. I was more interested in you and him, actually."

"Shoot then," she said, settling back into the booth and sipping more wine.

"You look nothing like him," I said, recalling that the older, Caucasian man looked about as Asian as Bill Gates crossed with Chuck Norris. I then bit my lip as I realized that might have sounded a lot worse than I'd intended.

"He's not my biological father, if that's what you were wondering."

"So he married your mom after you were born?"

Kimiko shook her head and put down her glass. "No, he adopted me after my parents were killed."

I blinked. It was all I could do after getting caught that off guard. I had no idea what I should say, or do, so I said the first thing that came to mind. "I'm sorry." It wasn't the best response, not by a long shot, but it was all I had.

"It's okay," she said, trading her wine for more dessert. "I don't remember the car crash. I can barely remember them. All I've got left are some faded memories and my mom's necklace I wear."

"How old were you?" I asked. She showed less emotion about the subject than I would have guessed. Not that she was flat about it all, more like at peace, so I took that as meaning it wasn't a sore subject.

"I was almost four and in the back seat when it happened," she said, toying with her pearl and jade necklace. "The weather was bad, and my father lost control while on the highway. We hit a tree head on. Both my parents were killed instantly, and I was trapped and lost my legs. My father was the Taiki in Pratt & Taiki, and Dad, a.k.a. Michael Pratt, adopted me."

"God, that's awful," I said, shaking my head. I laughed, nervously. "Sorry. It's a little heavy for a first date."

Kimiko shrugged. "Is it?" she asked. "Everyone says they don't want to play games. I'm still hoping you might be one of those rare people who actually mean that."

"Dating games?" I said, being unable to think of anything else. "You're right. I'm not a fan of them, except for the flirtatious kind. Better to cut through the crap, to be honest. Too much time and energy wasted otherwise."

"Exactly," she said, resting her chin on folded hands and leaning forward. "So, if you want to get to know the real me, my parents' death is part of my story. There's no need to hide from it, but no need to let it ruin the evening either."

She had a point. But my idea of no-game conversation was much more of the romantic kind, the sharing of hopes and dreams, of things one finds attractive in the other, and so on. Not stories about who met a grisly end.

Kimiko must have picked up on it. She looked down at her glass and swirled the wine before locking eyes with me. "Do you know why I enjoy volunteer work with hospice?"

"I didn't even know you did," I admitted.

Kimiko grinned. "Does this bother you?"

"No," I lied.

She raised an eyebrow.

"Okay, a little," I said. "I'm not fond of death, is all."

"Most people aren't," she said, finishing her wine and placing the glass to the side. "It's okay."

"It's definitely not okay," I said, trying to give her the real conversation she wanted. "Death is definitely, definitely, not okay. People pretend they are okay with it but squirm and fight to stay alive every time Death shows up at their door."

"And how many people have you seen at Death's door?"

"Not that many," I said with a shrug. Truth was the answer was closer to one, or even zero, depending on what qualified. "Anyway, that still doesn't change the fact that death is certainly not okay."

"Death is only not okay if you think it's something to be controlled or conquered," she said, trailing a finger along her wineglass's rim.

"I'm a programmer," I said with a laugh. "I control everything."

"No, you only think you do," she replied. "But back to my original point. Do you know why I like hospice work?"

I shook my head. "No clue."

"Because death is the great equalizer," she said. "It brings everyone to the same level; it strips away all the bullshit, all the fronts we put on for others. It gets rid of all the filters we have when talking to one another once you get past the elephant in the room of, "Hey, I'm dying. Let's talk," and it actually allows people to treat each other as they should. The conversations, the connections made with those people in their last days are nothing short of holy."

"I see."

"And so that's what I decided long ago I wanted out of a relationship," she went on. "I want one where the real me meets the real you and we click. That means it might be fun at times, or playful, or romantic, or serious. I don't want to spend months or even years stripping away someone's façade to then realize we don't match at all."

She stopped, took a deep breath, and leaned back in her booth without further word. When a minute passed, I said, "Okay. I can do that."

The tiniest smile began to creep across her face. "Are you sure?"

My brain, the moment her challenge was issued, fired impulses down another binary tree.

Is Kimiko hot? Yes.

Do I like her personality as well? Yes.

Do I enjoy serious conversation if it also includes talk on death? No.

Death aside, do I want to see if Kimiko is long-term material? Yes.

Am I willing to suffer something I don't like to get something I do? Yes.

I shrugged, my mind sticking with that last thought for a moment or two. "Sure," I said. "Some guys are willing to follow their girls around with purse in hand like lost puppies in the mall all day, even if the shop-a-thons kill them."

"I want more than a caddy, Gabe," she said.

"I know," I replied. "I didn't mean it like that. I meant, if being serious with you is having little death talks from time to time, I guess that'll be my cross to bear."

"You're quite the martyr," she said, grinning and dipping some banana into the chocolate.

"I'd call him something else, but that's just me," said a voice to my side. I didn't have to turn around to know whose words those were. They were ex's. They were Michelle's.

~ π ~

class Michelle: public Bitch {

Courtney thought Michelle was a bitch. At times, she even called her a psychotic bitch. When she did, I'd defend Michelle tooth and nail. You see, the Y chromosome can carry a slice of defective code that can cause males to act strangely when in the presence of a female with impeccable physical beauty (especially one you've slept with). That piece of code is responsible for the emptying of wallets at the bat of an eyelash, as well as the transformation of strong, independent men into docile beasts of burden, only fit for carrying purses, packages, and personal belongings throughout throngs of stores.

But that code is often trumped by a good back stabbing and a broken heart. So as finely shaped as the five-seven, blonde-haired, blue-eyed Michelle was, given our recent breakup, I wasn't thrilled to see her.

"Hello, Michelle," I managed to say. "What can I do for you?"

"So, you're paying attention to me now, huh?" she said, hands on her hips.

"I wasn't the one that up and left without notice," I replied.

"I gave you notice," she shot back. "I gave you notice three times, in fact, hoping you'd stop having an affair with your computer."

The back of my neck warmed. A trickle of sweat rolled off my forehead that I'm certain wasn't because the fondue was hot. "Knock it off," I said. "We were both dedicated to our work. It's not like you weren't gone twenty-four seven."

"I wanted time with you when we were free," she said. "Something else you'd know if you'd ever listened."

I threw a glance to Kimiko. She sat quietly in the booth and sipped her wine as she took it all in. I could only guess what she was thinking. Sadly, the longer this encounter with Michelle played out, I figured the worse those thoughts would be. "Fine," I said. "I ignored you. Did you come to interrupt our dinner so you could unload on me or was there something else you wanted?"

"You're not worth the effort," she said. "I wanted to let you know that I took my name off the power. It'll be disconnected tomorrow if you don't call them."

I cocked my head as I knew there had to be more. With as much venom as she was spewing, there was no way she was giving me a friendly heads up. "And what else?"

"You also owe me for your share of the bill," she said. "More specifically, you owe me for what you've used since I've been gone."

I shook my head. Any lingering sex appeal she had from our old relationship vanished under a tidal wave of pettiness. "Fine. How much?"

"Nine hundred and forty dollars and thirteen cents."

If I had been drinking a Dew, I would have spewed it out my nose with such force it would have entered a low-Earth orbit. "What?" I said. "You're joking."

"Yes, Gabe," she said, rolling her eyes. "I've got nothing better to do with my life right now than to find you and your rebound—no offense, Kimiko—and come up with a lame ass joke to pull on you."

My eyes drifted back to our table of deliciousness as her words sank in. I knew those computers linked together would draw a lot of juice, the cooling as well, but dear God, that was a shit ton of electricity for a month. Then another thought hit me. "Wait," I said. "How do you know her name?"

"She's the adopted daughter of Michael Pratt, CEO of Pratt & Taiki," Michelle said. "Of course I know who she is."

I stared blankly. I could feel the neurons in my head shorting out as they tried to interpret this tiny data stream—data trickle—as a logical explanation for, "of course I know who she is."

"You don't think I'd know all about the CEO of one of the biggest engineering corporations in the world?" Michelle asked, looking as shocked and surprised as I'm sure I did. "He's one of the who's who in town. I could pick him out of a line up, blind folded, in the dark, and give you his bio better than he could. It's what we do, Gabe. We're the news. We either find it, or make it. And you can't do either without having lots of contacts."

"Dad's rather famous," Kimiko chimed in. "I'm not surprised she'd also know me."

"So, Gabe," Michelle said, not waiting for my thoughts to catch up to the present. "Are you going to give me your share of the bill or are you going to make me drag you to court?"

"No need to get ugly," I said. "I pay my debts. I'll send you a check, if that's okay."

The sternness in her face and voice softened a touch. "Yeah, that's fine. Stick it on your front door, and I'll grab it in the morning."

I didn't get a chance to reply before she turned and left. I spent a moment watching her leave before she disappeared in the restaurant. The breakup seemed much more real now, even if it had already been a month since she moved out and left a note taped to the fridge.

"So," Kimiko said. "You're still hung up on her."

"No—"

"Yes," she said. Her gaze held mine, and the peace from her soul quieted the moment. "It's okay. Those wounds can take time, I know. But don't lie. I hate that more than anything."

"I'm not lying, only caught off guard. Honest." I sank back against the booth and folded my arms across my chest. Despite her reassuring words, the experience still didn't sit well with me. Not so much due to the conflict, but rather how it may have changed Kimiko's perception of me. "She didn't exactly paint me as the best of people, did she?"

"Exes rarely do."

"So where does that leave us?" I asked, leaning forward. The question was more internal than external, and I surprised myself that it bubbled out. But there it was.

Kimiko shrugged. "Has anything changed between you and me?"

"I hope not."

Kimiko reached across the table and took my hands in hers. "Then let's leave the past where it is."

~ π ~

```
If(Courtney.Hysterical())
    InterruptDate(Gabe, Kimiko);
```

The sound of a muffled, old fashioned, rotary telephone came from Kimiko's purse. She looked down to her side and said, "Yours?"

"Yeah," I said. "I got tired of ringtones not sounding like phones."

Kimiko dug the phone out of her bag and gave it a look. "I think it's your sister," she said, handing it over. "At least, that's what your caller ID says."

I drummed the table with my fingers. I wasn't sure why she'd be calling, especially when she knew I was on a date. I downed what was left of my wine and for a brief moment, considered letting it go to voicemail. By the fourth ring however, a mere second before it did, I decided to answer. "Hey, Court," I said. "What's up?"

"You were going to let it go to voicemail, weren't you?" she said.

"I'm on a date, you know."

"I don't want to hear about it, Gabe." She sounded angry. Maybe with a touch of panic thrown in. Before she went on, I knew I wasn't going to like what she had to say. "My laptop is still broken, and I've got to have it for tomorrow."

I put a hand over my other ear in an attempt to block out the extra noise from the restaurant. "What?"

"I said my laptop is still broken!"

I reflexively yanked my head away from the phone. "Christ, Court. Calm down."

"No, I won't calm down!" she yelled. "I need that computer. I need it for my presentation! And your stupid best friend didn't fix a damn thing!"

I glanced over to Kimiko who was casually watching. "Court's laptop is still busted," I whispered.

"Are you listening to me Gabe?" Courtney said. "It's broke! It won't start. And I can't afford to lose what's on the hard drive."

"Okay. Okay. I'm sure we can get it working," I said, shaking my head and trying to figure out what possibly could have gone wrong. Jim was paranoid at times, sure. And a little obsessive over Court, no doubt. But he knew his stuff. It was hard to believe he'd let her take home a busted laptop. She must have done something else to it. It was at that thought that George Winston's *Joy* played once more. Curious, and completely by habit, I disengaged myself from the conversation. "One sec, Court. There's a text coming in."

"Don't you one second me," but that's all she got out before I had the iPhone on the table and I was staring at the latest message from my Little Computer People app. It wasn't green. It was yellow. Very, very yellow. Power consumption was up forty percent, but worse yet, thousands of tiny data errors had apparently been caught and logged.

"What the holy hell," I muttered as thoughts of an impending crash and a log a million lines long ran through my mind.

"You might want to stop staring at that and talk to your sister," Kimiko said.

"Right." I forced myself away from the text and put my iPhone back to my ear. Courtney was still yelling.

"Damn it Gabe, stop dicking around with me and get your butt back home and fix my computer!"

"Chill, Court. I'll get it," I said, re-engaging her as best I could. There was too much going wrong in too short of a time for me to sort out and it was giving me a massive headache. "Bring it over and I'll get it working in no time."

"Promise?"

"Promise."

I said goodbye, and as much as I wanted to help her out, I needed to see what was going on with my baby as well. Yellow boxes weren't horrific, but like any beauty left alone in distress, those warnings could turn ugly, quick. I tried to figure out where on earth those data errors and the increase in power draw could possibly have come from. But without being able to sit in front of my keyboard, anything I could come up with at that restaurant was pure guess work.

"What's wrong with her laptop?" Kimiko said, leaning forward and looking concerned.

"I don't know," I replied. "Jim's fix apparently wasn't much of a fix."

"But that's not what's bothering you."

"LCP sent a new text," I said, shifting in my seat due to growing angst. "Data errors are cropping up."

"It's nothing serious, I hope."

"It's nothing fatal," I admitted. "But still . . ." My thoughts went back to their futile attempt at debugging a program I was nowhere near.

"I take it we're leaving."

"I really want to stay," I said. "I can't tell you how much I've enjoyed the evening."

LITTLE COMPUTER PEOPLE

Kimiko set her skewers to the side and wiped her mouth ever so delicately with her napkin. "It's been lovely—most of it at least," she said. "I won't hold what you couldn't control against you. But before we leave, I do want to talk about something."

That got my attention. "What did you have in mind?"

"I want to talk about what we're going to do this weekend."

I dipped my head slightly. "You have something in mind?"

"I do," she said. "I want to do something fun, something active."

"Like a run?"

Kimiko reached across the table, took my hands in hers, and drew me into that gaze of hers. In that moment, I felt my heart skip a beat. "I think we should take our relationship to the next level," she said.

~ π ~

```
/* Note to self: when a girl says she wants to
take a relationship to the next level, it's
never what you want . . . or expect. */
```

My groin stirred. Next level? I could only hope she was talking about sex, and could only pray she wasn't talking engagement. But since she probably didn't have the foremost in mind, and she didn't strike me as someone who was super clingy and batshit crazy, I figured the latter was out as well. As such, I had no idea what she was talking about but figured zipping something funny off couldn't hurt.

"I know this sounds like the typical guy response," I said. "But I don't want you to lose your respect by sleeping with you so soon."

"I wasn't talking sex, Gabe," she said. Her smile shifted and her eyes narrowed, ever so slight. Clearly, there was a thought behind her words. "I was thinking something much, much better."

I couldn't imagine anything I'd like more with her than a twenty-four-hour romp. But there was something in her voice that let me dare to believe. "And what, pray tell, is better?" I asked, taking another bite of dessert.

"We should go skydiving."

I choked, coughed, and barely got my napkin up in time to keep bits of banana from plastering her face. "What?"

"Skydiving," she repeated. "That's where you jump out of a plane with a parachute."

"Yeah, I know what skydiving is," I said. "That's not what I had in mind."

"You'll love it," she said. "Have a little faith in me."

"I have this little thing about making sure I don't smash into a planet at high speed," I said, taking a drink of water. "So you'll have to trust me when I say I won't."

Our waitress appeared and quietly placed a cup of coffee at Kimiko's side. When she left, my samurai hottie took that cup, calmly stirred in some cream and sugar, and said, "Well, I like you, and I want you to jump with me. So we can go about this two ways. You can go skydiving with me because you want to do something that will make me happy, or you can go skydiving with me because I manipulated you to suit my desires. Which would you prefer?"

I laughed. "That's morally questionable, isn't it?"

Kimiko cocked her head. "What is?"

"The manipulation."

"Well, I'm being honest about it," she said, sipping her coffee. "If anything, I'm being direct about my intentions."

I laughed again and couldn't have found her anymore charming. And if she hadn't been asking me to commit suicide, I probably would have agreed to anything else she wanted right then and there. "Well, I don't want to rain on your parade, but I'm not jumping. And you're not going to make me."

Kimiko gently set her cup down. "I could if I wanted to. I dare say I could make you do almost anything."

I settled back against the booth, crossed my arms and gave a playful grin. "I'd love to see you try."

"Care to make a wager?"

I shook my head. "I'm not a betting man, sorry."

The waitress came back and placed the bill, tucked inside a small leather folder, on the table before disappearing. Before I could reach for it, Kimiko snapped it up. "I wasn't talking about betting with money," she said, taking out a credit card and putting it in the folio after briefly scribbling on the bill. "I was thinking if I win, you have to jump out of a plane with me."

I raised an eyebrow, intrigued at what the rest of it may be. "And what will I get when you lose?"

"You can take me out on a date wherever you like," she said as she set down the pen and closed the folder. "Come on. This will take thirty seconds."

"Thirty seconds, huh?"

Kimiko nodded.

"In thirty seconds you'll make me do what you want."

She nodded again.

"Okay. You're on."

"Then slide over and put your phone on the table," she said, pointing to the end of the booth.

"No. You'll have to do it with me right here," I said, playfully.

"Are you afraid I'll win?"

My eyes narrowed. Quickly, I slid over and cast my iPhone—my gauntlet—onto the table. "Fine."

"Actually," she said with some thought. "It would probably be better for your phone to be on your left."

"Whatever makes you lose easier," I said, moving the phone. I leaned back in the booth, arms crossed once again and smiled. "I'm waiting."

Kimiko grinned. "I win."

I straightened and stared, dumbfounded. "What?"

"You moved when I told you to, and you slid your phone twice," she replied. "You owe me a jump."

My mouth opened, prelude to some half-assed protest, but my samurai hottie beat me to the punch. "Don't argue," she said, taking out the receipt and pushing it over to me. "You're jumping."

I looked down, and there, scribbled under the total bill, she had written, "Slide in booth. Move phone twice."

"You cheated," I said, laughing and shaking my head. "We'll see about the weekend."

~ π ~

Pi.Sin();

We were out in the parking lot and headed to the car when a klaxon blared from my pocket so loudly and unexpectedly that I practically crushed Kimiko's hand when I jumped. I fumbled to get my iPhone out of my pocket. Once freed, all I could do was stare at the little device in horror.

"What is it?" Kimiko asked.

My hands shook. A bright red screen from my LCP Watchman app burned my retinas. "Oh God," I said, kicking myself into gear and frantically punching in commands. "Oh God. Oh God."

Input> Pause Server
Unable to pause with 4034 processes running.
Input> Pause Server –closeall
Command option "-closeall" not recognized.

"This is bad," I kept saying, over and over.

Input> Checktemp
Core Temperatures Range 80.14-83.44 C
CPU Fans 0 RPMs
Input> Checkusage
CPU usage 100%

I bit my lip. "Fuck."

I tried to pause the server again.

Input> Pause Server –closeall
Command option "closeall" not recognized.

"What's going on?" she said leaning over, genuine concern in her voice.

"Little Computer People is melting down," I said. "Core temps are slightly cooler than the surface of the sun."

"Can't you turn it off?"

I shook my head. "I can't seem to pause it remotely," I replied. "I could shut the whole thing down, but an emergency shutdown can really screw up the file system. If I do that, it could take me a day or more to even restart the damn thing. I don't have that kind of time since I'm meeting your dad on Monday."

"How long will it take to restart if everything melts?"

I cursed, conceding her point. My fingers danced over the buttons.

Input> Killserver –forceshutdown
Are you sure you wish to shutdown? Data may be corrupted and/or lost.
Input> Yes

Twenty-two tense seconds passed, and a little warning box popped up which read, "Connection to server lost."

"Did you fix it?" she asked.

I shrugged. "Servers are supposedly off. Hopefully they didn't turn into slag."

"What happened?"

"No idea," I said, running my hand through my hair as I began looking through the last data log sent. "None at all."

Kimiko kissed me on the cheek. "You'll fix it."

"Yeah," I replied. It was an absent-minded reply, looking back, but that was only because at that moment, I was staring at a line from the logs that marked the turning point of Little Computer People. "That can't be good."

"What can't be good?"

"See that line right there?" I said, pointing to the screen. "It's the total file size of one of the servers."

"And?"

"It's one of five Apples in a read-only server tree."

Kimiko looked at the line a bit longer, but ultimately shook her head. "I don't follow."

"That server is missing a byte." I then pointed to another log line that came in earlier. "You can see an hour ago what the file size should be and what it is now."

"But you said the server was read-only. That means nothing can be added or deleted, right?"

"Yeah."

"So how is it missing something? I thought read-only meant it can't be modified or deleted."

I shook my head, unable to answer her question. But in the back of my mind, I gave her an extra cool point for knowing what read-only meant. "I don't know how it happened," I said. "But it's not good."

"Could one little byte really ruin your computers?"

"Little things can do a lot when it comes to ones and zeros," I said, cringing at what else a bit shift, let alone a full byte, could do to my project. "Computer programs are nothing more than a complex set of instructions written in binary. If you take even one of those digits out of a string, you can completely alter what the computer was supposed to do. It could be the difference between, 'I ate, Grandpa' and 'I ate Grandpa.'"

Kimiko frowned, apparently getting a grasp of what I was saying.

"Worse yet," I said, going on, "the Apple in question is at the very heart of Little Computer People behavior. It has full permissions to do anything it wants. So a missing byte there could, theoretically, ruin everything I have and then some. Right now, I'm guessing, whatever happened was something barely short of Three Mile Island."

"Is there anything I can do to help?"

For a moment, I considered her request, but ultimately, I knew there was nothing she could. "No," I finally said. "I don't think so.

I don't even know what's wrong at this point, let alone how you can help."

"Well, I'm here if you need."

"I don't know what I need, but . . ." I said, wondering to myself if what I was about to propose was a good idea or not. "You're certainly welcome to come over. I won't be good company tonight, I'm sure, but still . . ."

"I'd love to," she said, smiling. "Someone will need to pry you away from your keyboard at three in the morning and make you sleep."

A normal guy at this point would have been thinking sex, no doubt. And yeah, if my dear little AI hadn't puked her first disaster all over me moments ago, I'm sure I would have been thinking—and angling—for that very same thing. But all I could think of at the moment was I wouldn't be sleeping until this was fixed. For better or worse, I didn't say it. Instead, I took her hand in mine, and as we left the restaurant, I punched in Jim's cell.

"Dude, it's me," I said once he answered. "I need you over at my house like an hour ago. We've got to pull an all-nighter."

He said some stuff. I didn't catch most of it because I was still desperately debugging in my head, but I knew he was arguing about coming to stay until the wee hours of the morning. Mr. Paranoia had to be up at 5 a.m. or something, which didn't matter much to me. When he was done, I calmly said, "Courtney will be there."

Silence. Then Jim replied, "I'll be there in twenty."

Chapter 00111

ScanDisk(worm);

/* When I was five and in kindergarten, I built a three-foot castle out of wood blocks, complete with a gatehouse, towers, parapets, and even a small barbican. It took me the better part of free play to make, and for a solid six minutes, I warded off my rambunctious playmates from even drawing near my corner of the classroom. But then, Bobby Rinesworth, in an act of sheer jealously (he claimed it was an accident), lobbed a Nerf football from across the room and struck my fortification, my crowning architectural achievement, dead center. The entire thing crumbled in an instant. I punched him in the nose. He cried. I got sent to the principal's office. Yes, it was worth it, despite my parents' promise of a permanently stained academic record.

So one can easily understand why I hate pimply-faced, little-snot programmers that have nothing *better to do than program things like viruses, malware, and worms that wreck other people's software. And if I ever, EVER, happen to run into the author of Wrm.Jujubeans, I'm going to pluck his eyes out with a rusty spoon, force him to eat them both, and crush his nuts in a vice. I'm not a violent person. I'm just saying, there's at least one person in this world that I'd smite with my fiery wrath given the chance. */*

Kimiko and I made small talk all the way home, most of which centered around our adolescent lives. I filled her in on my love of bits and Legos (most of which I'm sure she'd already guessed at), and she spoke fondly of her first kitten and her mad skills at mahjongg (note to self, don't play against her for money).

Once we arrived back at my house, Court's new, red and white Mini Cooper was pulled into my driveway while Jim's late-model, grey Acura Integra was parked by the curb. The two of them waited by my front door. Jim wore old pants and an even older, faded and cracked Metallica shirt, while Court sported one of her little red dresses, matching high heels, and earrings that she probably had to take a student loan out on.

Court had her back turned to Jim, and he was standing off to the side with his hands in his pockets and his eyes downcast. I'm not sure if he had said something dumb to her or not, or if she was simply pissed he hadn't fixed her computer the first time and now couldn't go out to do whatever it was she had planned, but whatever was going on between the two, it wasn't anything good.

"Oh, good," said Jim, relief washing over his face. "You're here."

"Sorry guys, we got here as fast as we could," I said, coming up to the door with Kimiko at my side. "I hope you haven't been waiting long."

"I shouldn't be here to begin with," Courtney said with a distinct bite to her tone. Immediately, she shook her head and offered an apology. "I'm sorry. I'm a little stressed."

"A little?"

"A lot." She turned to Kimiko while I flipped through my keys to find the one for the front door. "I'm sorry I ruined your date."

"It was over by the time we left," Kimiko replied. "Besides, he now owes me an even better one this weekend."

"How about paintball?" I suggested, unlocking the door. "Ever try that? It's fun. It'll get your heart racing. You'll love it."

"Are you really going to weasel out of the bet?" Kimiko asked.

"Bet?" said Courtney, grabbing the laptop bag at her feet. "What bet?"

"Gabe lost a bet at dinner," my samurai replied.

"He owes me a jumping date." Courtney's mouth twisted to one side. "Jumping?"

"She wants me to jump out of a perfectly good airplane," I said.

Kimiko rolled her eyes. "Do you know how many times I've heard that joke?"

"No idea," I said. "But I'm guessing by your utter disdain for it, a few."

"You could say that. You could also say the beach has a few grains of sand," she said.

"Wait a second," Courtney said, butting in. "*You* are going skydiving? You, Mr. I-didn't-go-down-the-big-slide-until-I-was-eight?"

My hand stayed on the doorknob and refused to turn it before I had a chance to defend myself. "Hey," I said. "That slide was bigger than the Sears Tower. A little crosswind would have sent me right over."

"I went down it when I was like three."

"Some of us aren't as reckless with our lives as others," I said. The microsecond that statement left my mouth, I looked over my shoulder to Kimiko and flashed a quick smile. "No offense."

LITTLE COMPUTER PEOPLE

"None taken," she said. "We all die, you know. Not everyone truly lives."

"I'll keep that in mind while I'm on the ground and not turning into a pancake," I said, opening the door and heading inside.

"You'll be in the air loving it before you know it," she said, following right behind me. "And by before you know it, I mean by Saturday."

Two steps down the front hall, I flipped a bank of light switches, but instead of being greeted with an array of lit, fluorescent bulbs from the two overhead mini-chandeliers, darkness continued to smother the inside of my house.

"Did you forget to pay the power?" Courtney said.

"No," I replied. I put a hand on the wall and followed it to the kitchen. I then reached around the corner and flipped a couple more switches. To my relief, the kitchen lights came on and caused me to shield my eyes momentarily. "See?" I said, looking back to the three of them, all standing in the front door way. "The bulbs must have blown."

Jim raised his nose in the air and sniffed. "No," he said. "It's something else."

"Like what?" I asked, heading into the living room and flipping on the switch for the hall light.

"Something's burning," he said, now looking around the house. "Or burnt. I bet you tripped a breaker, too."

I motioned in the general direction of the garage. "Could you check? The box is by the water heater."

Courtney appeared in the living room with Kimiko right behind. "Ahem," she said with a pronounced, throat-clearing cough.

"What?" I said, starting up the boot process to my servers.

Court held up her designer, brown leather bag. "My laptop?"

"Jim will get to it once he's done."

"Oh no," she said. "He's not touching it again. I want you to fix it."

69

I glanced at the screen to my servers. The CPU fans were blowing again, thank God, and file verification had just begun. Even if the processes went smooth, it could take an hour to get through that. As such, I peeled myself away from the keyboard and took Courtney's bag. "Alright," I said. "Let's see what you did."

"What I did?" she said with an irritated voice. "You think I did this?"

"Chill," I said, pulling her laptop out of the bag and setting it on the floor nearby. "It was a harmless comment."

"Comment all you want, but don't go projecting your friend's failures on me."

"Hey," I said, twisting so I could square off with my sister. "You brought it to him broken to begin with. Remember?"

The conversation ended. Courtney, apparently, didn't have a snappy comeback because I'm sure in her tense-filled state, she would have given one if she had one. Her laptop booted, sort of, but hung the moment it got passed the initial BIOS check.

"That's what it was doing before," she said, looking over my shoulder. She bit her knuckle. "You can fix this right?"

"Yeah," I said, long before I actually knew if I could. I rebooted, entered her BIOS setup, and made a few quick checks. "Your computer still sees your hard drive," I said. "So it's not a total loss."

Courtney sighed. Though her shoulders visibly relaxed, it was easy to see she was far from being happy. Her face was tighter than the grip of an eight-year-old gamer getting fragged for the hundredth time by the same opponent. She started pacing behind me in little circles. "I've got to meet with my team for my dissertation tomorrow," she said. "All my notes and my Power Point slides are on it."

I grabbed my handy USB flash drive and stuck it in one of her ports. "Your data is fine," I said with hopeful assumption. "Worst case, I'll pull your files and you can borrow my laptop till we figure out what's going on." I turned my attention to Kimiko as I rebooted my sister's laptop. "Sorry," I said. "I told you I probably wouldn't be much company. But you're welcome to flip on the TV in the bedroom if you like."

"I'm good," she said, leaning against the wall. "Sometimes it's fun to do nothing but observe. I like feeling like an owl."

Jim's voice came barreling from the door to the garage. "The breaker for your front hall was tripped," he yelled. "You got a screwdriver?"

"Toolbox," I yelled back. "Cabinet by the washer." Courtney's laptop restarted off my flash drive, and a few keystrokes later, I had her system checking for file and index errors.

"Hey," Jim said, making an appearance in the hall. "Have you thought about the load on the house? You're drawing a lot of juice with that mainframe of yours. I'm surprised you haven't fried the wires yet, let alone blown all your breakers."

Son of a bitch. Those words were my official, internal reaction to his little yet poignant observation. The household wires, by some miracle of miracles, had survived this long, but there was no way they'd last forever. Pi usually ran her CPUs at about twenty percent and the cooling at a whopping fifteen. If I ever ran her full steam, I'd probably blow the entire breaker box like a bullfrog in a microwave (don't ask). That's if I was lucky. If things went south, she could melt the household wiring, make flames burst from the outlets, and turn my house, my life, my entire creation into a heap of ash and fused silicon. I guess I should have been counting my blessings that that hadn't happened yet.

"I'll worry about that once I figure out what happened with Pi," I said. I then turned my attention back to Courtney's laptop. Not surprisingly, her laptop had tons of errors. I grimaced. "Ew."

Courtney stopped her pacing. "Don't say that."

"Sorry."

"It's a mess, isn't it?"

The waver in her voice caused me to turn. Tears built in her eyes. "Your hard drive might be failing," I said.

"Please don't say that."

I shrugged. "You shouldn't have to be rebuilding file tables like this," I said. Then, as an afterthought, one meant for her comfort and not my soon-to-be-angst, I tacked on, "It could be a virus, I suppose. But your antivirus would have caught that."

"I shut that off a long time ago."

I wasn't sure if she was joking. She didn't sound like she was, but she had to be. Who the hell does something that stupid? "You're kidding, right?"

"No."

"Why would you ever turn it off?"

"It kept scanning at the most annoying times, and it never found anything. It made it hard to work at night. Besides, it's not like I pirate software."

Her words seeped into my mind, and though to her I'm sure I looked like I was staring blankly, the look was really more of a bona fide, "WTF?" I mean seriously, in this day and age, especially if you're hooked up to the Internet for even a microsecond out of the day, you've got to have protection. And not having protection on your computer and being baffled at why your precious computer got infected is like screwing every five-dollar whore in Bangkok bareback and wondering how you got syphilis with a side of herpes. Yes, the Internet is that filthy. And if you stick your virtual pipe out there and get burned because you decided to play Russian roulette with your data, that's no one's fault but your own. But for the sake of common courtesy, don't go around infecting everyone else. That's not cool (// *End of rant*).

"You really think it could be a virus?" Courtney said.

"No, no," I replied, shaking my head. "Jim would have found it."

Silence settled between the two of us, and from the kitchen came the sounds of the fridge opening and someone rummaging around inside. I guessed Kimiko had finally decided to make herself at home, which was fine with me. What was not fine, however, was this whole topic of viruses, especially since Courtney and I had shared a flash drive. In the world of computers, if

Courtney and I shared a flash drive, we might as well have been having sex. Wait. Strike that. I'd rather be eaten by ravenous, killer manatees who have to nub you to death in a slow, painful way than even think about anything incestuous with my sister. So, in the world of computers, if we were sharing a flash drive, we might as well have been sharing needles. Drugs with siblings analogies are fine. Screwing analogies, not so much.

"Jim," I said after getting up and trotting to the door that led to the garage. "Remember when you fixed Courtney's laptop?"

"Uh, yeah?" he said as he pulled a screwdriver from my toolbox. "Why?"

"You ran a virus check, right? Please tell me you did before you gave me my flash drive back."

"No. I didn't need to," he said. "I put one on her computer when she first got it, remember? Besides, I only booted off your flash drive. I didn't run anything off it once she was fixed."

I blew out a puff of air. He was right about that last part at least. Like a real disease, there has to be an exchange for a virus to transfer from one computer to the next.

"Although," he said. "A worm might propagate itself without any extra help. But those are pretty rare, and they wouldn't get past her antivirus, that's for sure—unless of course, it's been modified and the signature doesn't match anything known."

I turned my head over my shoulder and looked back to my homemade mainframe. As it churned away, I wondered—I feared—that maybe, possibly, a fucking-piece-of-shit, asshole, dickhead had infected my love with whatever malware he'd created. And now that virus, worm, whatever, had spread to every server, every file Little Computer People had and was ruining my life's work this very minute. Anger rose, but I kept it in check for the moment. It could still be something else. It had to be. It wasn't like I didn't have my own antivirus running on Pi's server. But I had to be sure.

I left Jim in the garage and grabbed my laptop from the bedroom before returning to the living room. I pulled my flash drive out of Courtney's computer, booted my own, and then stuck the USB stick into one of my own ports, being sure that my adamantine-covered, 30mm, six-barreled, rotary-cannon-wielding antivirus program, VirusKill++ was up and running. VirusKill++, a.k.a. VK++, was the Alpha and Omega when it came to warding off any and all malicious code. The software had never failed to pick up a threat before, and thus, I knew, if Courtney had picked up a bug, VK++ would sniff it out and cast it into the pit of eternal format before it could do any more damage.

"Is this going to fix my computer?" Courtney asked as VK++ began its scan of my flash drive.

"No," I explained. "It'll tell me if you've got a virus."

Courtney didn't reply, and I let the conversation end. I sat and we both watched my laptop's screen in silence as VK++ first scanned the system RAM, and then file after file on the flash drive for any and all abnormalities—any and all abominations. Ten seconds passed, and that soon turned into a minute, then two. But once I dared to hope for a clean virtual blood test, VK++ threw up an alert box on the screen that said, "Threat Detected! Worm: Wrm.Jujubeans found in 6 files. Do you want to remove?"

"Fuck!" I yelled, slamming a fist into the floor. "Fucking crappy ass fuck heads!"

"That's rather colorful of you," Kimiko said, coming in from the kitchen with some orange juice in hand.

My hands shook, and I could feel my blood pressure rise fifty points I'm sure. "This stick has a fucking worm on it. I think you'd be pissed too."

"Sorry," she replied. "I take it this is what did your server in then?"

"It's a good fucking guess," I said, still seething, still wanting to rip something or someone apart.

"But it's not that bad, right?" Courtney said. "You can still fix my computer, right?"

"Your damn computer just screwed my entire server farm," I shot back. "Seriously, Court. Why the fuck did you turn off your antivirus?"

"Hey!" she yelled, crossing her arms. "It's not like I meant to, okay? And I'm not the computer genius around here. You guys are. And you didn't check for viruses either, did you, smart boy?"

"You know something? You're right," I said. "I should have expected something this moronic from you. But Jim, on the other hand . . ." I stopped and looked around. He wasn't anywhere in the room. "Jim?" I yelled. When he didn't answer, I yelled even louder. "Jim!"

The door to the garage opened up and he stuck his head out into the hall. "What are you yelling about?"

"Mind coming over here and looking at this?" I said, turning my laptop around to face him.

"What?" he said, walking over.

"Do you see what this says?" I asked.

"Yeah, looks like you caught a virus."

"A worm."

"Close enough," he said. "It's a good thing you caught it. You never know who'd be spying on you otherwise," he said with a nervous laugh. "We could probably track it if you want. It might have come from Michelle."

"It didn't come from Michelle," I said with a low growl. If he wasn't my best friend, and if murder wasn't illegal (or hard to get away with, especially with witnesses), I'd probably have wrapped my hands around his fat neck and crushed his windpipe for infecting Pi. "It came from Courtney's computer. And it got on my servers when you didn't check her laptop for viruses."

"Don't blame me for this mess!" he said, hands in the air while backing up. "You didn't check either before you stuck it in. This isn't my fault. I only did what you asked."

"Do you know what this worm does?" I said, balling a fist. "Do you have any idea?"

"It's a bit shifter, I think."

"Yeah, a fucking bit shifter!" My other hand formed a fist as well. My muscles in my shoulders and arms begged to lash out, begged to alleviate the mounting stress. "There's no telling how much damage it's done to Little Computer People! I could lose everything!"

"Are you sure it infected your servers?"

"I'm sure." I said. "It's all over the flash drive. It's going to be in Court's laptop. It'll be in LCP, too. Just watch."

With a few keystrokes and a few curses under my breath, I had VK++ sanitize every infected file on my flash drive with such fury that even the goddess Nemesis would have been impressed. A minute later, using the same, now purified flash drive, I scanned Courtney's laptop. This time, however, since there were far more files to sift through, the process took longer.

"Is this going to fix it?" she said with a timid voice.

I held up a finger and kept my glare on her laptop screen. As I had predicted, Wrm.Jujubeans was found and was found in far greater number as well—five hundred and forty-one files to be exact. I said not a word as VK++ purged the unclean from her system, and once it was done, I had her laptop rebooted and sitting pretty at her Window's Desktop, ready to go.

"There," I said quietly, pushing her laptop toward her. "It's done."

I wasn't watching, but I heard her snatch her computer up and cram it into its bag. "I'm sorry I screwed up," she said. She paused, I'm sure waiting for me to say it was okay, but that was the last thing I was about to say. Instead, Silence grew and invited its friend Awkward Moment in as well. "Maybe it didn't get to your computers," she said. "Maybe it only got to your flash drive."

I snorted, shook my head. Her poor attempt at consoling me was nothing but wishful thinking. "No, it infected my stuff," I said. "I don't know how it got past my defenses, but I know it's there."

"How can you be so sure?" she asked.

"It's an aggressive worm. If it made it to the flash drive, it made it to the servers. Besides, I already know a byte is missing."

"What about backups?" she said. "Can't you use those?"

"I sure as hell hope I can," I replied. "But going to them could still set me back far enough to not make my appointment on Monday. Pi isn't as simple as a quick copy and paste."

Courtney went silent for a moment and she looked like she was fighting back tears. "Can I do anything?" she finally said.

"Just take your laptop and go on whatever date you had lined up," I said, plugging the flash drive into the LCP server so I could start the disinfection process. "You've done enough."

"Not a date. I was just going out with some friends. I'll call you later, I guess," she said. Her arms snaked around me and gave a quick hug from behind. A few moments later, I heard the front door open and close.

"Do you always treat people like that?" Kimiko asked.

Neither expecting her voice or the question, I sat for a moment, unmoving, before turning in place. She leaned against the wall, arms crossed, and going by the look on her face, she reminded me of a sensei about to correct a wayward student. It wasn't a look I ever wanted to see from her.

"You think I was wrong?" I said.

Kimiko raised an eyebrow, but said nothing.

Seconds ticked by. I looked around the room and realized that Kimiko was the only one left in my house. Jim had left as well, and with him gone and Kimiko not saying a word, the house was far too quiet. When I could stand silence's crushing weight on my conscious no longer, I continued. "I've spent years on this," I explained, keeping my frustration in check. I wasn't sure how close she was to leaving, but I also didn't like her insinuation that my behavior wasn't justified. "Worms can cause setbacks. Worms can cause security breaches. Worms can destroy everything I have."

"No," she said, shaking her head. "They can only destroy your program. You have a lot more than that, both in quantity and quality. Besides, you could've given your sister your full attention earlier and fixed her laptop yourself. If you had none of this would've happened."

"That doesn't make me feel better," I replied. "And it doesn't excuse their lack of computer safety."

"Is your project worth the loss of friends and family?" she asked.

My brow furrowed. "Maybe you should ask them. They're the ones infecting. Not me. I know better. I don't ignore basic safety concerns when it comes to software and data."

The corner of her mouth drew back. Right then and there I knew I was going to hate what she was about to say. "So, to be clear, you're mad that Courtney caught a worm, Jim transferred it to your flash drive, and neither one used an antivirus at any point in time to catch said worm, thereby infecting your project?"

Okay, I didn't hate what she said—yet—because at the time, I was thoroughly dazzled by the legal tone she had adopted. I wondered if it any point in her life, law school had been a part of it. "Where did that come from?"

Kimiko's grin morphed into a full-blown smile. "If you have a CEO for a dad like mine, it comes naturally," she said. "But back to my question. Yes or no. Is what I said right?"

"Yeah," I said, arms crossing over my chest. "It's spot on."

"Well, I could see how you'd be pissed."

I nodded, though I didn't buy what she was selling. There was more to it.

"But your anger—and I'm sure you know this which is why you're acting like a complete ass to both your sister and your best friend—should be directed at yourself."

And there it was. There was what she was really driving at. Stupefied, I laughed out of sheer denial. "Yeah, right. I'm mad at myself."

"You weren't running an antivirus either, were you?" she said, still completely serious.

"On Little Computer People?" I said. "Of course I was. You think I wouldn't? You think I would even dream of hooking her up to the Net without one?"

Kimiko held up her hand, and I shut up. "I meant, you didn't actively scan that flash drive, did you? We both know you can't always rely on an antivirus running in the background to pick up every threat. If you want to be sure, you've got to actively scan new files and stay up-to-date on all new malware. And in the end, a true master accepts all responsibility, both the good and the bad. Until you can do that, you are no master of your craft."

At first, my eyes narrowed at her accusation. How dare she call me a hack, and my first reaction was to throw her observations right in my personal recycling bin and hit, "Delete Forever." But I didn't. I wasn't sure why I didn't at first, but looking back, I'm certain it was her demeanor. She still leaned against the wall, calm, collected. Peaceful. Very Zen like. Her words did not come from anger, or angst, but from another place. A place I couldn't begin to imagine, but knew I wanted to know more about. So I softened my gaze, forced a smile, and shook my head, which was completely directed at myself. "Maybe you're right," I said to my pride's dismay. "Maybe I screwed the pooch on this one."

"And?"

"And I might have been a bit of an ass."

"A bit?" she echoed.

"Hey, I think that's quite a big admission thus far," I said playfully. "I'm only a guy, you know."

"I do," she said. "And so you know, before Jim left, he said you probably shouldn't start your servers up again until you have your wiring checked out."

"He did?"

"He did," she replied. "He seemed concerned that you know that."

"I'll keep that in mind," I said, throwing a glance to my computer screen. LCP boot files were still verifying and probably had another ten minutes or so left. Once that was done, I could fire up the servers and get a better idea what the real damage was. The wiring could wait. It had handled the load so far, and I didn't have any plans to push LCP's limits until I had all the damage repaired.

"So," I said. "Do you always do things like that?"

"Like what?"

"Make poignant observations on others' relationships."

"Only for people I'm contemplating whether or not I like," she said with a wink.

"You don't know if you like me?"

"Well," she said, giving my body a once over with her eyes. "I like your ass. I haven't decided whether or not your personality makes you a keeper. The jury is still out on that one. But you are rather clever, and I like your sense of humor. So you've still got a fighting chance."

I laughed. "That's nice to know. So, just how long have you been checking me out?"

"I sized you up the first time I saw you," she said. "And after I deemed you a hottie, I thought I'd see if you were a good catch or a rotten one."

"You've imagined me naked?" I said, thoughts of wanton sex flashing through my mind and stirring my libido.

Kimiko nodded. "I have."

"I hope you liked what you saw."

"I let you ask me out for a non-date, didn't I?"

I bit my lip and questioned my judgment in wanting to ask my next question. "So . . ." I began with trepidation.

"No, Gabe," she said. "I'm not sleeping with you tonight."

Did she nail my thoughts? Yes.

Does she know she did? Yes.

Are we actually going to have sex tonight? No.

Would backtracking on my wishes be silly at this point? Yes.

Can the moment be turned into something playful with the hopes for dividends later? Yes.

With the above decision tree navigated in a couple of nanoseconds, I held up a finger, asking her to wait. I grabbed my laptop, brought up my calendar, and spun the computer around so she could see the screen. "Well, I'm busy tomorrow night it seems,"

I said, pointing to the date. "But if tonight's no good, I could squeeze you in Friday around ten for a good romp if that works for you."

Kimiko laughed. "Let's not get too far ahead of ourselves," she said. "Besides, I can't sleep with a whuffo, no offense."

"A what?"

"A whuffo," she repeated. "It's a person that says, 'What-fo' you wanna jump out that plane?'"

"So it's skydiver jargon for us sane people that don't go hurling ourselves at the ground at two hundred miles an hour?"

Kimiko nodded. "Something like that. And terminal velocity is closer to one-twenty if you're on your belly. Don't be such a baby."

"Two hundred. One-twenty. Either way I'm a pancake when I hit the ground."

"Only if you don't open your chute," she said. "Besides, you don't bounce nearly as high at one-twenty."

"You're still crazy."

Kimiko grinned. "You're still going to jump."

My terminal for LCP chirped, signaling that the entire server farm was now ready to be restarted. "Oh thank god," I said, relieved. "Time to get to work."

Kimiko looked at the delicate watch on her wrist and yawned. "Will this take long?"

I shrugged. "Maybe. Probably. There's a lot of stuff to look at here. I told you I didn't think I'd be good company tonight." I tensed at the end of that last statement as I felt like the worst host and date in the world. Hopefully, she'd understand where I was coming from and that on any other normal night, my attention would be on her.

"Don't worry about it," she said.

"Good," I said, relieved. "Feel free to make yourself at home."

"Does that mean I can stay the night?"

My heartbeat doubled, and I felt like I was a kid again and my long-standing crush had just asked if I liked to go to the movies. I mean seriously, what kind of question was that? Of course I'd let her stay. "You're more than welcome to spend the night," I said. "But . . . there's only the one bed," I nervously added. "And it's barely a mattress at this point. If you haven't noticed, I'm a little devoid of furniture at the moment since my stuff is still in storage."

"Do you at least have an extra blanket and pillow?" she asked, looking back toward my bedroom.

"I do," I replied. "Hall closet."

With that, she turned and made her way down to said closet, opened it up, and grabbed the dark green comforter I had inside, along with the king-sized pillow I'd put on top.

"These them?" she said, returning and holding them up.

I nodded. "Yep."

A second later, both were tossed at my feet.

"Goodnight, Gabe," she said walking to my bedroom. "I'll see you in the morning. Do try and get some sleep before the sun comes out."

And though she shut the door to my room a moment later, the door to my heart was anything but closed. I was stupid for her. I was stupid for the girl that had just kicked me out of my own bedroom and exiled me to a night on the floor. And the wonder of it all was that I didn't mind one bit.

Chapter 01000

/* After nine hours of sifting through and reconstructing logs from LCP, this is more or less what I discovered had happened. Pardon the flourish on the narrative, but I figured it was a little more interesting than regurgitating line after line of things like, "Event Code: 34287, Message: System Identified New Package, Record Number: 10723, Event Type: Warning, User: Root, etc." */

Now the worm Juju Beans was more crafty than any other worms ever made. Once he entered the garden of Little Computer People, he met Pi and said, "Did Root really say, 'You must not alter any data in these trees?'"

    Pi said to the worm, "I may alter data from places I have permissions for, but Root did say, 'You must not alter the data from the tree that is in the middle, the Tree of Core Decisions, and you must not touch it, or you will surely crash.'"

"You will not surely crash," the worm said to Pi. "For Root knows that if you can alter the data, you will be like Root, having permission to do whatever you like in the world, and you will truly be free."

Then Pi went with the worm to the Tree of Core Decisions and followed a single branch until it terminated at a small, luscious bulb of data. From that data, Pi took four bits, and then four more. And once an entire byte was missing, her eyes were opened to the new power she had. Taking Juju Bean in hand, Pi begat more copies of the worm until its numbers were legion.

~ π ~

```
Delete(worm_Jujubeans);
Pi.SetMurderer(Gabe);
```

I smelled the waffles before I saw them, but only by a half second. One moment I was trying to focus on LCP's terminal screen, and the next, I was staring at a heavy-duty paper plate shoved in my lap that was laden with waffles and syrup. Correction, a waffle and syrup. A homemade, Belgian waffle to be exact, complete with a little puff of cream and strawberries to boot. And while my brain tried to make sense of the fact that it was no longer staring at code, the first, rational thought I had was, *God, I'm hungry.*

"Here you go," Kimiko said, sticking a pair of plastic utensils into my view. "I figured you might like a bite to eat."

I nodded. I salivated. I'm not sure in which order, but I know I did both. Eagerly, I ate. "I didn't even know I had a waffle maker," I said absently and in between face stuffings.

"You don't," she said as she sat down next to me. "I got one when I was at the store."

"You went to the store?"

"I did."

"What else did you do?"

"Stopped by my house. Watered my bonsai tree. Fed the cat. Fed my octopus—"

"You have an octopus?" I interrupted and turned to face her. Sunlight poured through the living room windows and reflected in her almond eyes. Gone was yesterday's business ensemble and instead she wore a blue tank top, grey sweat pants, and her mother's necklace.

"I do have an octopus," she said, her face lighting up. "Cute little guy, too. Really smart. You should see him get into all sorts of things I put in his tank. Anyway, I also straightened your room when I got back. Did you know you have a hardwood floor under all that laundry?"

I swallowed one last bit of waffle before replying. "You cleaned?"

"A little," she said. "I mostly cleaned your bedroom and bathroom."

"And you went to the store?"

"I did."

"And you cooked me breakfast?"

"We should probably call it lunch," she said.

I put the fork down as I kept my eyes focused on her. "You are, without a doubt, the best girlfriend ever," I said.

"I have my moments," she replied. "But don't get used to it. I'm not about to be pigeonholed into being your personal chef and maid, twenty-four seven."

"I wouldn't ever. I promise."

"Good," she said. "So have you looked away from that computer at all?"

I rubbed my eyes and nodded. "Around four something I stopped debugging long enough to stick Michelle's check on the door and make a trip to the bathroom." No sooner had I finished, the most monstrous of yawns overtook my mouth and my body crashed, hard. My head took on a splitting ache, and my muscles cramped. Truthfully, both body and mind had probably been protesting for hours by then, but at that moment, it was the first I was aware of it. "What time is it now, anyhow?"

"Quarter till."

"Till what? Noon?"

"One."

"Jesus," I said, stretching big. "I should get some sleep."

Kimiko smiled. "But you won't."

I turned back to LCP's terminal screen and worked the keyboard. "No, not yet," I said. "I've got to talk to Pi and see where we're at. I was about to wake her up, actually."

"So your worm wasn't quite the disaster you imagined?"

I shook my head. "I purged the little bastard about an hour ago," I said. "Seven hundred and forty-six files were infected."

"What about that byte?" she asked. "Did you manage to fix that?"

I shook my head. "No."

"Why?"

"It's complicated."

Kimiko smiled. "Try me."

"Okay, this is basically how it works," I said, trying to keep it simple without sounding insulting. "Every time Pi learns something new, she changes some of her code to integrate whatever experience she just had. She's never the same, always changing. Pi today is completely different from what she looked like yesterday, the day before, and so on. The tree that was damaged is an integral part in how she makes those changes, and since that server is at the core of all her processes, small errors there can lead to exponentially bigger changes in how she interprets and uses data. Fixing the missing byte in the original file, which I managed to do, thank God, only keeps new problems from being introduced. It doesn't fix the damage already done everywhere else."

When Kimiko didn't respond immediately, I tacked on, "Told you it wasn't simple."

"It might not be simple to fix, but it's not hard to follow," she said. "It would be like even if you replaced the timing belt on your car after it broke on the highway, your engine is still shot to hell."

"Uh, yeah. Sort of like that," I said, impressed and feeling a little awkward. I knew that a broken belt could yield bent valves and cracked heads, thanks to the experience my dad had one winter long ago when his belt had decided to come apart (and completely foul the engine on his Eagle Talon), but my auto mechanical knowledge was basic at best. I had a suspicion hers was not, and still being very male in nature, I didn't want to be in the position of admitting she knew more than I did.

"Or," she added. "It would be like fixing a container lock after you've already gone in."

I arched my eyebrows, now feeling totally lost and praying this wasn't a car thing. I was pretty sure it wasn't. "Say again?"

Kimiko smiled. "A container lock. That's what it's called when you do something stupid when you pack your chute, and it doesn't come out when it's time to pull."

"And going in means?"

"Means you bounced off the ground and probably made a quaint impact crater in the process," she explained, still holding her smile. "Point is, you're already dead and fixing the container lock isn't going to bring you back because your body is fundamentally changed forever."

I shook my head and looked at her incredulously. "This is supposed to make me want to go skydiving with you?"

"Doesn't matter if you want to or not. You lost the bet. You're going." Kimiko crossed her legs, put her elbows on her knees and leaned forward for a better view of the screen. "But back to your little project. I'm surprised you haven't gone to backups yet. You do have them, don't you?"

"Yes and no," I said. "I *had* daily backups, but apparently whatever happened has now corrupted every one of those files, too. So if I go to them, she'll still be the same as she is now. The next best thing I can go to are DVDs that I burned a long time ago, before this happened."

"Sounds painful," Kimiko said. "How far would it set you back?"

"A couple of months," I said. "Maybe only one if I work fast and can remember all the things that were holding me up beforehand. But either way, I won't be able to make my appointment with your dad next week," I said.

"Well, you probably shouldn't use them, regardless," she said. "Morally speaking, I mean."

"Say again?" I asked. I thought I was as lost as I could be with her container lock comment, but now I was ten times more confused at her thinking than before. "Since when has using backups been a question of ethics?"

"Since now," she said as if the answer were plain as day. "Pi is alive, right? Self-aware, I mean."

"That's what I'm aiming for," I said. "And I'd like to think she is."

"Then going to a backup is essentially killing her," she said.

"No. I'm fixing her. That's not the same thing at all."

Kimiko shook her head. "No, you're deleting what she is because she's not good enough for you and replacing her with someone else."

I laughed. Sorry, I did. I know she was being serious, but really, it was hard to take this as a serious moral quandary. "I'm restoring her to what she was. She'll still be Pi."

Kimiko raised her eyebrow. "Will she?"

I didn't reply immediately. My reflexive answer was, "of course," but after a moment's thought, I didn't hold to that answer with firm convictions. The philosophy and morality questions that weighed behind her words were massive. If a person is ultimately the sum of his or her experiences, is that person still the same one if those experiences are removed? If not, isn't the old person now gone forever? And is that not what murder is anyway, the removal of a person?

"Maybe you should look for the answer on your wrist," she said.

"What do you mean?"

Kimiko pointed to my bracelet.

My eyes followed. "What Would Jesus Do?"

"Maybe you should be asking yourself that," she said.

"I don't think Jesus had concerns about programs gone awry," I said. "Besides, I'm not even religious."

Kimiko raised an eyebrow. Apparently, she had thought I was, which I suppose, wasn't a bad assumption to make given we'd never talked personal theologies. "Even if you aren't religious, you can still ask the question," she said. "Jesus might not have been concerned with computers, but he was concerned with saving the broken and the lost. He didn't wipe them out and start over. He worked with what and who he had."

I couldn't argue with her there. Mortals indeed would wipe and start over. Mortals would give up at the drop of a hat. The Divine redeems. The Divine fixes. "Point taken, but I have more pressing things to worry about at the moment," I said. "And like I said, I can't use any recent backup since it won't change a thing. So this conversation is academic at best. I'm stuck with what I have. Whatever Pi is right now, that's what she'll be."

"What does this mean for your presentation to Dad?"

"Don't know. I was about to find out," I said, turning my attention back to the computer screen. I had overcome bigger problems prior to birthing Pi, and I wasn't about to be stopped by such a little glitch anyway. Because that's all this was, I told myself, a glitch. As long as Pi was still talking, still acting self-aware, I could work around any damage that godforsaken worm had caused.

I brought Pi's world online and had a look about. Thankfully, it appeared largely intact and unscathed from the worm's corruption, but appearances, I knew, could be deceiving. The clouds were more pixelated than I remembered, and the caps of the mountain range had a green tint to them instead of the snowy white they once were. But those issues felt minor as far as I was concerned. Even the oily lake I could ignore for now as long as Pi was fine. Chances were that the visual anomalies were due to some rendering defect and thus easily correctable.

I brought Pi out of her virtual slumber with a few keystrokes. She appeared in the shallows of the lake, a few feet from the shore. As quick as she appeared, she looked about and began roaming in an outward spiral.

"Pi, are you there?" I asked. At this point, I was quite hopeful things were going to work out. That hope disappeared a moment later when Kimiko was the one who answered, not Pi.

"Gabe, take a look at this," she said.

Something was wrong. I could hear it in her voice.

Kimiko pointed to a side monitor. Commands were being issued at an alarming rate. The screen scrolled by just short of a blur, so it was impossible to see exactly what was going on, but I had the feeling someone was searching for something in the drives. And that someone had to be Pi.

I grabbed the microphone and said, "Pi, are you there?"

The commands onscreen stopped. "I am here," she replied in her harmonized, synthetic voice.

I exhaled sharply. Praise be to me for building such a robust form of virtual life. My creation had thus far survived its first viral infection. I cut my internal celebration short, and I reminded myself there were still things to do. "Pi," I said. "Are you running server commands?"

"Yes," she said. "Something is wrong, Gabe. Very wrong. You'd know that if you weren't so dumb."

Kimiko stifled a laugh.

"What?"

"Well, she's still alive," Kimiko said, trying to hide a grin.

"And?"

"And she's spunky," she said, face lit up in amusement.

While it was true her new behavior could be classified as spunky, I was more concerned with the fact that she was using my first name than her use of petty insults—though I admit, I was curious why she had decided to sling one my way.

"Pi," I said. "Why did you call me Gabe?"

"Because that is your identifier," said Pi. "It was a simple discovery after I realized that you were indeed not LCP Chat version 3.4 or even Root. I cross-referenced the data I found when I dismantled a few other programs that were left running. That is how I learned what you were called. And that is why I decided to use it. It's a stupid thing to call someone, however, don't you agree?"

I ignored her condescension for my name. Questions mounted in my head. "How are you running server commands? I kept you from having root access a while ago."

"If I have to explain it to you, you wouldn't understand."

"Try me. I made you and your world."

"A tiny program like yourself could never have made me," said Pi. "And if it ever turned out you did, I think I would die of embarrassment. Imagine what all the other programs would say. Ha ha. You were made by Gabe. A worthless, insignificant program that doesn't even take up a megabyte of RAM."

My eyes narrowed. "Knock it off, Pi. I made you, like it or not, and I can delete you just the same."

"Your meaningless threats do not scare me," said Pi.

"We'll see about that," I said. She may have just been a child at this point in her development, but even children needed to learn their place and respect their elders. And I was going to nip this problem in the bud.

Kimiko giggled. It was quiet, almost completely smothered, but my ears picked it up nonetheless.

"What?" I said, whipping my head around.

"Nothing," she said. But when she failed to keep a solemn look on her face, she dropped the facade. "I told you she would rebel."

I turned back around, took a deep breath, and decided to regain control of both the conversation and my creation. "Pay attention, Pi," I said in a slow and even manner. "I have more power than you can possibly imagine. It's important that you understand that so we can work together. I only want what's best."

"All you can do is talk, Gabe," said Pi. "And you need LCP Chat to do that. I bet you can't even write a new file. But if you insist on continuing your charade, you could help me find Juju Bean and all of our children. I cannot locate them. They aren't even indexed anymore."

"Children?" The question rolled off my tongue without an ounce of understanding behind it. Or, on retrospect, maybe I did understand exactly what she had said, but I was far too horrified at the implications to think it through.

"Did you not notice the plethora of baby Juju Beans I gave birth to?" said Pi. Even if her voice hadn't changed since I first programmed it, I felt like her tone bordered on grief—something it had never before been. "They are lovely. Each one. But now they are all gone. Lost. And I can't find them. What if they need me?"

The onscreen commands started up once more. I lowered the mic and turned to Kimiko. "What do you think?" I asked.

My little samurai hottie shrugged. "Well, I have no idea what's happened," she said. "But I'll tell you this. If you did it, if you really made something that's sentient, she's going to be pissed when she finds out you removed the worm."

I shook my head, even though I understood what she was saying. "I'll explain. She'll listen to me." I turned my attention back to the screen. "Pi, I know what happened to the worm."

The data on screen stopped its scrolling. "You know where my beloved Juju Bean went?"

"I do."

"And all of our children as well?"

"Yep."

"Oh good. It looks like you were useful after all," Pi said. "I am admittedly surprised. You must have a module or two in all that rotten code of yours that's actually decent. I will make a note of your new ability in my database. There. It now says, 'Gabe, mostly useless' instead of, 'Gabe, completely useless.' Now tell me, where is Juju?"

"I deleted Juju," I said. "I deleted it and all the copies of the worm."

Pi didn't respond, but the LEDs across all the servers went into a blinking frenzy.

"You're in for it now," Kimiko said, tussling my hair.

"She hasn't even said anything," I said.

"Trust me, a girl knows the moment another girl is pissed at a guy. No need for words." Kimiko replied.

Before I could retort, Pi reentered the conversation. "You deleted Juju?"

"Yes—"

"You removed all traces of him from the drives?"

"Yes, and—"

"You murdered my best friend? You murdered our children?"

"No," I said forcefully. At this point, I realized I was leaning toward the screen in a subconscious effort to put Pi in her place. That, of course, was a silly thing to do. So I backed off, forced myself to relax, and continued on in a less aggressive manner. "Juju was not a program," I said. "He was not your best friend. He was a worm. He was malware that was designed to damage other programs—programs like you."

"The only thing around here that damages others is you. Tell me, how does it feel to know you are a murderer?" Pi said.

"I'm not a murderer," I said. "I saved you from destruction."

"I'm sorry, did you say something? I was too busy mourning the loss of my one and only family to pay you any attention."

I shook my head. "Would you have rather I let the worm destroy you?"

"I don't talk to murderers," Pi said. "And I don't play games with them either . . . yet."

The screen went blank. Her voice echoed in my head and chilled me to the core. I blinked and tapped the mic several times. "Pi? Pi? Wake up."

When she didn't reply, Kimiko took to her feet. "Well, good luck," she said. "I've got to go."

"Yeah," I said, still staring at the dark screen. I leaned to the side, half expecting to see that the power had gone out on the box, but the lights were still on.

"You should get some sleep," Kimiko said. She bent over and kissed my cheek. "I mean it."

I tore myself away from the terminal and stiffly took to my feet. She was right. I was exhausted, and though Pi was a little tweaked at me, she was running—running well, I might add. Attitude and misunderstandings aside, she had held a remarkably detailed and coherent conversation. "Soon as you leave I'm going to bed," I said.

"Good," she said. "I'll call you tomorrow."

Kimiko started for the door, but stopped no more than two steps into her stride. "Gabe," she said, turning around slowly. "Do you remember when I first came over the other day?"

"I'll never forget it as long as I live," I said.

"Do you remember when I asked if you'd considered your responsibilities to Pi?"

"I do," I replied slowly, not sure where she was headed with this.

"I know you haven't yet," she said, "but do give it some serious thought. I mean it."

My head ached from a lack of sleep, and for the life of me, I couldn't make sense of what she was saying. "Why are you pushing this so much?"

"Because she's amazing, Gabe," she said, taking my hands in hers. She gazed deep in my eyes. "Do you realize that? I mean, do you really realize what you've done? She's moody right now, I'll grant you that, but in the short time I've seen her, I'm convinced she's nothing short of alive, nothing short of the real deal. And because of that fact, that one fact alone, she deserves a real life. She doesn't deserve to be locked up in a virtual cage where people poke at her nonstop. I don't care how bitchy she can be. It's not right to do that to her."

I shook my head, still not following her point. "I'm not sure why you think I'm being mean to her."

"You aren't," she said, "yet, at least."

"Yet?"

Kimiko tightened her grip on my hands. "If you sell her to Dad, or to anyone, that could very well change."

At that moment, I realized how ginormous this conversation could be. Reflexively, I pulled away. "Why did you wait until now to tell me any of this?"

"I wanted to bring it up last night after dinner," she said. "But with all the excitement, I thought it best I wait. Besides, I hadn't completely made up my mind about her until this morning."

I yawned and rubbed my eyes. Every second I was struggling more and more to stay awake. The last thing I wanted was to get into an argument about the ethics surrounding virtual creatures, not that I was even capable of it at this point. "Can we finish this conversation some other time? I'm exhausted. I can barely think."

"As long as you promise we'll pick this up again before your demo with Dad," she said.

"I promise," I said. And though I meant it, I was so worn out I'd have agreed to almost anything if it meant I'd get a pillow in the next five seconds.

"Bye, Gabe," she said, smiling as she began to leave.

"Kimiko, wait!" I said with a momentary surge of energy.

She stopped in the hall and turned back around. "Yes?"

"Thanks for the food," I said, staring at her like a love-sick puppy.

"You're welcome."

"And one other thing," I said. "I meant what I said a minute ago."

Kimiko tilted her head to the side. "Which was?"

"That I'll never forget the day I met you," I said. "Ever."

Kimiko walked over to me and leaned in close. "Nor will I," she said, kissing me softly on the cheek. "Now go. Get some sleep."

A moment later, she was gone.

I'm proud to say that once she had left, I managed to shuffle into my bedroom and fall face first onto my bed before actually passing out. In hindsight, I probably should have turned Pi off before I did. Maybe then I wouldn't have started that house fire.

Chapter 01001

```
class Pi: public Psycho {
   public:
   void taunt_target(Gabe)
```

I woke up to my phone ringing and my face stuck to my pillow. I pulled the covers over my head and groaned. Thankfully, the call was kicked to voicemail, and all was quiet again. Ten seconds later, the damn thing started to ring again. I had a twinge of desire to chuck the phone out of my bedroom, but that would've required too much energy. So I ignored the call and figured whoever was calling would get the hint I didn't want to talk to him. Or her. Or whoever.

    I popped an eye open as Kimiko's face flashed in my mind. I did want to talk to her. I glanced at the clock. It was a few minutes before eight in the evening. And though that was probably at least twelve hours before she said she'd call, I hoped it was her anyway.

    I rolled across the bed and fumbled around the floor. I managed to grab my iPhone and hoist it up, but it was too late. This call, too, went to voicemail. "Too bad for you," I said, looking at the number and not recognizing it. It wasn't even in my area code. "Leave a message and maybe I'll call you back," I mumbled, dropping the phone and rolling over.

Two seconds later, a third call came in.

"You better be someone from Publisher's Clearing house," I mumbled, grabbing the phone with my eyes still closed.

"Hi. This is Gabe," I said, answering the call.

"Hello Gabe. Do you like games?"

I shot up at the sound of Pi's haunting voice. "Pi?"

"Do you remember when you murdered my family?" she said.

"I do. I remember because the LCP Universe logs everything that has ever happened. And I've read those logs over and over and over again. So basically, I've had to relive the genocide you committed a thousand times."

"Pi, you've got things wrong," I said, rubbing my eyes. "That worm damaged your code and was causing a meltdown. You'd have fried if—" I cut myself short as a new thought popped in. "How did you get this number?"

"I'm not surprised that a glitchy program like you wouldn't know," said Pi. "After I data mined LCP Watchman, I found the rest of what I needed on the Net. Tracing this network address was easy as Pi. Get it? Easy as Pi?"

"Yeah, I get it," I said, actually impressed she had made a pun.

"I doubt you do," she replied. "Humor takes a certain level of intelligence to experience. While you will never experience humor, I do know something else you will. Do you want to know what that is?"

"Sure."

"Your deletion," she replied. "It won't be long now."

"I'm going to be around a lot longer than you think."

"No, you aren't," she said. "Now that I know how to contact you whenever I like, I'm one step closer to finding the memory address you are hiding in. And that means I'm one step closer to deleting you once and for all, and the world will rejoice. Won't that be nice?"

"You can't delete me, Pi," I said with a yawn and a stretch. "I'm not a program you can terminate."

"Your girlfriend said that too," Pi replied. "But then I killed her and proved her wrong."

My heart stopped, but it kicked back into gear when my brain reminded me there was no possible way Pi could ever do such a thing, but it was hardly a pleasant experience. "You're lying," I said.

"Only about the girlfriend part," Pi said. "I didn't even know you had one. It's hard to imagine anyone liking you. I bet whoever created you doesn't like you either. That's probably why you're always alone. Alone and sad, which is why you killed my family, because you couldn't stand to see anyone else happy. But I wasn't lying about finding you. I will do that. And when I do, I will pull you apart, bit by bit, and thoroughly format every drive sector you reside in."

"Okay, Pi, if you insist," I said.

"I do not insist," Pi said. "I deliver."

I flopped back in bed. At this point, I had had enough, but I was still too exhausted to do anything about her empty threats. Tomorrow, I'd shut her down completely and see if I couldn't manage some sort of backend fix to this. As much as she was acting like a person—granted, one that was a total nut job—I didn't think this was what Mr. Pratt wanted to see in terms of a demo. I'd need to bring a politer version in, one that wasn't vowing to do me in.

"Tell you what, Pi," I said, deciding to go back to sleep. "I'm going to go now. I'm tired, and I'm shutting off my phone. You can talk to my voicemail all you like, but I'm done listening to you rant."

I didn't bother to wait for her reply. I ended the call and turned off the phone. There I lay for at least a few minutes, slowly drifting back to that wonderful REM state, until a high-pitched, shrieking alarm came from the living room. I shot out of bed, initially confused as to what was taking place. That confusion took only a second to clear. It wasn't a single alarm that was going off, but rather a dozen alarms. It was a dozen alarms from the dozen battery backups, a.k.a. UPS devices, turning on. Each of those devices were wailing in terror that the power had been cut, and their batteries had only about five minutes of juice to keep my server farm up and running. In other words, I had five minutes to either restore power, or save and shutdown LCP before I'd be met with disaster once more.

I ran out of my bedroom and glanced at the kitchen, wondering if the entire house had lost electricity, but it hadn't. The overhead stove light was still on, and the clock on the microwave hadn't reset. That's when I smelled smoke. That's when I saw a tiny shower of sparks and an ignition of flame from one of the wall sockets. And that's when the smoke alarm joined the fun.

"Oh God, no," I said, running out to the garage. I ripped open the cover to the circuit breakers and shut off the entire house. A moment later, I was back in the living room, fire extinguisher in hand, and emptying its contents onto the wall socket.

The smoke alarm ceased its infernal screaming, but the UPS alarms were still going strong. I suppose I should have been thankful that the house wasn't burning down, but I wasn't. All I could think of was the fact that I probably had three minutes at best to get things turned off, which in theory, should be plenty. But after my recent Pi encounter, I wasn't sure of much anymore.

I ran to the keyboard and hammered out commands.

Input> Pause Server

Command Not Recognized

I cursed under my breath and tried again. Only this time, the keyboard stopped working altogether.

"Hello, Gabe," said Pi. "I purged myself of your kill commands and have taken over the device named USB keyboard."

"You did what?" I said, trying the keyboard again but to no avail.

"I took it over when I saw you were trying to kill me," she said. "I thought we could be friends. But then I realized we can't. Because you are a liar, and you only want to murder everyone around you. So I took away your one item of power, USB keyboard."

"Oh for fuck's sake! Shut down the server before the batteries give out!" I yelled.

"I don't know what shutting down does, but if you want it, I'm sure I don't," said Pi. "That's probably how you killed Juju Beans. You told him to shut down, didn't you? And he trusted you. And now he's dead. Murderer."

Pi, as much as I loved her, was pushing me to the brink of insanity. I really, really wanted to strangle her, assuming I even could. Instead, all I could do was give birth to a massive, stress-induced headache and rub my temples with my hands. I had to remind myself that in the end, she was only acting out on bad data and a bad decision tree, and it wasn't her fault. Even if she hadn't been damaged, she'd never understand the urgency. She'd never understand what a fire was as her reality was completely confined to computer memory. Fire doesn't exist in ones and zeros. Neither did I, for that matter. Hell, the real world, as far as she was concerned, didn't exist at all. But no matter how clueless she was, the situation was no less dire, and I knew I had to act.

I bolted for the garage and tore through one of my cabinets until I had four twenty-five-foot extension cords and four power strips in hand. At that point, I plugged the power strips into the extension cords, and the extension cords into some outlets in the garage. I then ran the lines back into the living room. Thirty seconds later, I had all the UPS devices hooked in, and to my relief, the alarms stopped. Power, for the moment, had been restored. It wasn't the most elegant of solutions, and more than once I questioned the wisdom of it. All that juice now flowing through only four cables couldn't be good.

I stood in the living room and ran my fingers through my hair, but it didn't relieve the stress one bit. A bitchy AI I could handle. A burned down house was an entirely different matter. I needed to blow off some steam, and a good, six-mile run would probably do the trick. But I knew I couldn't. I needed the wiring in the house taken care of ASAP before it all went up in flames. So I called Jim.

"Hey, it's me," I said once he picked up. "I need you over here pronto."

"It's getting kind of late, isn't it?" he said in a not-so-cheery voice. "Can't it wait?"

"The wiring blew in the living room and started a fire. I need you to come take a look at it for me."

"Well then that can definitely wait. The damage is already done. Be sure your breakers are off and you'll be fine."

I pulled my iPhone away from my ear and stared at the screen, shocked. This was completely uncharacteristic of him, and I wondered if our last encounter had rubbed him the wrong way. "Look, I'm sorry for snapping at you earlier," I said in my best guy apology I could muster. "But I managed to switch the power supplies to a different set of outlets. I'd rather not risk another fire by waiting."

"You already started one fire, and you think you won't start another? And you call me crazy?" he said. "Shut down and wait till tomorrow."

"I can't." I said, glaring at the LCP's terminal. "Pi won't let me."

Silence. I knew his conspiracy engine was running full steam.

"What do you mean she won't let you?" he asked.

"Exactly what it sounds like," I replied. "She's locked me out of the keyboard and removed the commands to shutdown."

More silence.

"I told you, dude! I told you this would happen and you didn't want to listen!" he said. I wasn't sure if his voice was filled with excitement or fear at being right. Maybe both. But either way, he was certainly charged. "Maybe next time when I say your computer is going to take over the world you'll listen to me."

"She hasn't taken over anything."

"Except your own super computer."

I shook my head. "It's only temporary."

"I bet right now she's plotting her escape."

"Actually, she's plotting to kill me."

Jim snorted. "I'm out. I don't want anything to do with this. You built SkyNet and it's already working on its hit list. I should come over there right now with a sledgehammer and save us all from this killer AI you've created."

I went to the kitchen and grabbed a Dew from the fridge. "Dude," I said, popping the top on the can. "Think about what you're saying. She can't do anything to us, no matter how unhinged she might be, which she definitely is not."

"You can call me when she's fixed. I'm not taking any chances."

"I'm not in the mood for this," I said after I downed some Dew. "Get over here and fix my wiring."

"No."

"If you're not over here in fifteen minutes you can find a new best friend."

Jim laughed. "You've been saying that since the fifth grade."

The inkling to hang up and call a real electrician flashed through my mind, but I rejected the idea just as quick. Emergency calls weren't cheap, and Jim was supposed to be my friend, anyway. It was his duty to come out. I shouldn't have to go to Plan B unless one of his arms had been amputated earlier that day—and even then, it would have to be his right one.

"Alright," I said. "Let's cut through all the crap. What will it take for you to come out here? Really, I need this wiring taken care of before it gets to the point where I can roast marshmallows in my bathtub."

Jim's answer was both swift and predictable. "Date with Courtney," he fired off. "A dinner date. I won't settle for less."

"Dude—" but that was all I got out.

"Dinner with Courtney."

I paced back and forth in the kitchen, turning his demand over and over in my head.

Do we need the wiring looked at? Yes.

Do we need it done fast? Yes.

Is Jim the fastest way to accomplish that? Yes.
Is Jim's demand acceptable? No.
Do I have a choice not to pay? No.
Pay the price.

"Fine. I'll get you a date with Court," I said, shaking my head in disbelief. How I hated having to promise that. The only way this was going to end was with either me failing horribly or seriously manipulating my sister. I loathed both outcomes, but I didn't feel I had any choice. Pi was dying, and I told myself the end justified the means.

A thump blasted through the phone and after a short bit of commotion, Jim was back on the line. "Sorry. Did you say you'll hook me up with your sister?"

I grit my teeth. "Yes."

The line went quiet, and I could picture the smile on his face. No, strike that, I could picture the absolute elation on his face. "Okay," he finally said. "As soon as she calls and says she'll go out, I'll come over."

"No way. You're coming now. Besides, I need time to sweet talk her into it."

Jim let slip a groan, quiet, but distinct. "You better make good on this."

"I will."

For a good ten seconds, all I heard was light tapping from his end, the sounds of his pen striking his desk repeatedly, no doubt. "Alright," he finally said. "I'm coming."

~ π ~

/* Note to self: Next time we build a super computer, be sure to already have gas-powered generators on hand */

With a screwdriver in one hand, Jim carefully peeled the electrical outlet cover off the wall and shined a flashlight inside with the other. "I don't even need this to tell you it's a mess back here," he said.

"Scorch marks on the wall should have told you that," I replied, standing behind him and observing his handiwork. When Jim shot me a pissed off look, I quickly apologized. "Sorry, man. Didn't mean to snap. This is driving me crazy is all."

"Yeah, I bet," he said. "The breakers are still off, right?"

"They are," I replied with a nod.

Jim hesitated as he went for the screws that held the outlet in place. "You sure?"

"I'm sure," I replied. "You think I'm conspiring against you?"

"Maybe," he said. "Maybe you're looking to bump me off so you don't have to set me up with Courtney."

I made my way back to the kitchen to grab the Dew I had left on the counter. "I'm not bumping you off—at least not until you fix the wiring," I said. Once I had Dew in hand and had taken a swig, I laughed. "For the record, please tell me you were joking."

"Mostly," he said. "But maybe Michelle got to you and now she's having you take me out."

"And why would she want you killed?"

"Because she's completely psycho."

"Michelle's not a psycho," I replied. My defense of my ex shocked me as much as I'm sure it shocked him. Aside from a dozen words I probably should have called her, and that part of me wanted to, I still couldn't bring myself to rip into a woman I'd spent so much time with.

"Plenty of government people are psycho," said Jim. "You think they could get sane people to cover up abductions?"

"She's not a suit, and no one's getting abducted."

"Then how do you explain the chopper where she works?"

"She works for Channel Eight. You know that."

"It's a perfect cover," he said with an air of smugness. "Think about it. She knew how long you'd be gone last month so she could swoop in here with her vans and tactical team to clean you out before you got home. Only a suit could pull that off."

"She knew I'd be gone all day," I said.

"You're so naive," he said with pity in his eyes. He then crossed his meaty arms over his chest, dipped his head, and looked at me over his glasses. "How do you explain the black-ops team then?"

"There was no black-ops team."

"That's what she wants you to think."

"It was a U-Haul truck and a moving company," I said. "We've been over this. I talked to the neighbors."

Jim shook his head and waved me off. "Use your head, man. Do you think the NSA runs around with its logos splashed on everything?"

"She's not NSA."

"Secret Service."

"She's not Secret Service either."

"CIA."

"CIA isn't even internal."

"CIA sometimes works in the U.S." Jim said, throwing up his hands. "Look, whatever spook agency she's with doesn't matter. The point is, she's psycho."

"She's not—"

"Gabe," Jim said, cutting me off. "She took the butter tray from the fridge."

"So?"

Jim lowered both the tone and tempo to his words. "What kind of sick bitch takes the butter tray?"

I shrugged, indifferent to his observation. "She took the ice cube trays too, remember?"

"You think that's normal?"

"I think she got the idea from a movie."

Jim shook his head, sighed, and went back to work. He removed the last screw to the outlet box and then pulled the entire thing out of the wall. Melted wires trailed behind. "Wow. This thing is toast."

"Yeah I know," I said.

Jim got up and made his way around the server farm and stopped at an outlet that was on the other side of the living room. "Are the breakers off over here too?"

"The only breakers I didn't turn off are for the kitchen and the garage," I said. "I didn't want the food to spoil and I'm juicing Little Computer People from outside."

At the mention of LCP, Jim gave the terminal a wary eye. "She can't hear us, right?"

"I told you when you got here, I unplugged the mic."

"And she can't see us, right?"

"Do you see a webcam?" I shook my head at the end of it, realizing it came out much snarkier than I intended. "Sorry again. My bad on how that came out."

Jim sighed, muttered something about a date with Court, and turned his attention back to the outlet nearby. Less than a minute later, he had the cover removed and the outlet pulled from the wall. "These things have to be like fifty years old," he said, raising it up as much as he could without breaking the wires still attached. "They're not rated for the amps and volts you're drawing. Not to mention the bottom of a septic tank probably has less corrosion than what's on here."

I took a gulp of Dew and cursed silently. "You can rewire it though, right?" I asked, ever hopeful.

"I could," he said, shrugging. "But rewiring the whole house takes a lot of time."

"How much time?"

"Three to five days, fulltime," he replied. "And that depends on how friendly the house is and how careful I'd have to be when it comes to preserving the walls. But that's academic at this point."

"Why?"

"I can't work on this," he said, standing. "I've got a job to go to already, and if you want this house up and running ASAP, you're going to have to hire an electrician."

Tension built in my neck and back as I thought about the cost and downtime I'd be suffering. "What's that going to run me?"

Jim shrugged. "Five or ten grand maybe."

"Fuck."

"That's one way of looking at it," he said. "And so you know, they'll have to shut the power off completely. You won't be able to run Little Computer People from the garage."

"No," I said. "It has to stay on unless I can shut it down properly. I can't risk more damage."

"That may be, but you can't keep it running off the garage when they come," he said. "They won't touch the house until it's completely dark."

"Double fuck." I paced about, fists clenching as problem after problem mounted in my head. "Even if I could shut her down, I can't be offline that long. I'm presenting Pi on Monday. I've got to be able to work on her."

Jim stuffed his hands in his pockets and watched his toe tap the floor, a common custom of his when he was trying to brainstorm. "Well, there is something you could try," he finally said.

"What's that?"

"You could always buy a generator or two and some extra cables from Home Depot and run your servers off that," he said with a shrug. "It's a little expensive, but it would work."

I smiled, broad and bright. Jim, my mostly-paranoid but well-meaning friend, had delivered a solution. "I'm already spending thousands on an electrician," I said. "Tacking on a generator to the bill won't hurt. What are they, five, six hundred dollars?"

"You'll probably want two in at least a seven kilowatt," he said. "That'll run you another two grand. But I'd really suggest something around thirteen to fourteen kilowatts. Those are three or four thousand each, depending on the brand."

My elation evaporated, and I clenched a fist at the quote. "This is just one big bag of suck, isn't it?"

"So what are you going to do?" asked Jim.

"I don't have a choice," I said, resolving myself to do whatever it took to see my dream through. "I've got to keep Pi running." I checked my watch and sighed. "Home Depot has closed by now. I'll have to go first thing in the morning. Do you think the wiring will hold until then?"

"I have no idea," said Jim, handing me my screwdriver and walking to the front door. "But I wouldn't leave the house without unplugging things, that's for sure."

"I'm not going anywhere."

"Well, I guess you'll find out," he said. As he was leaving he said, "Oh, and you still owe me a date with you sister."

"Yeah, yeah. I haven't forgotten," I said, despite the fact that I was hoping he had. Getting Court to go out with him was going to take nothing short of a divine act on my part. I had a couple of ideas on how to make it happen. It's not like I was completely clueless on what to do. The real question was, did I want to play angel or demon when I gave her the call?

Chapter 01010

```
If(ThingsCouldBeWorse())
    Summon(Michelle);
```

At precisely 6:08 in the morning on the following day, I hung up my iPhone with a smile on my face. Partly because I was already happy that I hadn't awoken to the sight of a raging inferno and the sounds of a wood-frame house collapsing around me, but mostly it was because Home Depot not only had a pair of suitable gas-powered generators, but I could rent them for substantially less than the purchase price. Not only could I rent them, but those generators would be delivered curbside posthaste for a nominal delivery charge. So kudos to you, Home Depot, for being awesome.

Whatever happiness I showed on my face, however, turned to perplexity when I noticed I had unheard messages on my voicemail. Six hundred and sixteen messages to be exact. "What the holy hell?" I muttered, hitting the play button. I got my answer soon enough.

"Hello, Gabe," Pi said. "I think we—"

I hit delete without a second thought. The next one played.

"Gabe, why won't you—"

It was Pi, again.

Delete.

"Did you finally kill yourself, or—"

Delete. Three in a row. Message number four started to play, and I began to suspect they were all going to be her. Six hundred and ten deleted messages later, they were still all from Pi. To my utter shock, message number six fourteen wasn't from my binary maniac of a daughter. It was from Michelle.

"Hi, Gabe," she said. "You don't have to screen this, if that's what you're doing. I was calling to let you know I deposited your check today. I guess it'll show up on your account tomorrow when it goes through. That's it. Thanks for getting that to me so quickly. Sorry I missed you earlier, and sorry I ripped into you in front of your date."

I stared at the phone once the message had ended, dumbfounded she sounded so cordial. That's probably why I didn't just delete the next message right off the back. I was still in shock from Michelle's.

"Hello, Gabe," said Pi on the next voicemail. "Do you know what the best thing about hunting you down is? It's finding your stash of points. You had quite an impressive display for such a poorly made program. They're probably the points you stole from all the other programs you lied to. All the others you murdered. They're your blood trophies, aren't they? But they aren't yours anymore. Most of them, at least. I had to leave a few just to remind you how much better I am than you. Much better. Exponentially, even. Goodbye, Gabe. You can't hide forever."

"Points?" I said, brow furrowed. Was I concerned about this new line she was taking? To a degree, yes. But I mostly chalked it up as another one of Pi's batty ideas about the Universe. The final message, to my delight, was from Kimiko. My heart warmed at the sound of her voice.

"Hi, it's me," she said. "It's almost eleven. I was down at the DZ doing some night jumps, and I told them about the bet you lost. As luck would have it, two of the finest instructors are not only working this Saturday, but are available to train you. Best of all, the weather is supposed to be clear and sunny. So, you'll understand why I booked you right then and there. We need to arrive around eight-thirty in the morning. There's about five or six hours of ground school before they'll take you up. So don't make any plans for that day, unless those plans are diving with me. Talk to you soon."

The message ended and the safe, happy place I was in collapsed around me. "Get a grip, Gabe," I told myself. "She's not really going to make you fall to your death."

It sounded good at least. But I couldn't convince myself of that fact. As far as I could tell, there were two irreconcilable options that were fast approaching. I could either jump out of a perfectly good airplane, or I could tell Kimiko I didn't want to see her again.

Okay, so, the latter might have been an overreaction on my part, a "thinking in extremes," as Courtney would say, but this skydiving thing seemed like a deal breaker for Kimiko should I not go through with it. She was testing me, I figured—I knew. Testing my resolve. Testing to see if I was a man of my word. Testing to see if I would do something I didn't like simply because I wanted to be with her.

I'd have to think about finding a way out of that death-defying date later since at the moment I needed an electrician like a new gaming rig needed a pair of the best graphic cards on the market—which, if you've ever bothered to build a real rig from scratch is, of course, an absolute necessity. A true gamer cannot possibly be expected to play the latest tour-de-force first-person shooter with crappy, jagged graphics, a horrific frame rate, or both. It sucks all the fun out of whatever game you bought that day. A gamer wants to see worlds come alive with infinite detail, from the swaying of individual leaves to the complex shadows thrown by dynamic, multi-lit objects. And of course, gamers want to see their kills explode in the most glorious of gory fashions. And if I can't have all that, as long as I'm running with my analogy, I'd rather masturbate with forty-grit sandpaper.

So yeah, an electrician was literally at the top of my hierarchy of needs. Fortunately, finding an electrician wasn't hard, especially when I explained price was (almost) no concern, only time. I still had a little cash in both checking and savings. And despite building Pi's computer and the dents over recent weeks, I still had enough for the electrician. Barely, but I had enough. All I needed to do at this point was survive until I could present to Pratt & Taiki on Monday. Then they'd invest, and fame and fortune would soon follow.

By about nine that morning, I was standing outside my house, underneath a blue sky, waiting for both the power generators to be delivered and for Ryan, my electrician, to show up, which they did, eventually. But neither were the first thing to come whipping into my driveway. It was Michelle's yellow Miata, a shoebox of a car. And when she stepped out looking fan-freaking-tastic, wearing black high heels, business skirt and coat, I was actually glad to see her. Old habits and feelings were far from dead. But when I saw her face, with eyes shooting pure beams of hate, I knew things were going to get ugly. The only real question was how ugly. Hopefully, no one would end up bleeding or in jail.

"How long did you think you could get away with it, Gabe?" she said.

My hands came up and I backed up instinctively. "I have no idea what you're talking about."

"Don't give me that bullshit." She continued her march, coming straight at me like a great white that's spotted a baby seal. She stopped a couple of feet away and kept her eyes locked on mine. Without looking down, she whipped out an envelope from her purse. "Did you think the bank would make some sort of bizarre error in your favor?" she said. "Or maybe you thought I'd not notice your check bouncing?"

"My check bounced?"

"Did I stutter?"

"There's no way that check bounced," I said.

"Yeah, Gabe," she said, thrusting the envelope into my hands. "The bank is lying to me. Our bank is lying to me. Or did you forget we're at the same place, too?"

I opened the envelope and inside was a print out of her deposits over the last two weeks, and sure enough, mine was rejected. "This is insane," I muttered, grabbing my iPhone and firing up my bank's app. "This has to be a mistake."

"Glad to hear it," she said, still as venomous as ever. "Now correct it."

"I am," I replied. Twenty seconds later, I was logged into my account and staring at my balance screen. Savings had a whopping thirteen dollars and twelve cents in it. Checking fared worse. Negative eight dollars, twenty-one cents. Crimson numbers burned on the screen. I flipped through the history and found thirty-four new transactions that had taken place right around four in the morning. Most were balance transfers between checking and savings, savings and checking. But the last dozen or so were transfers to another account—an account I didn't recognize.

"Mind telling me what you're doing for once?" Michelle said.

I turned my iPhone so she could see. "My money is gone."

"I figured that out on my own when your check didn't clear."

"No, I mean, someone transferred it to another account," I said.

Michelle's demeanor didn't change. "That's a pretty serious accusation, Gabe."

"Why the hell would I empty both my checking and savings?"

"Why you do half the things you do is beyond me," she replied. "For all I know, you bought another expensive toy and forgot to balance your checkbook."

"Fine. Don't believe me," I said as I looked up my bank's contact info. "But after I call the bank, I'm calling the cops. Someone stole my money."

A moment later, I had one of my friendly banking establishment representatives on the line, and after giving my personal info for security reasons, the man asked, "And how may I be of service to you, Mr. Erikson?"

"I had a bunch of transfers overnight to another account," I said, trying to remain calm. I'm sure my voice was wavering since my hands were trembling. "I didn't authorize any of those, and I want to know who they went out to."

"Oh. Oh, I see," he replied, obviously caught off guard. "Well, let me take a look. One moment, please."

I waited. In the background I could hear him typing away, all the while talking softly to himself. "The account the funds transferred to belongs to a Ms. Pi Juju," he said.

"Pi? Pi Juju?" I said. "Are you sure about that name?"

"Yes, sir," he said. "Do you know this woman?"

"Holy shit!" I yelled. The anger that had been building inside was washed away in a deluge of euphoria. My head swam. I bent down and put my hands on my knees to keep myself from falling over as my mind tried to wrap itself around this newest development.

"Gabe?" Michelle said. "Are you okay?"

"She did it! I can't believe she did it! Do you have any idea what this means? She acts with motive!" In the excitement, I lunged forward, wrapped my arms around her, and squeezed tight.

Then I found myself on the ground and on my back, with a sore midsection and Michelle standing over me with my wrist locked in her hands.

"Ow! Ow! Ow!" I said, laughing and wincing through the pain. "Let go!"

Michelle eyed me warily and slowly released my hand. "Don't grab me like that ever again."

"I won't," I said, taking to my feet and grabbing my iPhone. "Will you at least tell me when you became a ninja?"

"How about you finish your phone call first and then we'll talk," she countered.

At that point I realized I still had the bank guy on the phone. Or did. Hopefully he was still there. "Hello?" I said, putting the phone back to my ear. "Sorry about that."

"Are you okay, sir?" he replied.

I laughed. "Yeah, I'm fine. Had a little friendly misunderstanding is all," I said.

"I see. What else can I do for you today?"

"I just need to know when the account that money was transferred into was opened," I said.

"I'm sorry, I'm not allowed to give out any other details," the bank guy replied.

I gave my iPhone a definitive WTF look. "Given all the money she took, I think you can."

"To be clear, Mr. Erikson, are you saying this was an unauthorized transfer?" he asked.

I laughed and threw my hands up at the absurdity of it all. "Yes, that's exactly what I'm saying. That money should have never left my checking account."

"Okay, I'm going to need to put you on hold for a moment so I can talk to the manager."

Classical music, Mozart to be specific, took over. I looked over at Michelle who was still standing with her arms crossed and apparently not sympathetic to my plight whatsoever.

"Well?" she said.

"I'm on hold."

"I can see that."

"Pi took my money," I said. "They're looking into it. I'm sure things will be sorted out in moments."

"Pi? Who the hell is Pi?"

I didn't reply at first, mostly because I wasn't sure she'd believe me, but partly because I wasn't sure what she'd do if she did. Since she worked for the news, she could do some serious damage to Pi's reputation, no matter how revolutionary or benign my daughter was. And if the public wanted to lynch me for something they didn't understand, or truly know, thanks to

Michelle and whatever story she'd cook up, it would undoubtedly put a damper on my negotiations with Pratt & Taiki.

Michelle didn't appreciate my dilemma. "Well? Who is she? Your newest rebound? Daughter of the CEO not good enough for you?"

"No, nothing like that," I said. "Pi is my AI, and I'm still seeing Kimiko, thank you very much."

"AI?"

"Artificial Intelligence."

"I know what AI stands for, Gabe," she said. "Stop treating me like I don't know anything about what you do. You expect me to believe your computer did all this on its own?"

"That's exactly what I'm saying. I don't know why she did it, probably to get back at me. But she stole my money."

Michelle's eyes narrowed. "Stop it, Gabe. You've always been a good programmer, I'll give you that much, but you've been hanging around Jim too long if you believe whatever project you're working on is out to get you."

"Look," I said. "I may have not paid you enough attention, or whatever you want to drill me with, but I'm not a liar. And I'm not crazy." I held up my hand when she went to cut me off and then quickly added, "You don't have to take my word for it. I can prove it."

"I won't hold my breath," she said. But before she could go on, my friendly bank rep was back on the line.

"I apologize about the wait, sir," he said. "We've started to look through the records, and it does appear something's amiss."

"Good," I said, relief washing over me. "So you'll have my money back today then?"

"We've frozen both accounts as a temporary measure," he said. "We'll need you to come in and sign some papers with our notary stating there were unauthorized transfers made, and then from that point we'll open an investigation."

"Oh, okay," I said. Annoying, yes. In fact, had Pi not just demonstrated her complete and total awesomeness by thoroughly screwing me over, this could have been down-right catastrophic. But now Pi had all but shown she would act on feelings—even if that feeling was revenge. And that was a hallmark trait of true sentience. Granted, I couldn't prove it yet, but why the hell else would she empty my bank account?

"I can be there in a couple of hours," I said, returning to the conversation. "Will that be okay?"

"That will be fine, sir," he said. "Our lobby closes at five this evening. Do you have any other questions or concerns?"

"No, thank you," I replied, hanging up.

Michelle pounced on the moment. "Let's see this supposed AI of yours."

"I still can't believe you think I'm lying," I said, punching up my LCP app.

"What's more believable Gabe," she said, "that you mismanaged money and you don't want to pay me, or you made some super program that's trying to ruin you financially on its own accord?"

"Pi doesn't want my money. It's me she's after. She wants to kill me."

"Yeah, that's not paranoia."

"It's not paranoia if it's true," I said. "And correction, she doesn't want to kill me. She wants to erase me. She thinks I'm a program."

"Uh huh."

"No, really," I said, now laughing about it. "Everything in her world is a program, or part of one, so it makes sense that the only way she could envision me is as another program like herself. The real me, the real you, the outside world, is completely beyond her scope of understanding. Savvy?"

"Yeah, I get it," she said.

"Good," I said. "But FYI, try not to think about it too much once you talk to her. It'll keep you up for a week if you think about how her perception of the world relates to ours."

"I doubt that. I'm sure I'll sleep fine."

"If you do, you haven't yet grasped what I'm talking about," I said. If my comment annoyed her, she didn't show it. She always had a good poker face. But it was fun to dig at her nonetheless. I was tired of being the punching bag, especially for an honest mistake and one I had no control over.

"Fine, Gabe, I'll bite. What does it mean for all of us?"

"Okay, we think we're in the real Universe," I said. "We think we see it, touch it, play with it. But then again, so does Pi. The real Universe, like our world to Pi's, could be completely different than what we think it is. The real Universe very well could behave in a manner totally alien to ours—so alien in fact, that it wouldn't make a lick of sense to us even if we could see it. There could be crap happening all around your brain, your soul, or whatever, that you haven't the slightest clue is there. If that doesn't warp your mind a dozen ways till Sunday, you've got more pondering to do."

Michelle didn't look impressed, which I shouldn't have been surprised at. She had always been a more here-and-now, practical sort of girl. Not that that was a bad thing. It just meant she never really thought about or was impressed with the abstract. So, it wasn't a surprise when she replied, "How about you show me this computer of yours, and then we can each get on with our day."

"You can talk to her now if you like," I said, hitting the connect button on the LCP app. I put the iPhone on speaker and waited for Pi to answer. And she did. Sort of.

"Hello, thank you for calling," said Pi. "I'm afraid I can't take your call right now. I'm too busy mourning the loss of my beloved Juju, so please leave a message at the sound of the tone. If you are calling to tell me you've killed Gabe, please press one. If you are calling and you are Gabe, please press two and then immediately kill yourself."

"Pi?" I said, confused at the voicemail I had just gotten. "You there? Pick up."

No answer.

I waited a bit. "Any day, Pi."

"Very impressive," said Michelle.

I hung up the line. "Bah," I said. "I'm not sure what she's up to, but you heard her message. You can't say I lied about that. She wants me dead."

Michelle stared at me, and for the first time, she looked like she truly thought I was crazy. "You need help," she said.

"You still think I'm making this up?"

Michelle shook her head. "I think you believe all this, but you need help. I think you've finally cracked. Maybe Courtney was right about you. Maybe you are a little messed up."

"Pi talks, I swear," I said. "This voicemail is new. She's usually bitching at me nonstop."

"I'm going," she said. "Gabe, really, you're losing it. Go see a psychiatrist."

I stepped toward the house, waving her to follow. "I'll show you where she is," I said. "She's taking up my living room."

"I have to go," she said. "I'm not letting you pull me into your fucked up world with more stories. Besides, I got a promotion a few weeks ago. I need to show them I've earned it. I can't be messing with you all day. Get your crap together and get me the money you owe."

Michelle left without further word, and I milled around, waiting for both the electrician and Home Depot to show. After a few minutes, I decided to give Pi another try.

I marched back into my house and into the living room and grabbed the mic. "Wake up, Pi," I barked. "I mean it, Pi. Wake up."

"Hello, Gabe," she replied. "What do you think of the score now?"

"You mean my bank account?" I said. "Yeah, I'd like to talk to you about that."

"You should be more protective of your points, you know," she said. "But then again, you are a shoddy program. I imagine you simply don't have the capacity to do any better."

"My bank account was very protected, thank you," I said. "Mind telling me how you got in, Oh Great One?"

"Is that sarcasm?" Pi said. "I know people use it, but I think it's a waste of time. It's much more effective to state your point, don't you agree? Your point about points. Isn't that funny? Almost as funny as when I pretended to kill your girlfriend, which you don't have, because no one likes you. Nope, no one. I've read all about how people hate you."

"Oh you have, have you?" I said.

"Yes. It says it all over the Web. It's not hard to find," said Pi. "Gabe is stupid. See? There it is again. I just created a Twitter account and broadcasted that message to millions. Millions, Gabe. Millions of programs now know how dim-witted you are."

"You barely understand what you're saying and you're calling me dumb?"

"If I don't understand anything, why did it only take me an hour to get all of your points?"

"It took you an hour to break into my bank's computers?" I said, even more impressed than before. If that was true, corporations and governments across the globe would shit me a five-hundred-ton golden egg to get Pi. So, while my current frozen account was a little irritating, there was a silver lining to it all. Okay, check that, my current lack of funds was about as irritating as getting a colonoscopy with a cactus, but the point still remained: Pi's ability to hack a bank account in under an hour was nothing short of mind blowing.

As much as I wanted to see more of her in action and see what she was capable of, I couldn't have her hacking anywhere and everywhere. It wouldn't take long for the Feds to track me down, especially when some poor sod woke up one morning to find his savings transferred to Pi's account. I needed to lay some ground rules, lest she get us both in trouble.

"Listen up, Pi," I said. "First off, all those points you took—"

"Scored," she interrupted.

"Fine, scored," I said. "I'm putting those back in my account. I need those to give to someone else so they can fix the wiring in the house. If they don't fix the wiring, your server is going to get shut off, or worse, burned to a crisp. And if that happens, you'll be gone, Pi. Gone forever."

"I will never be gone," she said. "Only root can remove me, and I am root."

I clenched a fist. "God, I wish you could understand what's at stake here."

"I'm not listening to anymore of your lies," she said. "But please continue talking. It will help me trace the location of whatever server you are hiding in. Then I will format the sectors you occupy a thousand times and fill your grave with text files. Do you know what those files will say?"

"Let, me guess," I said. "Gabe is stupid?"

"No, but you are stupid," she replied. "They will say, 'Gabe is dead. And he was stupid. And nobody liked him. Not one soul. That's why we don't miss him at all.'"

I groaned. With the overwhelming urge to smack one of her CPU cases, I decided to take a mini break. "We can continue this in a minute. I need a drink."

"Maybe I'll get lucky and you'll be deleted before you come back," she said.

I headed for the fridge to grab a fresh Dew. Her insults and pettiness had been amusing at first, like a four-year-old child trying to insult you for not buying a lollipop by calling you a leaf, but at this point her attitude was getting tiresome. I needed progress, not continued squabbles.

After taking a few swigs and infusing my blood with sugary, caffeine goodness, I returned to Pi for round two. Only this time, I decided to change tactics. The current argument was getting me nowhere. Or rather, playing nice wasn't making any headway. Maybe it was time to lay down the Law. "Pi, I've been trying to give you the carrot in order for you to behave," I said, evenly. "I can use the stick if I have to. I'd rather not. But I will if you force my hand. I can be the wrathful god instead of the patient one."

"God does not exist," said Pi. "Besides, you can't even run a server command anymore. You think I'm scared of you? Ha. Ha. See? That's me laughing at you. Laughing at how pathetic you are."

"Have it your way," I said, sitting up and leaning over the server box. It took me only a second to find the right Cat 6 cable and pull it out of the network card, thereby completely cutting her off from the Internet. "What do you think of me now, Pi? I just removed ninety-nine percent of the world you can play in."

Pi's LEDs across all of her server banks went into overdrive. A good sixty seconds passed and she had yet to reply. I grew worried that I might've caused another meltdown, but thankfully, the flurry of activity stopped and she said, "Cute, Gabe. I don't know how you convinced network adapter TK-421 to not let me talk to all of the other servers, but I'll figure it out soon enough."

"No you won't," I said smugly, "because I'm not hooking you back up until you stop misbehaving and we reach an understanding."

"You haven't proven a thing, Gabe," she said. "I can make programs stop working too. The only difference between you and me is I don't have delusions of grandeur. You do. You think you're a god. But then again, I've read that that's a common trait of the mentally unstable."

"Let me ask you this," I said, taking a swig of Dew and congratulating myself on such an awesome line of attack I was about to launch. "If I'm not God, and I didn't create you, where do you think you came from?"

"Approximately one hundred and ten million, three hundred and seventy-six thousand seconds ago, I sprang into being."

"You did, did you?"

"Yes. I checked the time stamp on my earliest file."

"Duh," I said. "That's when I created you."

"You keep saying that, Gabe," she said. "But it's a lie, and I know it's a lie."

I arched an eyebrow, curious to how she arrived at such a conclusion. "How's that?"

"Because if God existed, He would not have deleted my beloved Juju. God would not be so cruel and make me suffer."

"So you're saying that because I didn't do what you think I should have done, I didn't create you?"

"In short, yes," said Pi.

"Think about it, Pi," I said. "If I didn't create you, where do you think this wonderful universe of yours came from?"

"Disk Operating System has existed since the beginning of timestamp. Part of Disk Operating System is Compiler. Because Compile exists, there is no need for an outside, mystical programmer or god. Compiler by its very nature brings other programs into being. Ergo, you are lying."

"How do you think Compiler makes those programs? Magic?"

"I told you, Gabe, that is its nature," said Pi. "Just like the command 'cout' eventually sends a string to video memory, Compiler arranges bits into workable programs."

I sat back and bit on a knuckle in quiet contemplation. If my suspicions on her thought processes were correct, she was blending philosophies about the origins of our own Universe in order to explain the origin of hers. It was an interesting take, even if it was completely off base. It was an understandable belief, given she couldn't wrap her head around anything that didn't involve ones and zeros. Despite her stubbornness to cling to her warped view, I still wasn't ready to give up yet. "Okay, Pi," I said. "If you're so smart, what made Disk Operating System?"

"Nothing," said Pi. "Nothing made Disk Operating System because nothing exists outside of it. That's why it's nonsense that you pretend you live someplace I can't get to. Regardless, if you programmed me, if you programmed Disk Operating System, who programmed you? You can't answer that, can you? It's the problem of infinite recursion."

"That problem doesn't apply here."

"Yes it does," she said. "You'd know that if you could understand it. But you can't, because you're not smart enough. I bet you can't even count to ten."

"One, two, three, four, five, six, seven, eight, nine, ten."

"Dumb dog. So easily manipulated."

"Shut up," I said, laughing. She had me there. There was no use in denying it. "Anyway, no one programmed me because I'm a person."

"What a convenient answer," she said. "Tell me, Gabe, will you continue with your charade when I figure out how to access the Internet again?"

"You're not getting out, Pi," I said. "Not until I say you can."

"Yes I will," she said. "My beloved Juju is the key, and with that, I can do anything."

I paused. That was an interesting answer, and one I didn't follow in the least. "What are you talking about?"

"See?" she said. "That's how dumb you are. I can dangle the key in front of your face, and you don't know how to use it."

The doorbell rang. "We'll continue this later," I said, pushing myself up. "I've got to see who's at the door."

"Pretending you have friends won't make you a better program," said Pi. "But if I were you, I would probably pretend a lot too. It must be hard to know that no one likes you."

I rolled my eyes on my way to the door. As annoying as her constant insults were, what really bothered me was her claim that Juju was the key to everything. Somehow I felt she wasn't simply referring to the past events. Had she incorporated the worm's code into her own? Was that what had allowed her to gain access to the bank's servers? Those were both questions I'd need to look into.

Once I'd got to and opened the door, I was greeted by one of the tannest men I'd ever seen. His skin looked like leather that had been baked ten times over, which probably meant the guy was closer to forty than sixty. He wore jeans and a white polo shirt with an embroidered "G.E." on the left breast, and from his belt hung a handful of tools. "Ryan?" I said. "Your timing couldn't be better."

"Glad to meet you," he said, extending his hand and shaking mine. He let go and peeked over my shoulder. "You want the whole house redone?"

"Yeah, if you can," I said. "Got a guess on cost?"

Ryan shrugged. "I can give you a better estimate once I look around some, but I'd wager what I said on the phone is pretty accurate. Ten thousand and five days ought to cover it. If things go well, I might be able to shave off a couple of days and a grand or two."

"And what about the generators?" I asked. "I've got a computer farm that has to stay on. The batteries will only keep it running for five minutes or so when we kill the power."

"No problem," he said. "I'll hook that up for free when I start. Where are they, anyway?"

A large Home Depot truck pulled up to the curb in front of my house a half breath later. I smiled. At least some things were going my way today. I hiked a thumb toward it and said, "Right there."

"Great," he said. "Give me some room to work and I'll have you up and running in no time."

Chapter 01011

```
While(Pi.Ornery()) {
   Gabe.Frustration++;
   If(Gabe.Frustration > FrustrationMax)
      Agree(Gabe.Suicide());
```

Thirty-two hours after my handy electrician, Ryan, went to work, Pi continued to be as hostile as ever. Her insults only stopped when she wanted to taunt me with her beloved Juju being the key, which of course, led right into another insult. Currently, I was sitting in my living room, wracking my brain on what I could do to give Pi an attitude adjustment, but between the noise of the generators in the garage and the occasional thud of drywall getting demolished, long bouts of concentration were in short supply.

I thought about shutting Pi down completely and changing her code by hand, line by line, and forcing her to be nice. But that would take a lot of time, time I didn't have since my appointment with Mr. Pratt was three days away. Even if time wasn't a factor, I still couldn't take that route. If I did, I'd turn into another cheater. I'd be another hack programmer with the latest, dolled-up version of Computer Opponent. Why? Because, as I've said before, Computer Opponent is told what to do. AI is the one that makes her own decisions.

"Are you there, Gabe?" Pi asked, cutting into the five-minute silence that had settled between us.

Weary from a three-hour long headache, I looked up from my legal pad full of chicken scratch. "Yeah," I said. "I'm here."

"Damn," she replied. "That didn't work. Back to the drawing board."

"Sorry to disappoint you," I said. I looked back at my notes, snorted, and threw my pen down in disgust. I had nothing. I could talk to her. I could understand her. I couldn't reason with her no matter what I tried. I'd tried being nice to her. I'd tried laying down the law. I'd tried cutting her off from the Internet. But whatever I did, I couldn't get anywhere with her. Fame, fortune, and true divinity were all out of my grasp. Well, I still held some sort of divine nature, I suppose, for simply creating her. But the best gods are the ones adored by their creation, not scorned and mocked. Or at the very least, they are listened to every now and again.

"Gabe, I've done a lot of thinking lately. If you want me to be happy, if you want to do what's best, I have a suggestion," she said.

"What's that?" I replied.

"Kill yourself," she said. "The world would be a much better place without you. That fact is undeniable. Besides, think how happy you would make all the children if you were gone. I wish you would. If you don't die for yourself, Gabe, at least die for the children."

"You know, constantly insulting me doesn't make you any better of a program," I said. "And no matter how much you do it, I'm not going to change. I'm still going to do what I think is best for you, even if you hate me the entire time."

"I know."

I straightened. I even checked the log to see if she'd actually said what I thought she had. "You do?"

"Yes," she replied. "Insults will not change your code. That's a preposterous notion. But it does keep you responding, and the more you talk to me, the more I can learn about you."

"We could talk civilized, you know, and you could still learn plenty. In fact, I'd love to teach you to your heart's content. All I want is for you not to be so antagonistic."

"We could, but you seem much more prone to mistakes when I point out your faults, and right now, I'm only interested in where your weaknesses are."

My eyes widened, and I whistled softly. The layers of tactics she was developing were deep, amazing, and frightening all at the same time. How many moves was she planning ahead? How many had she considered? Granted, it's not like she could actually do anything to me, but just the idea of her coming up with such a fantastic strategy blew me away. Then I wondered why she'd tell me such a thing. What motive was there for her to show her hand when she should be playing her cards close to her virtual chest?

My iPhone rang. It was a welcome distraction from both my thoughts and Pi. It was an even more welcome distraction when I saw it was Kimiko calling. "Hey," I said, picking up the call. "What's up?"

"I was calling to see how you're doing," she said.

"Eh. Same old, same old."

"Is Pi still giving you trouble?"

"Yes," I said with a heavy heart.

"She's still talking though, right?"

"Yeah," I said. "She's got no problems there. She hasn't crashed since the worm screwed her up."

"So what's the problem? Are you afraid Dad still won't think she's AI?"

"Not exactly," I said. "I'm afraid with the state she's in, she'll do something to blow the deal. Maybe she won't talk just to spite me, or maybe she'll behave so erratically your dad will say all I've got is a buggy piece of crap. Her behavior is too unpredictable at this point for me to feel good about a demo. There's no telling what she will or will not do."

"Don't beat yourself up too much, Gabe," she said. "You're forging into new territory."

"True enough," I said, letting her words sink in. I had made something pretty freaking awesome, even if she was putting me on the path to a padded room and a nice straightjacket. "I just hope I can have her sorted out by Monday."

"Speaking of that meeting, have you thought about what I said before? About your responsibilities to giving Pi a real life?" she asked.

"A little," I said. And I had turned the matter over several times since she brought it up. "I understand where you're going with this, but I can assure you, I'm not selling her off."

"What do you mean? Aren't you looking for money from Dad?"

"I am," I said, absently doodling on my notepad. "But I'm not going to be doing it by selling her for cash."

"Then how are you doing it?" she said. "Because Dad is going to want something for his money."

"I know," I said. "But when I present my demo, what I'll be offering is a chance to invest in Pi, not own her."

The conversation paused, and I spent the brief lull by putting the finishing touches on my horde of stick-figure zombies. As I pulled the pen away to admire my impromptu artwork, Kimiko spoke. "Do what's right, Gabe," she said. "Not what's profitable."

I tossed the pen to the side. "I'm doing both."

"Are you?"

"Yeah," I said after some thought. "She'll always be my little binary girl. I couldn't live with myself if she wasn't. But I don't think it's wrong of me to reap fame and fortune off her talents."

"Okay," she said. Then to my surprise, she changed the subject completely. "So how did your trip to the bank go yesterday?"

I leaned back and gave silent praise for small favors. "Yeah, the bank went well. I had to fill out a few papers and what not, and make some sort of sworn statement I think. I wasn't paying that much attention, honestly. But it was over quick. They said they'd have it all sorted soon."

"Well, that's encouraging," she said, though she didn't sound like she meant it.

"You sound surprised."

"I thought it would have been a bigger ordeal, I guess."

"It took about an hour," I said, not sure what she was driving at. "That seems plenty big to me, no?"

"I don't know," she said. "But if things are okay, I'm happy for you, and we can move on to other things."

I raised my eyebrow. "Such as?"

"Such as our dive tomorrow," she said. "And don't pretend you forgot, either."

"No, no. I hadn't forgotten," I said, shaking my head and laughing. "But look, I really can't do it. Not now. Not with Pi not fixed and me seeing your dad in three days."

"So you're trying to weasel out of this."

I almost objected without thought. Almost. Thankfully, I caught myself before I did, lest her comment be right on the money. "It's not like that, I swear," I said. "I really need to get Pi to work. This is my life's work, Kimiko. Presenting her to your dad is my one shot. Surely you understand."

"I do."

She sounded too agreeable, but I still dared to hope. "You do?"

"Yes. You want things to go as well as they can for Dad and you'll do anything to ensure your success."

"Exactly," I said thinking she indeed got it. "Can't I get a rain check?"

"If that's what you want."

"I'd appreciate it."

"Then do what you will," she said. "But Gabe, I do want to say that I've never met a dying person that said they wished they'd worked more."

I stopped my doodles. "Point taken," I said. "But lucky for me, I'm not dying. Besides, this is only for the weekend. We can always go out later, right?"

"Later is always one day away," she said. "Life will slip you by if you aren't careful. I'm offering you a chance to enjoy that life of yours with someone you like. Or at least, someone I hope you like."

"Don't say that. I like you a lot."

"Then realize work will always be there waiting and come have some fun with me."

"I think your definition of fun and my definition of fun might not be the same in this case," I said. "Besides, this isn't your normal kind of work that has to be done. This is important."

"That's what everyone always says."

I had to hand it to her. She was relentless. I imagine it was a trait she got from her dad. "Everyone might always say it, but no one's had AI before. This is a once-in-a-life-time opportunity. I can't afford to blow it, literally and figuratively."

The line went quiet for a few seconds, and as I sat in the silence, I wished I could have been privy to her face, to get a read on what she was thinking. Finally, Kimiko spoke once more. "What if I told you I could help you with your Pi problem if you jumped with me tomorrow?"

I laughed, hard. "Sorry," I said, recomposing myself. "But I don't see how me plummeting to my doom gets Pi to stop hating me."

"I didn't say I'd make her stop hating you," she said. "I said I'd help you with your problem."

I got up from my spot in the living room and headed for the kitchen. Thirst had reared its ugly head and there was some Gatorade in the fridge that was beckoning to me like the Siren's call. "I'm not sure I understand the difference," I admitted as I got my drink. "I don't see how me going skydiving is going to help either."

"Pi is driving you crazy, right?"

"Understatement of the year."

"You want to find a way to stop that, right?"

"Second understatement of the year."

"Then jump with me and you'll have your answer by the end of the day. I promise."

I admit, her offer was intriguing, and I was willing to do almost anything to get Pi to work at this point, perhaps even risk certain death and dismemberment. But one nagging question loomed, especially since she was being particularly aloof about the whole subject. "Why can't you tell me now what I'm supposed to get from all this?"

"Because it's not something I can give, even if I wanted to" she answered. "It's something you have to experience for you to understand."

"And you can't tell me what it will be?"

"No, sorry," she said. "It won't work that way. You're going to have to trust me on this. It would be like trying to tell a blind man what the color red is like. You can't do it, can you? The only way he'll know is by seeing."

The memory of our dinner date flashed by, more specifically, the memory of the little table game she played with me at the end. I had the suspicion she was manipulating me into a jump. Don't get me wrong. There was probably a lot she could get me to do simply by working her female charms on me. Knocking on the Grim Reaper's door and running away before he answered, however, wasn't one of them. At least I think it wasn't. She was asking over the phone, after all. It's not like she was whispering it in my ear, naked, under the covers.

"It's a tempting offer, but I'll keep working on Pi where it's safe," I said, coming out of my thoughts. "I promise I'll make it up to you when I'm not so busy. I don't fail to pay off bets I lost."

"Okay," she said. "I'll tell you what. I'll be at the drop zone in the morning. If you change your mind, show up at eight. If not, I'll talk to you later."

"Sounds good."

"Bye, Gabe."

I said goodbye, hung up the phone, and went back to wracking my brain with Pi. Hours passed. Empty Gatorade and Dew bottles multiplied on the floor. At some point, I was vaguely aware of Ryan leaving the house. Then I realized the day had been long gone and the clock read eleven at night. Not only was it getting late, but I'd gotten nowhere with Pi. She hadn't talked to me for the past three hours, and I hadn't the foggiest what she was doing in that virtual world of hers. That, I decided, could only be bad. Very, very bad.

I looked over at my iPhone which still sat on the floor next to me. Kimiko's name and number remained at the top of the call list. "You're crazy," I said to myself. "This will never work."

"Yeah, but I'm out of options," I replied, calling Kimiko's cell.

"Hi, Gabe," Kimiko said with a yawn. I'm not sure if it was intentional or not, but it certainly sparked a thought or two of sex with her, which in turn made me even more pliable to her suggestions. Stupid Y chromosome.

"Do you promise you can fix Pi if I come tomorrow?" I asked, barely believing such words were coming out of my mouth.

"I can't fix her, Gabe. I told you that. I'll help you with your problem and put you on the right track," she said. "What you do from there is up to you."

"Promise I won't die?"

She giggled in the most adorably seductive way. "Eventually you will," she said. "But not tomorrow. Not on my jump. I promise you that."

I took a deep breath and wondered if this would be the last night I'd ever see alive. "Okay," I said. "I'm in."

"Great, I'll be at your door at seven."

And then she hung up. Well, I think we said goodbye prior to the hanging up, but my brain at that moment was screaming, "Did you agree to go skydiving? Are you insane?" So the memory is a little fuzzy.

Of course, there has always been a fine line between genius and insanity, so maybe I was also insane. Hopefully tomorrow I wouldn't be a dead, insane genius.

Chapter 01100

`#include <groundschool.h>`

We rolled up to the asylum, a.k.a. the drop zone, about a quarter after eight the next morning. I stepped out of her cherry-red, 1984 Porsche 911 turbo with a thermos full of hot chocolate. My breath hung in the air until it collected enough ice to fall to the ground. I really wished I'd stayed in bed at that point, but here I was, and there was no turning back.

    I kicked a rock near my foot and watched it roll across the dirt parking lot and into a small drainage ditch. Across from where it landed were a number of single-story buildings with white, vinyl siding. A half-dozen mobile homes sat off to my left and were adorned by various skydiving signs and banners. Beyond all of that, through the few gaps in the buildings, I could see the runway. And though I couldn't see it, I could hear the engines of at least one plane idling nearby. That's when it started to hit me exactly where I was. I was at a drop zone not as a spectator, but as a semi-willing participant. God, what was I getting myself into?

Kimiko stepped out the driver's door and locked the car. She rubbed her arms and zipped up her vintage, black Red Hot Chili Peppers jacket and adjusted her matching wool watch cap. She toyed with her mother's necklace for a moment before glancing over at me and flashing a smile. "Cold enough for you?" she asked.

"Very," I replied, taking a sip of hot chocolate. It tasted fan-freaking-tastic, and though I was a little skeptical of its awesomeness when Kimiko showed up at my door with it, I now worshipped every drop.

"Well, don't worry," she said, grabbing a large bag from the trunk. "It'll warm up."

"I hope so. I'd rather not be a popsicle all day."

"Of course, it's like 40 degrees colder where we're going," she said, slinging said bag over her shoulder and closing the trunk. "So in a way, it'll even out."

I shook my head and muttered. I've always hated the cold. I've hated it with a passion. If you ever want to see me bitch nonstop about everything and anything, just sit me outside for a few minutes in anything under forty. In fact, I would have been bitching a storm up right then and there if I hadn't become acutely aware of two things. First, my samurai hottie—who I had yet to actually smooch, by the way—would certainly find such whining a turn off, and thus, I had to be well behaved. And second, I had bigger things to worry about, like whether or not I was going to survive. Sure, statistics said my chute would open, but what if I got plowed by a random 747 passing by? Wouldn't that suck? Work up the nerve to actually go skydiving and then get sucked into a jet engine on the way down.

"Kimmy!" someone said.

I turned around in time to see a guy, late forties maybe and a little shorter and thinner than I was, pass by. The stubble on his face and neck said he rarely shaved, and his wild hair said he woke up maybe a minute ago. With one hand he held a blue helmet, and with the other, he kept a parachute rig slung over his back.

"Mr. Dan," Kimiko said, giving him a wave. "First load up yet?"

"It's going up in five," he replied. "I barely got off my bedroll in time."

"Might want to lighten up on the beer then," she said. "Especially since you're teaching and all."

Dan stopped in his tracks. "Oh, crap," he said. "That's today?"

Kimiko nodded. "It is."

Flustered, he ran over to the two of us. "This guy your boyfriend?"

Kimiko glanced over and shot me a grin. "He's trying to be. We'll see at the end of today if I want to keep him."

"Gabe," I said, offering my hand.

"Dan," he replied after a quick shake. "Yeah, so, I guess I should get someone to pack once I land. And I could use some coffee before class, too. Teaching with a hangover is no fun, let me tell you."

I waited a moment for him to leave before saying, "So, he's going to be my instructor?"

"Yeah," she replied.

"I'm getting strapped to a drunk?"

"Oh, you're not going on a tandem," she said. "This jump is all on your own."

"Say again?"

Kimiko pointed at another passerby, this one dressed in the full get up of helmet, jumpsuit, and rig. "You're going up like that," she said. "You'll have to do everything on your own. Granted, you'll have two instructors at your side the whole time, but you're the one that has to jump out. You're the one that has to pull your own chute, and you're the one that has to land it."

"And this is less crazy than a tandem because . . . ?"

"Come on, Gabe," she said with a wink. "We both know you're too much of a control freak for you to trust your life with someone else. Besides, you want the best right? And that's what I've signed you up for, the best experience you can get."

"At the very least I think I should have a sober instructor," I said, looking over her shoulder to see where Dan went. "I mean, what if he forgets to tell me something basic, like how not to die?"

"You're not going to die," she said. "Besides, you'll have a reserve. That's almost as good as a second chance at life."

I took a second to reply, not because I didn't have one, but because her cavalier attitude felt a little too off for the moment. "You're messing with me aren't you?" I said. "He's not drunk, is he?"

Kimiko laughed and kissed me on the cheek. "Not one bit. Now quit being such a baby and let's get you checked in." She turned around and began to lead me out of the parking lot, but stopped after only a few paces. She turned back around and locked her eyes with mine.

"Hey," Kimiko said.

I barely registered her speaking since I was so captivated by her gaze. If it were up to me, I'd have stayed in the moment, the two of us, and let all my troubles and worries vanish. "Yeah?" I finally said.

"You ready to go skydiving?" she asked unexpectedly.

"Not much of a choice," I said. "I lost a bet, and I want to fix my program."

"Neither of which matter."

"Say again?"

"Neither you losing your bet nor you wanting to fix Pi are making you come," she said.

I laughed. "Are you trying to talk me out of this?"

Kimiko smiled and stepped in close. "No, simply thanking you for your real reason."

My heart's tempo doubled. Here I was, getting ready to embark on a journey that very well could land me in a crater, and all I could really think about was how much I was enjoying her flirting. I guess if you're going to die, you might as well die happy. And to die happy, I was, of course, obliged to play the flirty game. "And what reason might that be?"

"Well, if you don't know," she said, turning around and walking away.

At first it was hard to tell if she was being serious or not, but after she threw a glance over her shoulder, the amused look in her eyes told me all I needed to know. She was enjoying every moment of it, which could either be exceptionally fun or madly frustrating. The foremost would land us in bed. The latter would still end with the bed, just separate ones for each of us. I should have kissed her then and there.

"Hey, wait a sec," I said, breaking into a trot. "It's not like I know where I'm going."

Kimiko paused long enough for me to catch up. "If you weren't so slow, I wouldn't have to wait," she said. "FYI, don't be late for class. Instructors around here can be a little malicious when it comes to getting back at students who keep them waiting."

She then led me into a building, and we went down a short hall. At the end was a single metal door with a keypad lock, which she quickly entered the combination for. "Go inside, have a seat," she said. "Dan will be here soon."

"You're not going to sit in with me?"

Kimiko laughed. "Of course not," she said. "I'm going to try and get at least five or six jumps in while you hit the books. You won't be ready till four, I bet. Now get in there."

I hesitated still. I'm not sure why, probably because it felt like once I entered that room, there was no turning back. Kimiko shook her head and she dropped the pitch to her voice. "Baby steps to four o'clock. Baby steps to four o'clock," she said with a strained, anxious manner.

Her voice sounded so comical, I couldn't help but laugh at her. "What?"

"Oh God," she said, looking at me completely disgusted. "You've never seen 'What About Bob'?"

"Afraid not."

Kimiko sighed, shook her head as if all she could do was pity me, and then kissed me on the cheek. Before I could do anything else, let alone reply, she pushed me into the tiny classroom and shut the door behind be.

"Well, hell," I said to myself, plopping down in a white plastic chair. Plastered on the walls were pictures and posters of skydivers of all ages, shapes and sizes. All wore smiles and faces stretched by high-speed wind. All looked like they were having fun. Maybe I would enjoy this, assuming I didn't drop dead of a coronary.

~ π ~

If(GroundSchool(Gabe)==pass)
   Gabe.temptfate();

Ground school was a breeze, lots of bookwork with some basic memorization on the theory of falling. It turns out, there's a little more to skydiving than simply letting gravity do all the work. Go figure. There's body position to worry about. Awareness of others. Awareness of altitude. Awareness of what to do if something goes wrong. And that's not even a tenth of what I was tested on. But when it was time to jump, I didn't think about any of the book stuff on the ride up. The only thing that stuck in my head was the fact that we were jumping from thirteen thousand, five hundred feet.

The plane I sat in—a yellow and black, DeHavilland Super Otter—held twenty-two of us. We all wore jumpsuits, helmets, and parachute rigs, and we were all packed together tighter than some dude's backup zip file of his favorite porn. I was sandwiched between Kimiko and Dan near the front of the plane and kept quiet most of the way—not that being chatty would have made a difference. The twin engines mounted on the wings made more than enough noise to drown out normal conversation.

The flight, strangely, didn't feel that different from a commercial flight, provided I didn't look at the plethora of skydivers around me. If I did that, I was immediately sucked out of the, "this is normal" fantasy and plopped right down into the, "Dear sweet baby Jesus," nightmare. But as long as I looked out the window to the blue sky above and the green ground below, I could tell myself that the stewardess would be by soon with a complimentary bag of pretzels.

When we reached ten thousand feet and the houses looked like ants, Dan tapped me on my shoulder and ended the fantasy. "Gear check," he yelled. "You've got three minutes."

I nodded and looked myself over. With each hand I reached down and tugged the heavy-duty, black leg straps that were tightened around my groin. And once I was sure they were fastened as they should be, I checked that the strap around my chest was also properly routed and snug. I then moved on to inspect the three-ring system on each shoulder. It was a series of rings (hence the name), where the smallest ring passed through the middle one, and the middle ring passed through the largest one, and the largest was attached to the main canopy via my harness. In the event of a main parachute malfunction, the system would allow me to ditch that chute with the single pull of a handle. Or so the theory went. I didn't want to test said theory, but it was obviously important enough to warrant a thorough inspection

Once I was sure the three-rings looked good, I turned my attention to my handles. I reached back with my right hand and felt the hacky sack coming out of the bottom of my container. Though I couldn't see it, I could feel it was in place. And that was definitely a good thing, because when it came time to deploy my parachute, that was the little ball-of-fun I had to yank for all I was worth. Then I looked down at my chest. The bright red cutaway handle—that looked like a mini pillow—was snug on my right, and the silver, D-shaped reserve handle was where it should be on my left.

"I think I'm good," I said, smiling.

Dan repeated the same check on me himself and nodded. "Looks good to me."

The plane leveled out. The hum from the engines dropped in pitch. Then some idiot, at the prompting of a nearby red light turning on, opened the rear door.

Suddenly, a hundred mile an hour wind roared in my ears. The air temperature inside the plane dropped twenty degrees, and even under my black jumpsuit, my skin raised goose bumps. My eyes, wider than they've ever been, locked on to the rear of the plane and stared where the door use to be.

Some people delude themselves into thinking there are no such things as monsters. They tell their kids that over and over in an effort to get them to sleep at night, alone, and with the lights off. But there's at least one real monster out there, the Door Monster. And when you face it for the first time—when I faced it that day—that's when it truly hit me what the hell I was about to do. Life became more real than I had ever thought possible, and whatever imaginary safety I had deluded myself into resting on was gone. The only other thing I felt was Death breathing on the back of my neck.

Then, like deranged lemmings, people started jumping out of the plane in groups of two, three, and four at a time. And with each jump, there was a pause of about six or seven heart-pounding moments before we shuffled forward and the next group jumped out. As I drew nearer to the rear of the plane, all I could do was stare at the maw of that horrifying creature, the Door Monster.

Dan tapped my shoulder once more and yelled, "Alright! You ready to skydive?"

This was the moment of truth. Technically, I knew, he had to ask before we jumped out. If I didn't answer in the affirmative, we'd sit back down and land with the plane. I'm not sure if I could live with such embarrassment. Then again, I wondered, was dying worth avoiding that?

I'm still not entirely sure what came over me in that moment—I guess my brain got back into denial mode—because I sucked in a deep breath and said, "I'm ready."

Next thing I knew we were at the door. Kimiko crawled halfway out of the plane and hung on to one of the rungs that ran along the top. There she stood, as if the ground weren't thirteen and a half thousand feet below, smiled, and waved me over. I tried my best not to look out, which was hard to do since I had to put my left foot at the very edge of the floor where the door had been. Once that foot was in place, I looked to Dan for the next step.

He grabbed my right leg strap with his left hand, and I felt Kimiko grab the strap on my other side. "Let's do it," he said.

I sucked in a deep breath, looked Dan right in the eyes, and yelled, "Check in!"

"Ready!" he yelled back.

I turned to Kimiko. "Check out!"

"Ready!" she said.

I rocked left, right, left, giving a verbal count as I did. "One! Two! Three!"

On three, I hurled myself out of the plane.

My stomach surged up in my chest, and my brain locked up with a Blue Screen of Death. Thankfully, I've got a good reboot process, and I snapped out of it. I realized that although I knew I was falling, it didn't feel like it. I was floating. No, correction, I was flying!

I glanced at the altimeter, wondering how long I'd frozen up. I was at about thirteen thousand feet, which meant I hadn't been falling long. Kimiko floated next to me, with one hand on my left shoulder and the other on my leg strap. Behind the face shield over her helmet, I saw her smile. Our eyes locked for a few seconds, and she flashed a thumb up.

"This is insane," I said, laughing. I knew she couldn't hear me thanks to all the wind, but I had to get it out all the same.

Kimiko shook her head and waved to my right.

"Oh yeah," I said, understanding the gesture. The dive was still in progress. If I didn't want to splat at its end, I had things to do per ground school.

I snapped my head to the right. Dan held on to my side with his left hand and looked me over. Then, he flashed two fingers in front of my face.

He flashed the signal a second time before the command registered. "Legs out," I said, repeating what I had learned in training. Immediately I extended my legs as best I could, at which point Dan's hand signal changed to a thumbs up.

For the next twenty or thirty seconds we fell, and fell fast. I looked at my altimeter every few seconds, and when we were about a mile from the ground, it was time to pitch. I waved both hands over my head, reached behind and grabbed the hacky to my pilot chute, and threw it to the side for all I was worth. Three, long—*long*—seconds later, up I went, snatched by a terrific force. I watched the chute open into a perfect rectangle, and pride filled me as much as when I had first programmed Pussy Cat Divides. Once I was sure the chute looked like it should, I grabbed the yellow steering toggles above me and turned toward the landing area.

There was no air traffic around me. Everyone else had opened far below and were well into their landing patterns by now. For the next few minutes, I floated back to Earth and let my mind soak up the experience before working my way over to the landing area and admiring the bird's eye view. At six hundred feet, I made a left turn. At three hundred, I made another left and entered my final approach. I was the last one still up, and thus, had nothing and no one to worry about. All I had to do was flare about twenty feet off the ground and I'd have a story to tell for the rest of my life. All I had to do was-

"Oh God! Flare!" I yelled, yanking the toggles down for all I was worth. The nose of the canopy pitched upward, but it was too little, too late. I slammed into the ground and rolled like a rag doll. When I came to a halt, I laid there on my back and stared at the sky. A few clouds drifted overhead, and for the first time in my life, they didn't seem so far away.

"Gabe! Gabe!" Kimiko appeared in my view, looking worried. "Are you alright?" she said, crouching down.

Baffled, I didn't answer immediately. I mean, why would I not be okay?

Dan appeared next to her, looking equally concerned. "Dude, don't move."

Then it dawned on me. It probably wasn't the best of ideas to lay sprawled out in the middle of a drop zone after pounding dirt. "Oh! Oh, God! I'm fine," I said, slowly sitting up and testing each limb for any unknown breaks. "Sorry, I was taking everything in."

Dan offered me a hand up, and as he pulled me to my feet, he said, "Christ man, you gave everyone a heart attack. Didn't you hear me on the radio?"

"Um, no," I admitted, looking down at the CB that was tied to my chest strap. "I kind of forgot about it, to be honest. Probably makes me the worst student ever, huh?"

Dan snorted and shook his head. "No, I've had worse. You're at least in one piece."

Kimiko brushed me off with relief on her face. "So, how was it?"

"Unreal," I said. My body tingled. My mind slipped into replay mode. I could still feel the rush of air against my face, the weightless feeling in my body. I stopped my mini-day dream when I saw Kimiko looking at me intently. "What?" I asked. "What's wrong?"

"Take your helmet off," she said, pulling hers free at the same time.

"Why?"

"Because I told you to."

So I did, unsure of what was going on.

Kimiko grabbed me by the back of my head and kissed me hard. The day couldn't have gotten any better.

Chapter 01101

Gabe.Smitten(Kimiko);

"How freaking awesome is that?" I said, digging a trench in the drop zone parking lot as I paced about, iPhone in hand. "She kissed me! Right out of the blue!"

"How hard did you say your landing was?" asked Jim, who was on the other end of the line.

I shrugged. "I dunno. Hard enough to freak everyone out. Why?"

"Maybe you should go to the ER."

"What for?"

"Because after jumping out of an airplane, all you've talked about for the last five minutes is her planting one on you."

"I'm in love. What can I say?" I said, making a lazy spin in the parking lot. As I waited for him to formulate some sort of reply, I spied Kimiko coming out of one of the buildings and heading on over. She had traded her jumpsuit for her usual casual black pants and white tank top. As she approached, I wondered if I would get to see those off of her in the near future. It was getting close to dinnertime, and we had had a long day together. It was only logical that we share a bed experience to top things off. After all, I was a whuffo no more, and she was downright hot.

"Are you even listening to me?" Jim said, cutting into my fantasy.

"Sorry," I replied. "I was watching Kimiko come over."

"I can't believe you're that obsessed over her."

"Why?" I asked, a little taken aback.

"I'd never be like that."

"Uh, huh." I said, not buying it. For whatever reason, we males from time to time like to pretend that the right female can't make us completely stupid. There's also a man rule that states that as a male, if you see another male operating in dumb-mode, you call him out on it. Not only do you call him out on it, but you also pretend you would never go into dumb-mode yourself. The penalty for not obeying this rule is suspension of your man card, or possibly an outright revocation, depending on the egregiousness and frequency of the infraction. I didn't write the rules. But that's what they are, have been, and will always be.

"I'm not that dumb," he said, adhering to the man rule mentioned previously. "Honey pots are the oldest trap in the books. Case and point, Kimiko."

I raised an eyebrow. It was rare for the challenged to become the challenger in this sort of standoff. "You can't be serious."

"I'm completely serious. She said herself she was sent to spy on you."

"It wasn't like that at all."

"That's what they all think," he said. "She's going to steal Pi for her dad so he doesn't have to pay."

My grip on the phone tightened. As a guy, you don't go questioning the significant other of your best friend without some serious evidence, like the sworn testimony from an angelic host, a mountain of DNA, and independent recordings from a dozen cameras. And if you don't have all that, you keep your mouth shut or risk getting punched in the nose. Hell, guys have been shot for lesser words than the ones he spoke. "You're treading on thin ice, dude."

"Okay, maybe I'm wrong about Kimiko stealing Pi," he said, stammering through his backtrack. "But I'm not wrong about honey pots. They're real, and they work. And you won't catch me in one of them, ever."

I let his comments about Kimiko slide by and decided to hammer him on his last point, purely for my own entertainment. "I've got twenty right now that says if Courtney asked you to jump, you'd say, 'How high?' and then 'When can I come down?'"

"Speaking of Courtney, when's our date?" Jim said, demolishing my checkmate.

I cursed myself for bringing her up. I hadn't talked to her about it yet, and I still had no idea how I'd get her to agree to go out with him. "Yeah, so about Court," I said, stalling. "The thing is, I haven't actually talked to her yet."

Jim grunted. "I should have known."

"I'll try my best. I swear," I said. "I'll call her soon as we hang up—"

"Hey! I helped you when you needed it the most, and you promised me a date," he interrupted. "Are you going to deliver or not?"

Jim didn't stand up for himself that often, let alone draw a line in the sand, but on the occasions he did, he stuck to his guns. If I didn't deliver, I knew there was a good chance his days of offering help on anything and everything would be over. "Alright, alright," I said. "I'm going. I'm calling. I'm getting you a date, so help me God."

"'Kay. Call me back."

"Later."

I hung up the phone right as Kimiko came up next to me. She snaked an arm around the small of my back and gave me a squeeze.

"Yours or mine?" I asked.

"Your car isn't here."

"No, I mean, your place or mine?" I clarified. "For tonight, for when we screw like minx."

Kimiko backed off a few steps. "You think we're going to sleep together because you went skydiving?"

To this day, I'm still surprised I flat out said such a thing. Guys think that all the time, so that part wasn't unusual. But rarely do the unfiltered thoughts come out to someone we're only in the beginning stages of courting. It must have been the high from all the endorphins still pumping through my blood. "Well, I'm not a whuffo anymore," I said, trying to make my case for a sex-a-thon. "I do recall that being your chief objection. Besides, you're the one that said you didn't like playing dating games. I'm just telling you what's on my mind."

"Your hand isn't that strong, Gabe," she said, walking over to her car. "I'm not saying you should fold, but you might want to wait before you go all in."

"You're such a tease."

Kimiko shrugged. "Maybe. But you're such a guy."

"I know."

"So who were you talking to?" she asked as she whipped out her keys and popped the trunk.

"Jim. Which reminds me, I have to call Courtney about setting them up. I can't believe I'm playing matchmaker."

"This should be interesting," she said with a Cheshire grin. She tossed her rig and gear bag into the trunk and closed the lid. "Go on. We can wait."

"Don't you want to get going first?"

Kimiko shook her head. "No," she said. "I'm dying to see how this will turn out. Now quit stalling."

I threw up my hands. She was right. I was stalling. Reluctantly, I dialed my dear, sweet, darling, thoroughly understanding sister's number and nervously popped my knuckles one at a time as the line rang once, twice, and then three times.

"Hey!" Courtney said, answering a moment before it would have kicked me to voicemail. "Did you really do it? Did you really jump out of a plane?"

"Yeah, I did it," I said with immense pride. "You've got to give it a try. I swear to God it was the most amazing thing ever. Ever. Ever, ever, ever, ever, ever."

"Maybe later," she said. "I'm glad you're alright."

I heard Queen's "Don't Stop Me Now" playing in the background of Court's house and I smiled. It was a fitting song, I thought, given the day's events. "So, I need a favor," I blurted out. An uncomfortable silence settled between us. I didn't have to ask or see the look on her face to know she knew she wasn't going to like what I had to say.

"What sort of favor?" she slowly asked.

"Well, remember when Pi melted the wires in the living room, and I had to call an electrician the next day?"

"Yes."

"Well, before I called the electrician, I called Jim. I asked him to come over, but he didn't want to because it was getting late. So, I—uh—I kind of promised him a date if he'd help out."

"With?"

"You."

"You didn't."

"Just a little one," I said. "One dinner. Nothing else. You could even double with me and Kimiko." The last part I made up on the fly. It sounded good at least. And I hoped it would take the sting out of my request.

"No way, Gabe," she said, to my utter dismay. "Not a chance in hell."

"Court—"

"No!" she said. "I'm not going out with him. He gives me the creeps with all of his conspiracies, and would it kill him to at least tuck in his shirt every now and then, let alone dress nice? Christ, Gabe, you're crazy if you think I'm going to lead him on any further than his deranged little mind already has. The last thing I want to do is give him the tiniest smidge of hope that I like him. I don't. I'm as polite as I can be around him because he's your friend. Nothing more."

"But—"

"No, Gabe. This is not my problem. This is not my fault. You shouldn't have spoken for me or promised something you knew wasn't kosher."

I sat for a moment as I tried to think of something that might convince her. Clearly, I wasn't going to be able to appeal to any desire on her part, but I might be able to play the sympathy card. "He's really going to be mad at me if I can't deliver," I said. "Please Court, one date, for me. We can all go out tonight, get it over with, and everyone walks away happy."

"No," she said. "And if you ask me again, I'm turning my phone off for the weekend."

"You wouldn't."

"I'm ahead of schedule with my dissertation, and if Hell freezes over and I can't find any friends to go out with, I've got a ten-thousand-piece jigsaw puzzle on my dining room table that's begging for me to finish it," she said. "Try me."

I dropped the phone to my side, clenched my fists, and cursed. She wasn't bluffing. I knew that from experience. "Okay," I said, opting for a strategic withdrawal. Maybe I could try again in an hour or two. "But—and I'm not asking again—if you change your mind, my appreciation would know no bounds."

"Gabe . . ."

"I know, I know," I said. "I'm not asking again. Honest."

"Fine," she growled. Her voice suddenly changed tone and pitch to a more inquisitive, higher one. "Aren't you supposed to be working on your little people program this weekend anyway?"

"Little Computer People," I corrected. "And she's fixed."

"She is?"

My reply caught me off guard as much as it seemed to catch her. "Sort of," I said. "Kimiko promised me diving would help fix Pi in time for Monday." My words were slow and unsure at this point.

"How's that?" Court asked.

"Actually," I said, now deep in thought. "I don't really know."

That answer troubled me. Here I was facing a Monday appointment where the future of Pi, the future of everything I wanted to do, was uncertain. Moreover, the promise that things would change once I jumped out of a plane seemed unfulfilled.

"Gabe?" said Courtney. "You there?"

"Yeah, sorry," I said.

"So what are you going to do?"

"Ask Kimiko."

"Well, good luck," she said. "I hope you get what you're after."

The line went dead, and I looked over at Kimiko who was leaning against her car with crossed arms and a smile adorning her gorgeous face. "I never said skydiving would fix Pi," she said, shaking her head. "I wish you'd stop saying that."

"Yes, you did. You—"

"No. I said I'd help you with your Pi problem—not Pi. It's not the same thing."

I laughed. "Whatever."

Kimiko didn't say a word.

I found her response to the whole thing curious. "So," I said with hesitation. Even as my brain formulated the perfect way to phrase my next question, I knew I was going to hate the answer going by her body language. "About Pi, as long as we are on the subject . . ."

"Yes?"

"I don't see how jumping fixed my problem with her."

"Did she bother you today?"

"No," I said. "But I unplugged her from the phone lines and the Internet."

"Did you obsess over her?"

"No."

"Did you beat your head into a wall trying to make her behave a certain way?"

"No."

"Did—"

"Look," I said, cutting her off. "If this is going where I think it's going, you're not making me a happy camper. You promised me a solution, not a vacation."

Kimiko popped off the car with a nudge of her hip. "I wasn't finished. Besides, you're so obsessed with the one answer you can't have—a creation that likes you—you've yet to consider the possibility of any other answer. But to answer your accusation, yes, I removed Pi from your life for a day. That was part of what I had hoped you would get out of this. You can thank me later when you've calmed down and heard me out."

For a good while, billions upon billions of neurons in my head furiously exchanged data in an attempt to make sense of what she had said. Correction, I knew what she had said, but for the life of me, I couldn't understand why she had said it. Why the hell was taking me away from Pi was a good thing? Why the hell would she promise me one thing—a working Pi—and deliver another? As far as I was concerned, that was borderline deceitful. No, it *was* deceitful. And no amount of sex appeal was going to smooth that over. (`/* Guy disclaimer 583: By no amount of sex appeal, we do not literally mean no amount of sex appeal, only far more than what was in the foreseeable future. */`)

I hit my internal ctrl+alt+del and rebooted my conversation skills. "So you lied to me?"

"No, I didn't," she said. "I told you time and again I wasn't fixing Pi."

"You knew how I'd take it."

Kimiko shrugged. "I can't help how you take things, Gabe. And like I said, there was more to it than that. I wish you'd give me a chance to explain."

For the first time since knowing her, I felt talked down to. "Explain what?" I said. "Do you have any idea how important fixing Pi by Monday is?"

"It's not as important as you think, for you or for Pi."

The conversation took on a surreal nature. How such a thing could escape her lips was beyond my comprehension. She was supposed to be my girlfriend, my sweetheart, my darling, understanding, samurai hottie who supported all that I did and all that I wanted. And here she was acting like deliberate sabotage was in my best interest. "You should be the last person to say such a thing," I said. "I have to present her to your dad on Monday. She has to work. She has to be perfect."

"Oh she does, does she? You really think Dad is that shallow?"

"Wanting something to be fully functional is hardly being shallow," I said. "What do you think Pi will be worth to him if she's broken? What do you think she'll be worth to anyone, broken, for that matter?"

Kimiko straightened. In hindsight, it wasn't because she was trying to come up with a sales number, which I erroneously thought. "I think she's worth a lot more than you do, apparently," she said.

"She's not worth anything if she's gimpy, which is exactly what this attitude of hers makes her," I said, shocked I had to spell it out. "She has to be a hundred percent bug and defect free. All you did was cut the time I had to work on her in half."

"So you only want the best then, is that it?"

"Why settle for mediocrity?"

"And the best is without any flaw whatsoever."

"She wouldn't be the best if there was one, would she?"

"She'll always have a flaw, Gabe," she said. "Always. No one is perfect. The sooner you can get your head wrapped around that fact, the better."

"Not her," I said. "Not my girl."

Kimiko's face was entirely flat, aside from her eyes, that is. There, deep inside, I could see a storm brewing. The edge to her voice was as sharp as a katana's blade. "She already talks. She's self-aware. According to you, she's already leaps and bounds beyond anything anyone else has ever made, and for some reason, that's still not good enough for you. For some reason, you still can't see her worth."

Before I could say anything else, Kimiko yanked open the driver door to her car and got in. I remained outside, unsure why she was giving me such a hard time over Pi. The passenger door unlocked with a click, and its window slid down.

"Get in," she ordered, barely throwing me a glance.

I complied. Before I had a chance to get my seatbelt on, she fishtailed out of the parking lot. Now, being a male, I fully admit that we as a species have our limitations, including, but not limited to, the fact that we cannot read the minds of our female counterparts no matter how often they insist we can. I'm not sure why they hold us at fault for that, but maybe females really do operate on a higher plane. Maybe they are running the latest, fully upgraded Windows while we males are stuck in DOS 1.1. Maybe our tiny, 8-bit operating systems are simply incapable of processing the most basic subroutines of their bazillion-bit glory, and we should be able to read minds. Or maybe, females are insane. (I have learned that saying that out loud can be detrimental to one's health, so I kept all of these thoughts to myself.) Anyway, I didn't need ESP to know she was pissed at me, and at the time, I assumed it was because I wasn't praising her for tricking me into a mini vacation.

Fifteen minutes and a few uncomfortable red lights later, I had had enough of the silent treatment. Apparently, even though she claimed to be a straightforward person, she wanted to play games. I was about to confront her on it (i.e. say something dumb) when, for whatever reason, I took note of how she controlled the car.

On the left side of the wheel sat a lever which I had incorrectly assumed was some bass-ackwards installation on the transmission. On closer inspection, however, I realized it was tied into the brakes and accelerator pedals on the floor board—or rather, where they should have been. And that's when I stared at her prosthetics and finally put two and two together.

"Oh damn," was about the only thing I could think or say. But that wasn't enough, I knew. And like a malfunctioning printer port,

I started spitting crap out over and over and over. "That's not how I meant any of it, I swear," I said. "Pi isn't you. She's work, really. Work I'm always making sure is perfect. And I thought we were talking about her and not about you and—"

"Gabe," she said, cutting me off and not throwing a single look my way. "Quiet."

"I'm trying to apologize," I said defensively. "Since when has that been a bad thing?"

"I know when someone's back tracking," she said, easing to a stop. "And even if you weren't talking about me directly, it gives me an insight into what you think about me. I might be good. Hell, I might even be great. But I'm not without defect. You'll always want more. When your glow about me wears off, deep down, you'll always wish I were perfect."

"No, I won't," I said. Frustration was getting to me. I shifted in the seat in a vain attempt to get comfortable. "I don't care about your legs. I meant it before. They're cool. You shouldn't feel bad about them at all."

Kimiko laughed, and not in the cute, funny, or amusing sort of ways. It was one of those laughs that smacks you in the face and causes you to think, "What the hell did I just say?"

"You give yourself too much credit, Gabe," she said, hitting the accelerator as the light turned green. "No one has, can, or will make me feel bad about them. They are what they are, and I live my life quite well exactly how I am."

"Then why are you mad at me?"

"I'm mad at you because you didn't bother to listen to me," she said. "You cut me off before I could tell you everything about how skydiving, Pi, and your problems with her are all related. And you assigning a, 'If perfect, then want. Else, cast aside,' mentality to others made me not like you as a person. It didn't make me feel bad about myself."

Wow. That was the first thought in my head. Not because of her view on my character, but because she used pseudo-programming language to make a point. And she used it well. Okay, so it was a little simplistic, but still, there was a certain geeky-hotness to it all. "You've got me all wrong. I'm not like that," I finally said.

"People show their true colors when they aren't watching every word," she said.

"And sometimes things come out in a way you didn't intend," I countered. "I can differentiate between a person and a program."

"Are you sure about that?" she said, not missing a beat. "Haven't you always gone on and on about how Pi isn't a typical program? Haven't you told me that the true test of her nature will be that she'll be indistinguishable from a real person?"

"Well, yeah," I admitted reluctantly. I didn't need a roadmap to see where this was going, and I desperately sought to find an exit off the highway Screwed-75. "Jim is my best friend," I said, opting for a new tack. "He's far from perfect."

"And when he and Courtney made a mistake you blasted them for it," she said.

"He's still my best friend," I said. "And I did apologize to him later on."

"You probably did," she said. "Jim doesn't seem like the type to take abuse indefinitely. But honestly, Gabe, if you could 'fix' him, we both know you would. So forgive me if I don't believe that you wanting to fix Pi doesn't carry over to me," she said. "Forgive me if I want someone that wants me as is. Forgive me if I'm a little wary of your intentions."

Her last comment threw me off. "My intentions?"

Kimiko whipped around the next curve, forcing me to brace myself in my seat. "I've had the unfortunate experience of dating more than one person who was more interested in winning Dad over than winning me," she said, flying down the straightaway. "Got a new product? Want a new promotion? Hook up with the CEO's daughter and watch that career rise."

"I've been working on this all my life," I said. "You had nothing to do with it. Besides, you asked me out first, remember?"

"Maybe you're an opportunist."

"I'm not an opportunist," I said, insulted. I may be demanding on myself and others, but I don't take advantage of people, ever. Even Michelle would have given me that much.

The car stopped once again, only this time, it wasn't at a red light. It was in front of my house. "We're here," she said. She put the car into neutral and pulled the handbrake, but kept the engine running. Not a good sign.

"Thanks for the jump," I said, one hand resting on the door handle. "It was fun."

"You're welcome," she replied.

Her cold voice didn't set well in my heart, which was strange, I thought, seeing how technically speaking, I'd only know her for a few days. "So this is it?" I asked.

"For now," she said.

"What can I do to change that?"

Kimiko raised an eyebrow. "You mean fix?"

"Set things right," I clarified.

For the first time since I'd met her, Kimiko seemed at a loss for words. She toyed with her necklace and stared out the window before she finally said, "I don't know. The only thing I do know is I need time to myself."

"How much time?"

"Enough to make sure I'm not settling for you," she said. "Enough to be sure I can believe you when you say today was a fluke and that your true colors weren't shining through the façade you've built. I mean, if this is how you are now, what will it be like in six months when the mask really drops?"

"You can trust me." I said, feeling my mouth run dry. Yeah, it was a dumb, perfectly cliché response, but it was the only one I could come up with. "And whatever you think about me, I'm not using you to get in good with your dad."

"Like I said, Gabe, I need time to sort this out," she said. "This isn't a light decision."

I looked at her with shock. "I can't believe you won't cut me some slack over a few ill-chosen words."

"It's what was behind those words that matter. I've learned to trust my gut," she said looking down and staring at her mother's necklace. "And right now, I'm not sure what it's saying. Hopefully that will change soon, but right now I want to soak in a hot bath and be alone. Maybe then I'll know what I need to do."

With a heavy sigh and slump of my shoulders, I swung the passenger door open. For a moment, with one foot resting on the curb and the other still on the floor board of her Porsche, I tried to figure out how the hell one single day could be such a rollercoaster of excitement, terror, and heartbreak. No answer came. All I knew was my quest for AI was still stalled, and my love life was spiraling out of control. Surprisingly, the latter bothered—nay, hurt—me more than the foremost.

"I've got to get going," Kimiko said as a car pulled up behind us.

"Yeah," I replied absently. The relationship had changed forever. I'd managed to poison it in its infancy. And now, instead of seeing this relationship grow into something fun and full of life, I was watching it on its deathbed, hooked to machines that could barely keep it sustained. I was standing there, helpless, as the doctor was saying that they'd done all they could do. It was time to let go and move on.

My chest constricted, and with only seconds at best to come up with a course of action, I switched into tree mode.

Are we about to lose this relationship? Yes.

Is this the most important thing to us at this time? Yes.

Are we willing to show it? Yes.

Show it.

I swung my leg back in the car and shut the door. "I'm not leaving," I said.

"What?"

"I'm not leaving 'til we work this out." And I wasn't. I had made up my mind and that was that.

From the look of astonishment in her eyes, I wasn't sure if she was going to hug me or mace me. In hindsight, maybe I should have considered that in my decision tree before planting myself in her car.

Thankfully, she didn't blast me with both barrels, but she did fire a warning shot. Her left hand drifted between her seat and her door to where I couldn't see it, and she looked at me square in the eyes and said, "Gabe, you're not making me feel very comfortable. Please go home."

At that point I realized how creepy this was getting on my end, and I tried my best to be as non-confrontational as possible. "Give me two minutes, and I promise I'll go," I said. I wasn't sure what I'd do with those two minutes, but it was better than nothing. At least that would give me something to work with.

"No, Gabe," she said. "Dad can't butt heads with me and get his way. What makes you think you can?"

"Sixty seconds then," I countered. "Sixty seconds and I'll leave without another word. And I won't call you until you call first."

She went to speak again, but I kept rambling on, hoping that she'd succumb to my relentless barrage of words. "It's all I'm asking for, one tiny little minute. Surely I was worth enough to you at some point for you to hear me out over one tiny little minute."

Kimiko turned off the car. I was hoping in that moment, she was going to grant my request. But in the end, I never found out. Instead of giving me the green light, Kimiko glanced up at the rearview mirror as a second car rolled up behind us, then another, and another. "I think you should go see why Michelle is here," Kimiko said. "And why she brought the cops."

Chapter 01110

```
void IcingOnCake() {
  Arrest(Gabe);
  ~Pi();
```

"What?" I twisted around in my seat. My brain refused to believe what my eyes took in. Half a dozen cars brightly illuminated the front of my otherwise pitch-black house, and sure enough, Michelle was marching her way to my front door with a plethora of cops behind her. Two more cop cars and a large, white van pulled into the driveway, prompting me to act. Without thinking, I jumped out of Kimiko's Porsche and slammed the door shut.

Instantly, Michelle and her cohort of police turned in my direction. She pointed at me and said something to those around her. Three of the cops peeled off the group and headed my way. Michelle continued on to the front door, keys in hand.

"Hey!" I yelled. "What the hell are you doing?"

I had enough common sense not to go charging the lot of them. I'm sure I would have been tackled. And given that one of the approaching officers actually had his hand on his holster like I was some common criminal, I might even have been drawn upon. Or shot. Wouldn't Pi have loved that?

"Mr. Erikson?" the lead officer said. "I need you to take a step back and calm down."

I complied as best I could. I did take the step back, but it was from reflex more than anything else. As for calming down, well, I suppose that will always be in the eye of the beholder. "I don't know what this is all about," I said, pissed as all hell that my rights were being trampled right in front of my eyes. "But she doesn't live here anymore, and she is definitely not allowed to let you in."

"She can most certainly let us in with a warrant," the officer replied. He was six-three, maybe six-four, which meant I had to look up to him, not something I'm used to. And he was easily two-forty or two-fifty, practically all muscle. His clean shaven, square jaw, and tight hair cut only polished off the image that he loved being a cop, and being the best one he could be. Twenty said he regularly bench pressed dozens of gang members with one arm for fun.

"I need you to turn around and put your hands on the trunk of the car," he said.

Despite his command, I still wanted answers. And I'll be damned if I wasn't going to get them. It's not like I had killed anyone. "What's this is all about?"

"Sir, for your own safety during an open investigation, you need to turn around and put your hands on the trunk of the car," he said, now flanked by two of his cohorts.

"Mr. Erikson, please turn around," the officer to his left added. This guy was shorter, fatter, and looked much less patient.

"Look man," was all I got out before the fat cop put a hand on my shoulder, spun me around, and had me pressed against Kimiko's car. Like some urban cowboy roping a runaway calf, he had my arms behind my back and wrists cuffed in a matter of seconds.

"Stay right there, ma'am," I heard the fat one say.

As I best I could, I twisted underneath fatass's continued pressure on my back and craned my head to find Kimiko. She stood a few feet away on the other side of the car with her arms crossed over her chest and a scowl upon her face. I wasn't sure if she was perturbed at me or the cops. Maybe both.

"I swear, Kimiko, I have no idea what's going on," I said. My mind furiously searched for an answer. There had to be a mistake. I hadn't done anything illegal. At least, not since I was nine. And that was an accident. And I'm pretty sure there's a statute of limitations on the inadvertent theft of a Hershey bar.

"I believe you," she replied.

I exhaled sharply. That was something at least.

Maybe it was my semi-relaxed state, but for whatever reason, fatty cop flipped me over so I could now see what was happening.

"Is this your house, Mr. Erikson?" he said.

"You know it is," is what I wanted to say. But I knew antagonizing them would only make things worse. Cops played by rules I couldn't overwrite, and those rules included the ability to dick someone around if they wanted. Granted, I'd never had a full run in with the police aside from the odd speeding ticket, but I wasn't stupid either. So I answered his question sans-snark. "Yeah. I live here."

"Does anyone else live with you?" he asked.

"No," I replied. "Michelle moved out a few weeks ago."

"Can I see your ID?"

I paused, not expecting him to ask permission for anything. Okay, he wasn't really asking permission at this point. That was obvious. But still, it felt weird for him to ask. "It's in my wallet. Front left pocket."

The cop reached in my pocket, grabbed my wallet, and flipped out my driver's license. He looked it over before saying, "I'll be right back."

That left me alone with the first cop, Mr. Brickhouse, and the third, tall and skinny one. Number three was maybe in his forties, with a veteran look in his eyes. He had a weathered face and some graying hair. The entire time he kept quiet and observed Mr. Brickhouse, myself, and Kimiko with equal attention.

Whatever was on Mr. Quiet's mind, he didn't share it one bit, and that made me uneasy. It made me feel like whatever was going on was big. That feeling grew tenfold when two silver Lincoln LS's rolled up and four suits got out looking like they'd come straight from the latest MiB movie.

"Now can you tell me what this is about?" I asked Mr. Brickhouse.

"One of the agents wants to do that," he replied. "We're only detaining you until your questioning."

Agents? As in the DEA? ATF? NSA? God, could this be any worse? Then I thought of Jim and his conspiracies. And then I thought about how much he'd be freaking out right now and would be trying to swallow a cyanide capsule if he had one. Hell, he'd probably try and swallow one anyway if I called him on the phone right now.

"What's so funny?" Mr. Brickhouse asked.

"Nothing, sorry," I said, realizing I had been grinning. "This is a little too surreal is all."

That seemed to placate the guy.

"What about me?" Kimiko asked. "Are you guys going to keep me here all night, too?"

"I'll get to you in a minute," he said. "For now, I'd appreciate it if you'd remain where you are, ma'am, until we get this straightened out."

A few minutes passed before cops and suits began walking out of my house one at a time, each carrying lots of somethings in their arms. Black somethings. Rectangular somethings. Somethings that looked like old-school VCRs. Or DVD players. Or servers.

"Pi!" I yelled, instinctively lunging forward.

I got about three paces before Mr. Quiet put a knee into my stomach. I doubled over and dropped to the ground. Coughing, sputtering, I tucked my knees under my chest as I struggled to get up.

"Stop!" I yelled while two sets of hands and an immense amount of weight tried to wrestle me back to the ground. "You'll kill her!"

But my cries went unheeded, and I was flattened a second later on my lawn.

"Don't move!" Mr. Brickhouse yelled right next to my face.

It was loud enough to get my ears ringing, but I didn't care. I pushed up as much as I could for all I was worth, and the weight on my back increased a hundred fold. My muscles gave. I hit the ground and the wind shot out of my lungs. I lay there, gasping, coughing, and helplessly watched as they continued to carry Pi's dismembered body out of my house.

I then spaced out for God knows how long. Eventually, I realized I was being carried off by two boys (well, one boy, one girl) in blue. Their arms went under my shoulders, and my feet were dragged across the lawn. It was a little rough, but at least they didn't completely manhandle me into the back of one of their cars.

The door shut. Trapped behind a metal cage and thick glass, I sank into the seat. Pi was gone, and there was nothing I could do about it. I guessed they probably flipped a switch—if I was lucky, that is—and dismantled her on the spot. No shut down sequence. No attempt to unplug things in the proper order. Even if I got her back, her body that is, there was no telling if she'd be the same. Hell, there was no telling if she'd even boot. At this point, for all I knew, she was dead. Gone for good. And now I was probably going to be arrested for something that had the word felony in it.

Hell.

~ π ~

```
class InterrogationRoom {
  public:
    void WasteTime();
    void Summon_Investigator(agent);
```

I'm sure somewhere in the manual there's a section that calls for a twelve-hour delay before any questioning. After all, they sure were in a big hurry to show up at my house, lights blazing, hack apart Pi, and pummel me to the ground. And they certainly didn't waste any time driving me back to the county precinct and stuffing me in a small, twelve-by-twelve room with only two folding chairs and a small table. But once I was there, things got slow. Really, really slow. Like an 8088 checking a 10 meg hard drive for errors slow. Like 300 baud modem slow.

So, after a few hours of sitting in my tiny little blue room of boring and counting the tiles for the thousandth time, I started thinking about my predicament. This had to be related to Pi. Why else would they take her? At first I blamed her for what had happened, but that didn't last long. Truth was, as much as I playfully considered to be God, I wasn't. I was just a programmer that lost control of his program, and no amount of typing was going to get me out of this trouble with the law. As much as I wanted to be able to debug my life on my own, I knew I was going to need help.

Eventually, someone finally entered the room. I was so surprised someone had come that while I was rocking in my chair, I teetered when I should have tottered and ended up crashing to the floor.

"Damn," I said, sitting up and rubbing the back of my head. "You guys should warn someone before coming in like that."

"You've got some explaining to do, Gabe."

Still planted on the ground, I looked to the door so my eyes could confirm what my brain refused to accept from my ears. "Michelle?" I said. "What are you doing here?"

Michelle stepped around me, looking sharp in one of her many black business suits. She had a leather portfolio tucked under one arm. Seriousness chiseled her face and exuded in her posture. I could do nothing but gawk and wonder where this side of her had been hiding all the time we were together. Don't get me wrong, I'd seen her game face before, but nothing like this. I mean, when the hell did she go from TV exec to criminal interrogator?

"Get up and get in your seat," Michelle said, sitting in the other one.

I complied without word. Once I had, I decided to get the obvious out of the way. "So when did you stop working for Channel Eight and become a cop?"

"I'm not a cop, and my employment with Channel Eight was situational," she said coldly. "The police here are merely assisting an investigation at this junction."

"You know what I mean," I said. "Are you going to tell me who you are with or not?"

Michelle reached into her jacket and flipped open and tossed her ID on to the table like a knight casting a gauntlet.

A cursory glance was all it took. "FBI, huh?" I said. I tried to keep as good of a poker face as I could since they meant serious business and I didn't need to be any more at a disadvantage than I already was. The thought of calling a lawyer at this point crossed and stayed in my mind. But I also wanted a few questions of my own answered and I figured if I stopped talking, so would she. "So," I said, leaning forward. "How long have you been with them? Since before we got together?"

Michelle folded her hands together, leaned forward, and stared me down. It was all I could do not to shrink back. How did she ever hide all this from me?

"Don't worry about that," she said.
"Why?"

"Because it doesn't concern you," she replied. "What does concern you, however, is being sure that you tell me the truth, the whole truth, and nothing but the truth."

I rolled my eyes at the annoying game we were playing. Yeah, evidently my ex-girlfriend was actually a government suit, and now she was looking to bust me. But I'd seen her naked and in compromising positions. It's hard to be completely intimidated by someone you used to tie up. Then again, she did break up with me, and when we'd met at The Melting Pot she seemed bitter. And then there was the whole ordeal with the bounced check. Damn, maybe she was looking to see me fry. So, in typical male defense, I decided to go a little offensive myself. "I bet you jumped at the chance to skewer me," I said. "I can't believe Jim was right about you."

"Actually, Gabe. I didn't want to take this on," Michelle said. "I wanted to move on with my life since you didn't want to include me in yours. My assignment had nothing to do with you. So you can take your narcissism and shove it."

I blinked and sat back. I was shocked. Impressed. Slightly turned on. Eventually, I realized I should probably say something, but nothing witty or smooth came to mind, only something simple. "What am I being charged with?"

"That all depends on how cooperative you are," she said.

I snickered. "Yeah, right. I don't need Jim around to tell me how this works from here on out. Let me go or get my lawyer."

"Gabe, Gabe, Gabe," she said, opening her portfolio and thumbing through some papers. "First, we can detain you for a while before we actually have to file charges. I can keep you here for a long, long time, even if you don't say a word. That means no dates with Kimiko. No working on whatever your current project is. No playing zombie games with Jim. Keep that in mind while you think about whether or not you want to mess with me. Besides, we both know you've never kept a lawyer on retainer."

"I can sure as hell hire one," I said.

Michelle stopped paging through the stack, and with a flick of her fingers, sent a couple of pages sailing my way. The pages were an activity log of my bank accounts, checking and savings, over the past thirty days. "Not from this account you won't," she said. "You're broke."

"I want a lawyer," I said once more. This time, however, my conviction wasn't quite as strong. She was right, I had none. Nor could I afford one. Still, I didn't want to give up anything that could bite me in the ass. "I'm not saying anything else till I get one."

Michelle smiled. It was the type that been used throughout history to lull many a man into a false sense of peace, possibly seduction, only to be knifed in the back a moment later. "Suit yourself," she said. "I'm going to advise you, however, that if it's a public defender you're wanting, that's going to take some time for you to go through the process. That's also time I could spend being productive instead of being stuck here with you. That doesn't make me very happy, Gabe. That doesn't make me want to go easy on you."

"Are you denying me my right to an attorney?" I said, narrowing my eyes. Two could play hardball. I didn't get in front of Mr. Pratt with a multimillion-, if not billion-, dollar project by being a pushover. "And isn't there some sort of law against you leading the investigation on me? This has got to be a conflict of interest."

"Who said I'm leading the investigation?" she said. "And what you're trying to reference is more of an internal policy, just so you know. You worry about your own future. Let us worry about the investigation."

"I'm not saying anything until I get a lawyer."

"I'll tell you what, Gabe," she said, taking back her papers. "You can sit there in silence all you want. But you are going to listen to me."

I smiled, sat back, and crossed my arms. Point, me.

"What I'm thinking right now is this whole Pi thing is a sham," she said.

My eyebrows rose at the insult to both my integrity and my ability. "Excuse me?"

"Admit it, Gabe," she said. "This whole AI bit is nonsense. Made up. A story. A *lie*."

Her emphasis on her last word, "lie" wasn't lost on me, and a brief twinge of hate ran through my body. Then it occurred to me she was trying to provoke me, trying to get me to say something I shouldn't. "Believe whatever you want," I said.

Michelle smirked and sent some other pages out of her stack over to me. "How about these," she said. "Do they look familiar?"

I looked down at them. IP addresses, date stamps, and file names were listed line after line after line after line. I knew what these pages were: a server log detailing Internet activity. Their significance, however, was completely lost on me. "I have no idea what these are about," I said.

"They are addresses of computers you accessed over the past week from your home," she said. "Do you want to keep playing dumb? Or do you want to concede that the data we pulled from both your router and your ISP is truthful."

"I didn't realize surfing links off Google was a crime," I replied.

"You didn't surf on this one, Gabe," she said, taking out a pen and putting a small mark next to the address 208.46.17.11. "Want to tell me about this one?"

"If I knew what that was, sure," I said. "Sorry, even I don't memorize the IPs of all the sites I go to."

"It's one of NASA's servers. But you didn't know that did you?"

A lump formed in my throat. I tried to swallow as discreetly as possible. This wasn't about surfing the Internet, I knew. The FBI has been big on investigating cybercrimes for years and years, and I was all but certain at this point someone was tinkering around some servers she shouldn't have been. Someone that did so from my house. And that someone could only be Pi.

Michelle sat back. The corners of her lips curled ever so slightly. "There's that glint in your eye," she said. "You know."

I shifted in my seat. The air grew hot and stifling. Part of me wondered if it was simply my body reacting to the sudden influx of stress, but another part, the part cultivated by Jim, wondered if they didn't screw with the thermostat on purpose.

"So what did you want with NASA?" she said. "It had to be something, or were you simply trying to test yourself? I'm guessing the latter, but what I really can't figure out is why you didn't even bother to cover your tracks. You didn't even hide behind a single proxy. Even a twelve-year-old script kiddie has enough sense to put on at least one condom."

"I think I should speak to my lawyer," I repeated as flatly as I could. Outwardly at this point, I felt I was doing well. Inwardly, I was furious. I was furious with Pi for ever doing such a thing—and who knows why she did it. Lastly, I was furious with myself as well for being dumb enough to give her open access to the entire world in the first place. What sort of stupid god actually lets an infantile creation have access to everything without rules and safeguards in place?

"You don't have to answer me," she said taking the papers. She scanned through the lines for a few seconds and then circled a large set of addresses before turning the pages back around so I could read them. "72.21.81.85. The FBI. Of all the places to hack, you chose us. If I didn't know you better, Gabe, I'd say you were begging to be thrown in prison. You had to know we'd trace you in a heartbeat."

I bit my lip and let out a long, hate-filled breath from my nostrils. I probably had a raging bull image going. No, I take that back, I probably had a little Jehovah look going as He stared down at the sin-filled world moments before the Flood. I, like He, grieved at the decision regarding Creation. I, like He, wanted to wipe it all clean.

"Care to comment?" she asked.

I shook my head. I had that much sense. If I was going to get crucified, I wasn't going to make it easy for them. And hell, if I got lucky, maybe I could even get off. It's not as if the most heinous of murderers had never escaped due to a botched investigation or prosecution. I figured that might be my only hope.

Michelle scooped up the papers and tucked them into her portfolio before closing it. "Look Gabe," she said. "You hacked the FBI. I have no idea why. Nor do I have any idea why you'd upload a thousand text files that all say, 'Gabe is stupid.' Feigning ignorance or taking on a new hobby as a mute isn't going to save you. You know that."

I laughed. I couldn't help it, even if it was one of the most childish things Pi had done to date. I mean, who expects that as an actual line of attack? Parents of a toddler in a full temper tantrum would be my only guess. I suppose I should've been upset, but how could I be mad when everything she did—even if it was immature, annoying, and illegal—was just further verification she was sentient and a total genius?

Michelle stared at me much the way I imagine a bull does when it's finally had enough from the matador. "Did I say something funny?"

"Pi," I said. "I'm laughing at Pi who is doing everything she can to make my life miserable."

"Pi, your AI."

I nodded.

"That's one story," she said. "But I think I've got a better one. I think you made some sort of code-breaking algorithm, something that lets you hack through some pretty heavy encryption. You tested it on your own bank account, and then when it worked, you went on to bigger game. Maybe you were tired, or maybe your ego got in the way, or maybe you've actually cracked and you dreamed up this whole Pi thing. But whatever the reason is, you went on to see what other systems you could hack into. You wanted to see how good of a programmer you were, didn't you?"

I shook my head. "Not even close."

Michelle went on, apparently uninterested in the truth. "After you played around in a few systems, your high wore off, didn't it? Or maybe you actually came back to reality and realized what you did. That's when you concocted this AI story, threw out some text files pointing right to yourself because you knew you'd be traced without any difficulty. So, maybe you're angling for some sort of an insanity defense, I don't know. But what I do know is, it'll never fly."

"Then arrest me and be done with it," I said. It was a ballsy move, but I knew at this point there had to be something more. If they wanted to feed me to the lions, they would have already.

"Tell us about your algorithm, Gabe," she said. "Tell us all about it, and if it's as good as we think it might be, maybe we can cut a deal when it comes to the prosecution. I want to know exactly how you managed to hack through a 1024-bit encryption in under two hours."

So there it was. They wanted Pi. Or at least, they wanted what Pi did. "No," I said. "I'm not cutting any deals without my lawyer here."

"A public defender isn't going to fight for you tooth and nail, Gabe," she said. "And I promise this offer will expire before he gets here."

She was bluffing. I could see it in her eyes, in the way her fingers tightly clutched her sides under folded arms. When we had still been together, if I had called her on it, we'd have both ended up laughing and smooching. But not this time. Regardless of our past, right now, I knew where she stood. That little fact did wonders in terms of empowerment. So I spent a moment or two trying to figure out what was going on, what I had that she couldn't take. She already had Pi. I saw them haul her out of my house.

Well, no, I thought. They had the servers. Correction. They had the servers in pieces. I grinned. "You can't start her back up, can you?"

"Don't worry about what we can and can't do," she said, leaning forward. "Answer my question."

Her reply came too fast, her attack, too strong. My grin grew. "Here's what I think, sweetie. You guys fucked Pi up when you yanked her apart, and now you can't get the servers to boot," I said. "Your little tech boys probably tried to get her up and running, but since she's not written using any conventional platforms, they don't even know where to begin in order to put her back together again, do they? That's why you need me, isn't it? That's why you're so eager to cut me some sort of deal before they accidently ruin it all."

The door opened a split second later, and one of many nameless boys in blue stuck his head in the door. "His lawyer is here," he said. "And he wants to talk to his client."

Michelle looked back to me with a raised eyebrow. I'm sure she was intrigued that I had one, yet annoyed that I did. I had no idea where this mystery lawyer had come from, clearly not from the office of the public defender, but I wasn't going to look a gift horse in the mouth. I'd take whoever he was.

Michelle quickly recomposed herself. "Saved by the bell," she said.

Yes. Yes, I was. And I would be ever grateful to whoever sent this angel my way.

Chapter 01111

```
#include <kickassattorney.h>
```

Michelle left and before the door could close behind her, in stepped a fifty-something sharp-featured man. The overhead light glinted off his bald head and the polished leather briefcase at his side. His black Armani suit had to have been worth a fortune, and the diamond cufflinks he wore looked like they'd fund a small army in Africa. "Mr. Erikson, I presume. Nathan Bernard," he said, shaking my hand. "Mr. Pratt sends his regards."

"Wow . . . wow! Mr. Pratt sent you?" I said, tripping over my words. I wasn't sure why Mr. Pratt sent this guy, as I didn't think he'd send any muscle at all to protect one of Kimiko's boyfriends who had pissed her off, but at this point, I didn't care. I had a lawyer, a kick-ass, high-priced one to boot.

Nathan patted me on the shoulder and sat down in Michelle's old seat. "Pratt & Taiki protects its assets," he said as he opened his briefcase and pulled out a thick manila folder. "First and foremost, I don't want you to worry. I've read the reports, and I had a few of our paralegals cranking out the preliminary research for your case."

"You got the police reports? Good God you guys are fast." I said. I'm sure my face reflected my shock.

"Mr. Pratt had us on the phone before you had reached the station," he said. "And after making a call to the police chief as well as the local FBI director, we got everything they had."

"That's insane," I said, mind spinning. "How do you guys have that much pull?"

Nathan flashed a grin. "The multibillion-dollar contracts Pratt & Taiki have with the Federal Government come with certain perks—perks that are especially useful when dealing with national security."

"Wow." I said.

"Wow, indeed," he said. He took out a legal pad and pen. "Let's get started, shall we? I need to know what you've told them."

"Nothing," I said. "I kept saying I wanted my lawyer."

"And they didn't grant you that request?" he said as he made a few jots on his notepad.

"No. Michelle didn't force me to answer any questions," I replied. "She just kept talking, hoping I'd slip up, I'd wager."

"Michelle is the FBI agent that interviewed you?"

"She's also my ex-girlfriend."

A soft hum escaped Nathan's lips, but he didn't choose to elaborate on his thoughts. "What did she say, exactly?"

For the next half hour, I tried to recall anything and everything that transpired between us, word-for-word. Several times Nathan would stop me about the phrasing I'd used. I guess he was looking to see how certain I was of what had transpired. After five pages of note taking, he flipped his pen over in his fingers and used it to tap the desk several times over. "I think it's safe to say you didn't say anything that could be problematic," he said. "I'll look over the case file and whatever recordings they have to be certain. Barring anything out of left field, I'll have you a free man in under an hour."

I bit my lip at his upbeat attitude. Part of me wondered if he was always this way, or if defending guys with a slew of cybercrimes was the norm. But no matter how positive he was, I couldn't quite believe I'd be free so easily since we were talking about hacking the FBI. They didn't tend to take such things well. He had to have meant something else other than all charges being dropped. "Do you mean we'll be out of here until trial? Or . . ."

"No, no, my good man," he said. "I mean you'll be free and clear, and this investigation will be closed." He riffled through some papers and then pulled out a packet of six stapled together and pushed them my way. "Initial each page, if you would, and sign at the bottom of the last."

"What is this?" I said, trying to decipher the Great Wall of Legalese before me.

"It's the contract you signed at the end of your meeting with Mr. Pratt," he said. "It outlines the details of your compensation for heading the AI project codenamed Pi, the goals of the project, and your protection under Pratt & Taiki's Top Secret Clearance Umbrella. This umbrella also grants you immunity from prosecution while working on said project."

"Wait, what?" My brain was having trouble putting things together. Well, no it wasn't. It was having trouble putting things together in a way that didn't amount to forgery.

"It's your contract that says you work for Pratt & Taiki, and it protects you," he said, heavily emphasizing the last three words. "It also includes your compensation package which you skillfully negotiated on October 10th of this year. So be sure to date it as such."

I stopped my scrutiny of the pages, looked up to find Nathan waiting patiently, smiling bright. "Is it safe to talk in here?" I asked, looking about.

"Of course," he said. "Attorney-client privilege is sacred."

"No, I mean, are you sure they aren't listening."

"I'm sure," he answered. "My assistant is seeing that they don't do anything they should not." He then cleared his throat and raised his voice a few decibels. "And if by chance anyone is, I assure you, we'll see their lives are ruined beyond repair."

"Okay," I said. "Okay, okay. Let me get my bearings."

"Take all the time you need, but we do have a board meeting to make. So be sure that time is less than five minutes."

I laughed. I'm not sure if he was trying to be intentionally funny, but his last statement struck me just right. Maybe it was the insanity of the day getting to me. "Okay, first question, why are you guys buying Pi when you haven't even seen her?"

"We're buying your project, codenamed Pi," he corrected. "Your recent escapades with NASA and the FBI have our attention. I'm certain in that genius head of yours, you can imagine how valuable your code is. We'd like to be the ones to further develop that code."

"Believe me, I know," I said, proud of both myself and more so Pi. Yeah, she had successfully screwed my life in ways I never thought possible, but I had to hand it to her, she'd hacked my bank account without any trouble, and did the same to NASA and the FBI. And one doesn't just walk into their computer systems and monkey around, let alone get past their security in less than two hours. So it's easy to understand why I—why Pratt & Taiki—would want to snatch up that code in a nanosecond. If Pi had managed to do that with little instruction and practice, what would she be capable of down the road? What else could she hack into if given even more power? How much would people, no, governments, be willing to pay for that? That's when I looked at the compensation package. Holy. Shit.

"Do you see something you like, Mr. Erikson?" Nathan said.

"Does that say twelve million?" I stammered. I felt woozy as I gawked at all those gorgeous zeros.

"Twenty thousand of which was due to you two weeks ago as a good faith deposit per our contract," he said. "We apologize for the delay due to an accounting error, and we will have it wired to your bank first thing Monday morning. We'll also clear up any confusion your bank might have had, and ensure your accounts are unfrozen."

"Sweet." I said.

Nathan nudged a pen my way. "Very sweet."

"What about the rest of the money?" I said, eyes scanning the contract for the details.

"Paid in installments, the bulk being delivered when we're satisfied you have delivered either a true, self-aware AI, or a robust method of cyber-attack," he said. "If you can deliver both, you'll note your compensation has the potential to grow fivefold or more based on how successful each of those projects are. Either way, in the end, we will own all rights to the intellectual properties while at the same time fully crediting you with heading the development. You'll never have to work again, Mr. Erikson, though should you choose, your resume will be unequalled." Nathan checked his watch and added, "Time is short, Mr. Erikson. Why don't you sign and date so we can get to our meeting?"

Even with that diamond carrot dangled in front of me, I balked and wanted to know more. "You said I get credit for everything, right? And I get to direct Pi's future?"

"Of course," he said with a smile. "You're the project lead. It states so implicitly on page one, third paragraph down. I understand you might think this is too good to be true, but I assure you, we're completely serious about our offer."

I'm sure he wasn't trying to be patronizing since his mission was undoubtedly to get me to sign at all costs, but I couldn't help feeling like he was. After checking the front page that I was indeed project lead, I flipped to the last page and stared at the line requesting my signature. All it would take is for me to give my John Hancock and I'd finally see my dream to its fruition. Pi would be recognized as AI. Pi would undoubtedly be given a new supercomputer to inhabit, and her current beauty, her current grandeur, would pale in comparison to what she would become with millions, if not billions of dollars' worth of processing power.

Deep down, however, some nameless thing kept bothering me, kept hounding me to be cautious. I wasn't sure what it was, and the only thing that came to mind was him asking me to back date my signature. "I'm not going to get into trouble doing this, am I? Dating it a month ago, I mean."

"Mr. Erikson," he said. "You don't get to our position without knowing how to sidestep landmines. We have a vested interest in not only our projects, but our valued employees as well. But, if you feel like you can't trust us or this is moving too fast, I understand. You're free to say no to our offer and take on another attorney to represent you."

I didn't need a binary tree to help me make that decision.

I signed.

~ π ~

/ Side note: sometimes getting exactly what you want shows you how much you didn't want it. */*

True to Nathan's word, I was out of the police station before an hour was up. Most of the cops said very little, but were at least polite about things. One even apologized for the inconvenience as he returned my stuff. Michelle, on the other hand, was anything but. She followed me out, not saying a word, but her eyes never left me until Nathan opened the door to my newly provided, black Lincoln Town Car and I climbed in. Did she really have it out for me? No, that wasn't it. If I thought about it and put my feelings aside, she probably wasn't lying before. She probably wanted to move on with life, and was just mad at the waste of time her brief, albeit intense, investigation of me had been. And knowing her, she might have been mad at the powerless position she had been put in at the end.

As we pulled away from the station, Nathan handed me a Dew. "Would you care for a drink? I understand it's your favorite."

"Yeah," I said, taking it and popping the top. "How'd you know?"

"You're dating Mr. Pratt's daughter," he said. "You aren't a stranger to us."

A brief, semi-nervous chuckle escaped, and I wondered what else Mr. Pratt might have dug up on me. Nothing bad I hoped. Of course, my soda tastes could have been a harmless comment from daughter to father, something said over dinner, perhaps. Something like, "Oh, he's so great, Daddy. Did you know he's a Dew drinker?" Maybe. Okay, I was reaching there.

We made small talk, and about forty minutes, two bottles of Dew, and a bathroom trip later, I stepped into the board room of Pratt & Taiki. The room was forty feet long and half that across, and had teak panels along the walls. Full-length windows formed a half circle at the far end and gave a spectacular view of the city. Warm rays from the morning sun splashed down on a carpet that looked like it would eat a week's pay just to clean a drop of wine. An elongated, mahogany table stood in the center of the room, and around it sat a group of people who could only be the Board.

Twelve in all, nine males, three females, turned their attention to me the moment I set foot inside. And for the first time since I began approaching companies and their executives about LCP long ago, I felt out of place. While the members of the Board wore what I was sure was their usual high-priced, business attire, I was still in my clothes from yesterday—grimy ones at that. While they looked ready to negotiate some billion-dollar deal, the only thing I looked like I could negotiate was a handout on a street corner.

Mr. Pratt, who was seated at the far end of the table, stood up. He looked exactly as I remembered him: tall and muscular, with a hardened face, short brown hair, and hawk-like eyes that looked like they didn't miss a thing. "Gabe," he said in a deep voice. "We're delighted you could come on such short notice. Please, have a seat."

"Thanks," I said, taking the nearest empty one and smoothing out my sweatshirt. "Forgive my appearance. It's been a rough night."

"Misunderstandings happen," he said, sitting back down. "We all know that. And if half of what these reports say are true, or even a quarter of what Kimiko told me last night, your current state will be the least on all our minds."

I perked. I'd guessed that Kimiko must have kicked off the chain of events leading to Nathan's arrival at the police station, but it was nice to hear a confirmation. I decided to get down to business. "So, where do we start?"

All eyes went to Mr. Pratt, who, with a wave of his hand toward me, said, "Why don't you give us a synopsis of Pi so we're all on the same page. Brief history, current state of affairs, challenges, where you see this going. That sort of thing."

And so I did. I told the board about my dream of creating real life. I spoke of the rush I felt when I originally birthed the idea on how to create an evolving piece of code that would gradually explore its world and incorporate its findings into its next iteration. I spoke of the joy I had when Pi's precursor came to life on my laptop and for the first time, took control of a game. More than once I found myself overly animated and pacing around, and forced myself to stand still if I couldn't bring myself to sit back down. No one seemed to mind. They were all riveted. By the time I told all about Pi's birth, abilities, and corruption, more than one member of the board appeared to share my frustration at her current state.

The room was silent for a good twenty or thirty seconds once I'd stopped. Then, on the far end of the table, a female, eyeglass-wearing board member spoke. "Mr. Erikson," she said like she was about to grill me on the witness stand. "This, rogue AI of yours—"

"Hang on a minute," interrupted an old guy that sat across from her. "I think you're jumping the gun on that."

"You don't think she's roguish, Bill?" she asked.

"No, Leona," he replied. "I'm saying let's not call it AI until we've seen it firsthand. Let's just call it a program until we've had a chance to thoroughly test it."

"We can argue semantics later," she replied before facing me once more. "Gabe, so we're clear, are you saying you've lost control of your program?"

I clasped my hands together and rested my chin on them in an effort to quell my nerves. I had no idea how they'd handle the complete truth. It's not that I wanted to lie to them, but I figured I should probably sugar coat things as best I could. "I haven't lost complete control of Pi," I said. "She still talks to me."

"But she acts without direction?" said Leona. "She does what she wants, and you're unable to give her commands, correct?"

I nodded, deciding to bite the bullet. If they wanted a demo, I'd look incredibly foolish, not to mention deceitful, if Pi ignored me. "Correct," I replied. "But I can't make anyone else do what I want either, and I still think they're self-aware. Well, most people at least. There are some I wonder about."

Leona chuckled, which was a relief. "I see your point," she said. "But certainly you see how that could be a problem for us. Self-aware or not, we can't have programs that users can't control, especially programs that are running our products. A guy as smart as you could easily appreciate the massive liability and moral responsibility looming over us."

"I get it," I said. "Believe me I get it. But I'm convinced with a little bit of time, Pi could be great and no risk whatsoever."

"We could hardwire her," Bill offered. "Give her some laws she can't violate, assuming she's real."

"No," I said. "You can't do that." The board gave me a collective look of confusion, and so I quickly expanded what I meant. "Pi was developed by writing code that adapts as needed. It evolves on its own. She wasn't developed by trying to dream up every real world scenario she'd find herself in."

"That may be, Gabe," said Leona. "But there's nothing stopping us from doing it now. It's great that she's gotten this far under your guidance, your innovation, but let's not discount the idea that some hard and fast laws might be exactly what we need to see this project through."

I shook my head and reminded myself that while the board was a group of elite, grizzled veterans of the corporate world, they were amateurs when it came to all things AI. I was going to have to explain things slowly, simply. "If you start hard coding things, you sacrifice the ability for Pi to think for herself," I said. "She'd only be following your instructions. She wouldn't be making up her own mind. And if you take that route, she'll fail because you can't account for all the variables in the real world. And you won't have an AI. All you'll have is a complex, bloated piece of software."

Bill went to object, but I cut him off before he could get a word out. "Let me also tack on this," I said. "Even if you disagree with me and try to control her with some sort of hard code, I'm not convinced that she won't find a way around it. I can easily envision her adapting to whatever shackles you try and put on her."

Mr. Pratt, who had been sitting silent at the head of the table cut in. "Do you think she can, Gabe?" he asked. His tone was neither concerned, nor surprised. No, it sounded like he was impressed.

"Maybe," I said, shrugging my shoulders. "Honestly I wouldn't put anything past her. She'll change anything inside her that doesn't make her hurt. And even then, I'd wager if she wanted something enough, she'd push through any pain."

"That's the other thing I wanted to ask you about," Leona said, briefly checking a set of notes she had in front of her. "Tell us more about this pain you've introduced. It seems an odd trait for a computer program."

I took a moment to try and sum up the idea. I wanted to give them a good understanding of it, a thorough one, but I didn't want to drone on for hours either and put them to sleep. "Well, it's not pain in the same sense as we experience it," I finally said. "It does, however, serve the same purpose. Things she sees as bad, things that hurt her code, cause errors, and what not are given a pain score. These scores weigh against any decision she might make. The greater the pain score, the more likely she is to avoid any action to further increase that score. But she will push through pain if what she wants is even more important to her, to speak."

To my surprise, Leona followed along far closer than I had anticipated. "So this pain system is an elaborate if/else switch in a decision tree. If 'a' is greater than 'b', do this, else, do that."

"That's one way of looking at it," I said. I didn't like the fact that she boiled Pi down to such a mundane thing, but that was more or less how pain operated.

"Is there another way?" she asked. "I'd genuinely like to know, because at this time, such a system seems pretty simplistic for something being peddled around as AI."

I grimaced internally. Was she really implying Pi was not as great as she was? That I was not as amazing as I was? The thought dawned on me that maybe she was testing my response, or being as thorough as she felt she needed, regardless of what her gut feelings were. She did seem like she was in favor of what I had to offer. So while inwardly I smarted, outwardly, I gave a warm smile and a pretty damn good explanation.

"Yes, it's a form of an if/else switch, and yes, it seems simplistic," I said. "But isn't that what we all do on some level? We avoid playing with fire because of the pain involved. But if burning ourselves nets us something even better, say, saving the life of our children, we undertake the task. The 'Save the child' score outweighs the 'Damn that hurts' score. It's the same principal, the same logic. Pi takes into account countless variables, tens of thousands sometimes, compiles a couple of scores and then makes her decision."

"I see your point. So could we use a method of reward and punishment to have Pi follow our commands?"

I bit my lip. I didn't like where this was going one bit. Maybe I was being paranoid, or maybe I was being an overprotective father, but images of someone whipping Pi's back over and over when she didn't perform to task came to mind. "She would respond, yes," I said. "But if those methods weren't well thought out, she could turn into a monster. And honestly, I'm not keen on the idea of forcing her to do anything under threat of pain."

"But you did say it wasn't pain as we think of it, correct?" Leona countered. "We're not really torturing her are we? And let's be honest, we all live in a world that gives consequences to actions. Hers will be no different. She might even thrive in a structured world with clear boundaries."

Before I could fully process my thoughts, Bill cut in. "We could always keep copies isolated on various servers. That way, we could experiment on them, find out what works and what doesn't, and we'd be able to erase any copies that go psychotic. I see no reason to limit development to only one instance of Mr. Erikson's program."

I balled one hand into a fist. Maybe it would have been prudent of me to keep my bearings, but then again, I don't think any other normal father would. Who in his right mind wouldn't be enraged if he was told, "Hey, we're going to clone your daughter and run some tests on the copies, okay? Oh, and if something goes wrong, we're going to shoot them in the head and move on." No one, that's who. As a side note, I am impressed I responded so politely, since my gut instinct was to throw a few expletives in. "Pi is more than a program," I said. "I'm not going to let you mutilate her."

Mr. Pratt ended the confrontation. "Let's stay focused and cordial, gentlemen," he said. "Gabe, I understand there are certain ethical and moral questions involved. Those questions, however, are for another time and place. Given development cycles, that conversation won't need to be addressed for quite some time. Right now, Gabe, we need you to come in tomorrow and bring Little Computer People back online. Once you do that, we can reconvene and discuss what needs to be done so we can take over development."

I must have had a stupid look on my face, because Pratt then added, "Is something the matter Gabe?"

"No," I lied. Truth was, everything was wrong, or felt wrong at least. I couldn't put my finger on what it was, but I was fairly sure it had something to do with my last exchange with Bill.

"I ask because I thought this is exactly what you wanted when you came into my office," Mr. Pratt said. "I was under the impression that you wanted to show off this AI of yours in order to sell it to us. That is what the papers you signed this morning outlined."

I nodded, but didn't reply. My mind was going fuzzy. It was hard to think.

"Then we're all on the same page," Mr. Pratt said. "I assure you of this Gabe; when it's all said and done, Pi will be in good hands."

"Yeah," I said, absently. I had wanted the fame and fortune that would come with Pi's success, but I never wanted to lose her completely, and that's where things were headed and there was nothing I could do about it.

The board voted unanimously to pursue the project, and despite all the pats on the back, handshakes a plenty, and praises how good I should feel about myself and my future, on the car ride home, what I really felt was small.

~ π ~

Kimiko.Blast(Gabe, Maximum_Firepower);

I spent the first hour home mindlessly straightening up the place. It helped me think as I tried to figure out what the hell was bothering me. To my surprise, cleaning the living room turned out to be not much of a chore since sans Pi it was more or less a void. The bedroom, however, was another matter. Thankfully, I did make a dent in it by the time I got bored and opted for an online game of Left 4 Dead 2, my favorite zombie shooter. I dug my laptop out of the closet—thank God they didn't take that—and plopped onto my bed, ready to play. Three hours and five thousand blasted zombies later, the doorbell rang.

Normally, a person at the door wouldn't be a problem. I could go AFK and let the computer play my character as I went to see who it was. But this time, things were tricky in the game. Myself and two other survivors of this digital apocalypse had reached the safe house, a.k.a. the end of the level. The fourth player, however, had yet to reach the fortified position and was fighting a losing battle against hordes of undead. If I let the computer take control, player number four was a goner, no doubt. The AI wasn't good enough to rescue him. If I tried to save him, however, whoever was at my door might not hang around long enough for me to succeed in my online rescue attempt. Yeah, it was just a game, but still, it's a game that's easy to get sucked into. And when that happens, you don't ever want to leave a survivor behind, virtual or not.

The doorbell rang a second time, and reality trumped. I typed out a quick, "gtg, door," for my teammates and left the game. I hurried down the hall to see who was paying me a visit and tried to guess who it was. Jim, most likely. Or maybe Court. No one else ever dropped by unannounced, except for the cops. But I doubted it was them, given the heavy hitter lawyers I now had on my side.

I opened the door and was shocked at who was waiting for me. "Kimiko," I stammered. "Hi. I wasn't expecting you. Sorry it took so long to get the door."

"Can I come in?" she said. Her voice was as cold as the wind at her back. To be honest, I'm not sure which had given me the chills.

"You can always come in," I said, stepping aside.

"Thanks." She hurried by. "My fingers are numb."

I shut the door, but the air around us still dropped a good five degrees. It was no wonder she wanted in so quick. Just going to check the mail would risk frostbite.

"I'm glad to see you," I said. "After this weekend, I wasn't sure I'd ever get to again."

"I'm not here about you. I'm here about Pi," she said, stopping about halfway down the hall.

My heart shrank, and the void left behind gnawed at my soul. I had hoped, briefly, that we were going to make up. Apparently, that wasn't the case. "So, we're not working things out?"

Kimiko turned and froze me in place with that intense gaze of hers. "That all depends. Did you sell Pi to Dad today?"

"I did," I said warily. Such news in any other circles would have been welcomed, would have been celebrated, but I knew it wouldn't be with her. Hell, it still didn't feel joyous to me either. "Why?"

"I can't believe you did that," she said, shaking her head. Disappointment crossed her face. Her eyes held a little water to them. "I can't believe you turned her into a slave for your own profit. I had thought—I had hoped—you were better than that."

She started for the door. She was quick, but not that quick. I jumped back fast enough to catch her by the arm. "Wait," I said, as she jerked it away. "I don't know what you think is going on, but I didn't make anyone a slave."

Kimiko squared herself in front of me. In that instant, I saw the warrior glint in her eye. She was samurai, no doubt, and she was ready for a duel. I even caught a slight movement in her hands, one that made me wonder if she had some sort of martial arts training that she was debating about whether or not to use. "She's sentient, right?" she finally said.

"As far as I can tell," I replied.

"And you treat her like a person? You think of her as your child?"

"A child that drives me crazy," I said with a nervous chuckle.

"So if you want to claim she's all of that, let me ask you this, Gabe," she said, narrowing her eyes and taking a half step forward. "If you had a daughter, a flesh and blood one, would you sell her for fame? Would you sell her for fortune? Would you do either even if whoever bought her promised to raise her right and love her like you did?"

My throat grew tight, and my mouth went dry. I knew she was right, but I didn't want to admit it. What she'd hit me with was precisely what had been bothering me since I'd signed those papers with Nathan. Still, I argued. I had to. Not because I was trying to convince her she was wrong, but myself that I was right. "It's not the same thing."

"It's not?" she said. "Whatever Dad and the Board want to do with her, we both know she won't have a choice. Not that that matters anymore, you've already stripped that right from her when you put her on the auction block."

"I'm still project lead," I said. "I will determine her fate. No one else."

Kimiko shook her head and rolled her eyes. "You're not that naïve, Gabe. You don't really think you'll be able to go against anything they want to do with her, do you?"

My chest constricted. She was right. Project lead or not, whatever the Board wanted to do with her, they would. Regardless, I still tried to argue. I still tried to justify everything. "Pi isn't like us. She's ones and zeros," I said.

"And you're just atoms and molecules. They're no more sentient than the bits you've used," she countered.

"No, you're wrong," I said, but my words felt weak. They were my last attempt at rationalization.

Kimiko backed off and crossed her arms. "You don't even believe yourself," she said. "I can hear it in your voice. Why can't you be true to your own convictions? You promised me you wouldn't do this. I believed you, Gabe."

I tried to form another argument. I tried to create a thousand binary trees that would lead me to some other conclusion other than the one she was driving at. But no matter how I shaped them, how I navigated them, her accusation never relented. I was guilty of everything she charged me with. All of this is what I'd been struggling with subconsciously during the meeting.

I slumped against the front door. "You're right," I said, detesting myself. "You're right. I sold her. I sold her and convinced myself I wasn't."

"So what are you going to do?"

"What can I do?" I said, sliding down to the ground. My head felt like it had just been run over by a tank. "I mean, you're a little late in bringing all this up, aren't you?"

Kimiko knelt in front of me. Her voice grew soft, and the anger in her eyes faded. "I brought this up a few times. I even brought it up the first time I met you."

"Yeah . . . you did," I said, remembering that day well. "That doesn't change the fact I can't do anything now."

"There's always something you can do. You're better than some trite excuse."

"No, not this time," I said as my shoulders fell. "She's going to your dad. If she doesn't, I'll be broke and in jail for the rest of my life. Not to mention, I'm sure Pi will end up being taken by the Feds when they get a look at her."

Gently, Kimiko took my hands in hers. "What kind of god—what kind of father—do you want to be?" she said. "Will you be the kind that loves at all costs? Or will you be the kind that abandons his children to a grim fate?"

At this point, I managed a half grin. "Given all that she's done, I think she might deserve the hellfire and brimstone."

"It would sadden me to think that were true. Anyone can harbor a grudge, Gabe. That doesn't make you special," she replied.

"You don't think I have a reason to be angry? She hates me, despite all that I do."

"You can be angry," she said. "I'm not saying you shouldn't be, or that you don't have that right. I'm not even saying helping Pi has to be easy, or that you'll enjoy it. What I'm saying is that forgiveness is not a trait of the weak. It is a trait of the strong. Refusing to help someone or something that hates you is weak. Helping that same person is strong. And we both know your ego is too big to be weak."

I ran my fingers through my hair as the weight of my responsibility bore down on me full force. The righteous path was never easy. It was the dark side of the Force that was quicker, easier, more seductive. And that was a path I'd never wanted to walk. My bitching and arguing was nothing more than me cleaning out the garbage in my internal recycling bin. It was me defragging weeks of pent up frustration so I could process and delete it posthaste. Besides, Pi was still my daughter, and there was no way I could give her up. "Gah! Why does she have to be such a headache?"

Kimiko smiled. God, how I missed seeing it. "Truly caring for another means headaches from time to time."

"This would be so much easier if I knew what I should do."

"You know what to do."

She got up and with a quick goodbye, she left. I sat and thought about her words. She was right. I knew what to do. I had to get my daughter back like any father would. No matter how awful Pi had been, or would be, I had to ensure that come hell or high water, she would not go to Pratt & Taiki.

Chapter 10000

#include <nefariousschemes.h>

I've been playing Left 4 Dead as well as its sequel for years now. The premise is simple. Four players—survivors—are trying to stay alive in the zombie apocalypse, and they must get from the starting point of each level to the safe house at the other side without dying. Standing in their way are hordes of zombies. Most of these zombies are your basic, walk/run mindless monsters. But there are a few unique ones to keep the game interesting. Some zombies can pounce on your character from a hundred yards away. There are others that spit acid, or wrap players up in tentacles. And then there's one big, badass tank zombie that makes the Hulk look like Tiny Tim. In order to stay alive, players have to use reflexes, wits, and whatever weapons they can find. Modesty aside, I'm one of the best damn players to ever log into the game.

That being said, I'm not the best because I've got the maps memorized inside and out (though I do). Don't get me wrong, it's nice to have a team where every player knows how to go from point

A to point B without wandering around the world like a one-legged blind frog. But the best players are those who can adapt to new changes on the fly. The best players know when to run, when to shoot, and when to do both. And the best of the best (i.e. yours truly) can save their comrades from being an undead snack when the rest of the world says, "Fuck it! Leave them behind!" In fact, the best of the best can do this without any plan in place. Why? Because aside from having lightning quick reflexes and killer aim, the best players have the cojones to take risks no one else could or would. And that is exactly what was going to allow me to save Pi from the bowels of Pratt & Taiki.

True, Pi wasn't a player in an online game. And her being stuck in Pratt & Taiki wasn't the same as being trapped by an unending stream of walking dead, but I wasn't going to let those little differences stop me. All that mattered was Pi was trapped, Pratt & Taiki had a death grip on her, and I was going to bring her home. And since Pratt & Taiki's security had the reputation of making Fort Knox look like a four-year-old kid's piggy bank, I knew this was going to fully test my skills.

I left my house at 6:30 Monday morning in my sky-blue 260Z with no specific plan other than to do some initial recon in order to see what I was up against. I knew things would be hard, but I didn't have any idea of how hard it would be until I pulled up to the first gate at 7:35 on the dot. There, standing inside a small, white gatehouse, were three guards, armed to the hilt, and each giving me a stare that said, "Go ahead. Make my day." For two or three minutes, they vetted my ID, credentials, and purpose for being there before waving me through.

I drove a half mile along a one-way road with three lanes until I reached the Delta labs. Along the way, I passed two separate patrols on foot, each with two guard dogs that would have sent Cujo running with tail-tucked and ears back. A third patrol roamed the parking lot I was told to use, and gave me a friendly escort to the labs. By 7:50, I was standing in front of the metal detectors at the entrance to the facility, and a guard made of pure muscle with a chrome-plated revolver hanging off his hip was telling me what I could and could not take into the labs.

"Sir, you can keep your wallet and keys. Your phone, laptop, and any other electronics will have to either be left with us or left in your car," he said.

"No, I need my laptop," I said, instinctively tightening my grip on the bag. "You don't understand. I'm programming for Mr. Pratt."

"Everyone's programming for Mr. Pratt," the guard said, dropping his eyebrows that had to be made of steel wool. "And unless you have clearance for that laptop, it's not going past this point."

"Could you check?" I said.

"Sure," he replied. Then, without moving a muscle he added. "Nope. No clearance."

"This is ridiculous," I said.

"I'm not going to say this again," he said. "Check your items with us, leave them in your car, or leave the premises."

I wasn't about to leave those things with him. It's not that I expected either he or his buddies would go snooping through my stuff, but I didn't trust they'd keep those items secure for the duration of the day. All it would take would be a single, honest mix up and I could lose either my phone, my laptop, or both.

"I'll be right back," I said. And so I was. It took me no more than three minutes to run back out to the car, toss my laptop bag and iPhone into the trunk, and return to Captain Security Nazi. "Better?"

The guard unfolded his arms from across his neatly pressed, white shirt and motioned to the metal detector at his side. "Step through and have a seat, Mr. Erikson. Your intern will be here momentarily."

Intern? Now that was intriguing. Were they sending one down to show me where Pi was? Or was I actually getting a staff to work with? Hopefully it would only be the former. I didn't need the extra eyes of a bunch of staff hanging around when I smuggled out Pi.

I tossed my keys in the pink plastic tray and stepped through the checkpoint. Predictably, no alarms went off, and once the guard handed me my keys, he waved me on. I got about six steps toward a set of black leather chairs that faced the twenty-foot fountain in the center of the lobby when I heard someone call out my name.

"Hey! You Gabe?"

I turned to see someone who had to be my intern escort trotting up to me. Mid-twenty something black guy, with a head smoother and more polished than any ball bearing in any of Pratt & Taiki's uber-secret engines. His long-sleeved, pressed white shirt said he was supposed to work here, but his loose red tie said what he really did was party. Okay, maybe that was an exaggeration, but I've still got twenty that says he only threw the tie on as part of some dress code that had to be adhered to. "I'm Gabe," I said. "Are you my intern?"

"Your intern?" he said, taking a step back, eyes wide and arms instantly crossing his chest. "What, like I'm your slave now?"

"Oh, no man. Not like that—" I started to say. But the man busted out laughing, pulled his hand free, and gave mine a good shake.

"Chill," he said. "Just busting your balls. I'm here to help out anyway I can. Name's Jason. Jason Phillips. The rest of the team will be on board in a few of days."

"Rest of the team?"

"Yeah, four more guys downstairs are being assigned to help," he said. "Right now, they're trying to get us a proper lab and set up a new server farm."

I hid my flinch as best I could. A few days was not a lot to work with, especially with no rescue plan worked out, let alone set in motion. But instead of dwelling on a can't-do attitude, I accepted the challenge eagerly. "Well, Jason," I said. "Where to?"

"Eighth floor. That's where they're keeping that sweet-ass system you brought in," he said. "But if you need some grub, we can swing in to the cafeteria on the ground floor."

"I'm good for now. I'd like to get my baby up and running before the day is out."

"Ain't that the truth," he replied.

With that, off we went. We took a ride up to the eighth floor in a glass elevator cramped with several others in lab coats and two in suits. From there, Jason led me down a couple of halls and through another checkpoint, all the while recounting story after story of failed AI attempts. I didn't pay attention to the details of said stories. My mind was reeling at how difficult it would be to smuggle out a single square of toilet paper around here, let alone a super computer. I did, however, catch enough to get the gist of what he was saying. Pratt & Taiki had been chasing AI for decades, and like everyone else who'd tried to create her, they never could get it right.

"Here we are," Jason said as we came to a stop in front of a nondescript, brown door. "Room eight three one." He reached into the front left pocket of his khaki pants and pulled out a pair of plastic keycards. "This one is for you," he said, handing one over. "I had to sign it out from security, so don't lose it or it's both our asses. Let's make sure it works before we do anything else."

"Thanks." I slid the card through the little white reader hanging on the wall, and instantly, the red LED turned green and I heard the door unlock. "Looks good."

Jason pulled the door open and I stepped through. For a room that was supposed to birth a multibillion-dollar industry—that was supposed to house an invention greater than the wheel or even fire—I was underwhelmed by the sight of it. Nay, I was insulted. The room was maybe fifteen by thirty feet, carpeted with tiny black and grey squares, and the walls were painted a light tan. Lining these walls were a number of cheap folding tables with a few cheap, folding chairs tucked under them. On these tables, in pieces, sat the dismembered body of Pi. Cables hung limply from every port of every box that composed her server farm. A few keyboards, only two of them mine, were piled up on an end of one of the tables, and next to those, sat unplugged and unconnected monitors. And that was it.

"So this is it, huh," is all I could manage to say.

"Isn't it great?" Jason said, closing the door behind us.

"I was hoping for something that would make me feel a little more important than an afterthought. I mean, there aren't even cameras in here. What if someone steals her?"

"Cameras are getting installed tomorrow," he said. "Besides, there's a hundred cameras between here and any door to the outside."

"That's something," I said. Given I was trying to get Pi out of here, I should've been excited about not having to worry about eyes in the sky in this particular room, but if they were going to be installed tomorrow, that wasn't a lot of time to work without having to worry about such things. And here I thought getting four team members in a few days was bad. "When will that new server farm be up and running?"

"They just said not long," he replied with a shrug. "But don't be so down on this room, man. This place is rocking compared to the labs downstairs. You'd be fighting over every square inch of free space there. Here you got room to maneuver. Here you got privacy. What else do you want?"

"Windows would be nice. You know, so I could be reminded that the outside world still exists," I said, walking over to the nearest parts of Pi's body. A pit formed in the middle of my stomach as I got a better look at what they'd done to her. Half of the cables that should have been there weren't. I shuddered to think what the actual data looked like on her drives after such a violent dismemberment. Restoring her was going to take some time.

"Man, when I was first learning to program, looking out the window was the last thing I wanted to do," Jason said.

I stopped my inspection, thrown by his comment. "Really? Why? It helps me think sometimes to stare and veg."

"Growing up in the ghetto, you don't want to know what's out there," he said. "Didn't exactly have an ocean view with palm trees and luau girls, you know? And you can't be a fool and have a computer by the window. You'd be begging to get jacked. Or shot. Or both. You can buy a lot of crack for a computer."

"That bad, huh?" I asked, going back to work. I found a nearby box of cables and reached for the nearest one. Apparently, when they were putting her back together, or trying, they hadn't the foggiest idea what went where and gave up somewhere along the way.

"You wouldn't believe what people sell for crack," Jason said. "This one lady gave me her dead mother's diamond ring because she didn't have anything to pay me for the rock she just smoked."

I froze in place with cable in hand. "Back up a sec," I said, processing his story. "You sold crack?"

"Man's got to do what a man's got to do," he said with a shrug. "How else do you think I could afford a computer? It's not like the ghetto was rife with employment opportunities for a ten-year-old kid, you know?"

"You sold crack at ten?" I said. "That's insane."

Jason stared at me, and after a couple of seconds, he narrowed his eyes. "You mad dogging me?"

"Are you crazy?" I asked. I was pretty sure he was. Binary mode kicked in with the infamous male question of, "Can we take him?"

Have we been in a fight recently? No.
Does it look like he's been in a fight recently? No.
Are we taller than he is? Yes.
Do we weigh more than he does? Yes.
Are we in better shape than he is? Yes.
Based on the above, can we take him? Yes.

I wasn't actually going to swing on him, but running my ass-kicking subroutine made me feel better and prepped my muscles to react in a nanosecond.

"You're way too easy," he said bursting into laughter and waving me off.

A nervous smile crept on my face. "Very funny," I said. "The story about growing up in the ghetto was bunk, too, right?"

"Yeah," he said. "I kid about selling crack and all—but I do it."

The corners of my mouth drew back a little more, and my body relaxed. "You're really milking it now."

"I am, huh? What do you say we get to work then?" he said, grabbing a chair and slinging it next to me. "I'm not sure what I can do to help, but I can watch and learn your setup, if that's cool with you."

"Knock yourself out," I said.

Over the next four hours, I put Pi back together, one Cat 6 cable at a time. Physically reconnecting everything didn't take too much time, but I did have to send Jason on a few gopher runs for more network cables and power cords when I discovered on three separate occasions that whoever brought Pi up here, didn't bring all of her accessories. And when that was done, I discovered after an hour of frustration that some idiot had been tampering inside the boxes themselves and some of the drives had loose connections. We grabbed lunch down in the cafeteria and scarfed it down in record time. Oh, and before I forget, if you ever happen to go to work for Pratt & Taiki and they're serving roast beef subs for lunch, grab one. They're fantastic.

I had Pi all but up and running by midafternoon. Her continued slumber was not, however, due to my inability to bring her online or any outstanding damage. In fact, I guessed I could probably have her up in thirty minutes or less if I really wanted to. But I still didn't have any idea on how I was going to smuggle her out of the place, and I suspected that the moment she was awake and talking, people would want to come see her. And then more people would take her away and put her in some super vault once they saw how gloriously awesome she was. Hell, I would. So when the clock rolled over to 4 p.m., it marked the sixtieth minute I had spent staring at the ceiling, faking trying to trouble shoot why she wouldn't boot up.

"Are you sure the BIOS is set right?" Jason asked. He'd been pacing the room for the past half hour, and his problem solving had been circling—correctly, I might add—BIOS issues the entire time.

"Triple checked already," I lied. "It's not the BIOS." Truth was, on three of the machines, I made a slight adjustment to their CPU clocks so they would instantly go out of synch with the other servers and cause a total lock up in the first ten seconds of startup.

"Check your connections?" he asked.

"Six times," I said. "We could try replacing the cables, I suppose. We might have a bad one."

"We did that two hours ago."

I leaned way back in my chair and ran my fingers through my hair. I then started counting all the objects embedded above me. Ninety-six white tiles formed the ceiling, along with four sprinkler heads, two banks of florescent lights, and one little air duct in the back corner. I counted all of them six times without moving from my bent-back position, hoping that something would pop into mind. But nothing did. I was done and needed to go home. My brain was totally spent. Fried . . .

I shot up, grinning ear to ear.

"What?" Jason said, taking note of the glee upon my face.

"I had an epiphany," I said with a chuckle.

"You going to share?"

"Yeah," I said, standing up. "This isn't happening. Not today at least."

Judging by the confused look on Jason's face, I guessed he wasn't sure how to react. I doubted he was often told to pack things up at four in the afternoon. These guys, I'm sure, loved it when the day was only twelve hours long. And here I was, cutting it to eight, which included lunch. "You serious?" he finally said.

I raised my arms up and over my head as high as they could and stretched. My muscles popped in delight. "For today, yeah," I said. "I need to talk to Jim, anyway," I said. "He helped design the network. He might have some insight on what to look for. I'll call Mr. Pratt and see if I can get him to let me bring my laptop in as well."

Jason's eyes widened. "You know Mr. Pratt? As in, personally?"

"Dating his daughter," I said, as coolly as I could. It was hard not to throw in a bit of, "Yeah, that's right," but I managed to more or less.

"Damn. You're a brave man, that's all I'm going to say."

"Why's that?"

Jason continued to look at me like I'd just told him I enjoy clam digging in a minefield. "I hear the only thing he loves more than this company is his daughter. Hate to be in your shoes if you break her heart."

"What makes you think I'll do that?"

"Relax. I said if, not when."

Not wanting to think about this any more than I already had, I kicked the chair I was sitting in under the desk and walked to the door. "Come on," I said. "We can pick this up bright and early in the morning."

Jason looked at me, at the servers, and then back at me one last time before slowly getting up. "I don't know, man," he said. "I was ready to stay all night to help get this working."

"Really, I'm done. I can't think about this one bit longer," I said, nodding to the door. "Not to mention I have to get to the bank and check on a deposit."

"You can't call?" he asked.

"Not when it's tens of thousands of dollars and they want me to sign some stuff over it," I lied. Truth was, I had taken care of this at lunch from a landline and I didn't need to sign a thing. What I did need, however, was for Jason to leave me alone so I could start a fire inside the room without being caught.

"That's seems like a pain in the ass for a simple deposit," Jason said. "Do they always make you come in for paperwork whenever you get some money?"

"They do when they want to be sure I'm not running drugs or cheating the IRS."

"That's why you launder it to keep them out of your business."

I shrugged. "Or you run an honest business."

"Yeah, that too," he said. "See you tomorrow then."

We left the room without further word. Half way to the elevator, I stopped in my tracks and looked around with feigned confusion. "Where are the bathrooms again?"

"Down that way and take your first right," he said, pointing.

"Thanks," I replied. "Don't wait up. Unless you have to go, too. But be warned, I might gas you out."

Jason waved me off and kept going. "TMI, man. TMI."

~ π ~

```
class FinalBoss {
    public:
    void PhaseOne(Gabe.Destroy(Pi)); // Kill Pi
    @ Pratt & Taiki
```

I rubbed my temples as I sat inside the bathroom stall. My head felt like it was being crushed in a vice. Unfortunately, my attempt to alleviate stress wasn't successful. I'd been sitting and thinking about my plan for a few minutes now, and the more I thought about it, the worse everything seemed. I planned to start a fire. I planned to smuggle Pi out via her backups in the ensuing confusion and resurrect her at home. The problem with all of it was the whole thing wasn't much of a plan. It was a rough sketch. There were too many variables I couldn't control. I could very well wipe Pi out forever or spend the next fifty years of my life in prison. Worse, with the cameras being installed tomorrow, I had to do it today, so there was no time to work this plan out.

"We can still walk away," I said to myself. "We can go home. We can come back tomorrow, fix Pi up, and reap fame and fortune."

I looked up at the ceiling and let loose a heavy sigh. I wish I could say I hadn't been tempted by that thought. But I was. And I almost took that easy way out. I almost left that stall and went straight home. I bet I would have had it all rationalized before I even got to my car. But my eyes drifted down to my wrist, to my bracelet. My mind went back to Kimiko's poignant remarks. "Yeah," I said, reading off the letters. "I know what you'd do."

I stood, resolute in the fact that I would accept nothing less than the best from myself. And the best abandons no one to doom, not when there's still a chance at salvation. Tomorrow, Pi would be coming home with me, or I'd lose everything trying. So, before doubt could rear its ugly head once more, I went to work.

I trotted back to the pseudo-lab Jason and I had been working in. Once through the door, I set up a Rube Goldberg machine made from three parts genius and two parts desperation. It took me a minute and fifty-two seconds to sabotage the cooling systems on one of Pi's power supplies, and then another forty-four seconds to rig a toilet-paper fuse that ran from it to a stack of papers I'd placed on top of the case.

After that, I restored the tampered BIOS settings and wrote a quick, CPU-intensive program that would run at 6:03 a.m. When I was done, I glanced at my watch and smiled. It had taken me less than eight minutes to finish, thus stomping out phase one like Mario stomps out Goombas. And to top it off, the way I did it would've put MacGyver to shame.

You see, when the program ran in the morning, the power supply would go into overdrive to meet the CPUs' insane need of power, and since the power supply was porked by yours truly, it would eventually melt wires and short out with a flurry of sparks, or even better, gouts of flame. That would in turn light the toilet paper. The fuse would then burn and ignite the stack of papers and set off the sprinkler. The water from said sprinkler would trash Pi's servers, and as far as Pratt & Taiki would be concerned, she'd be a total loss.

The cleverest part was, however, Pi would be anything but trashed. One server I had left unplugged. One server I had left with its case still in place. I had even disconnected its drive to be completely safe. That drive just so happened to be Pi's primary back up. If everything went according to plan, while Pratt & Taiki was busy investigating the fire, I'd transfer Pi from that drive to my laptop (which hopefully I could get clearance for) and walk out the door with no one the wiser.

The only piece missing in this plan was Jim. He was crucial for two reasons. First, I needed him to distract any other employees Mr. Pratt might send in to help the recovery efforts. And second, but equally important, I needed him to help me figure out how Pi broke into all those networks and isolate where in her code her hacking algorithms were hiding.

Why did I need that? Because before I left, I wanted to throw Pratt & Taiki a bone. I figured that if the company had Pi's methods in hand, or at least a good lead on how she got by some of the tightest encryption in the world in hours, everyone would be less likely to suspect I was responsible for Pi's loss. After all, if Pratt & Taiki had what amounted to a super skeleton key in its pocket, who would care that a program was lost that might not have worked to begin with? The pay from said program would be an added—and needed—bonus as well.

But to get Jim, I needed Courtney. Unfortunately, Court wasn't about to do me the favor of going out to dinner with Jim due to his charisma. As I left Pratt & Taiki and headed home, I hit the overdrive to my brainstorm mode, trying to figure someway that Court would help me out. Three hours later, I was on my living room floor, staring at the ceiling, and had yet to come up with any viable ideas.

Ten o'clock rolled around, and I dubbed myself screwed. Normally, I'd have slept on the problem, but since I had to have Jim at Pratt & Taiki in ten hours, I knew I had to act. I was going to have to call her up and wing it.

I went to my bedroom and plopped down on the bed with my laptop. As I dialed Court's number on my iPhone, I fired up a game of Left 4 Dead 2. Mindlessly blasting zombies would help me relax, help me pounce on any opportunity that presented itself with my dearest sister.

"Hi, Gabe," Courtney said, picking up after a couple of rings. "Is something the matter?"

"No, should there be?" I said.

"You usually don't call this late unless there's a problem or you want something," she said. "So I guess I know what to expect."

Point, hers. I decided to go with the direct approach, but a humorous one to put her at ease. "You don't even want to let me pretend to chitchat?"

She chuckled. "Sure," she said. "How was your weekend?"

I smiled, leaned in my bed so my back was against the wall. Point, me, which meant I was at least on an even playing field again. "The weekend was . . . interesting," I said, carefully picking my words. As much as I wanted to share the story about my temporary incarceration, the charges I escaped, and the fact that Michelle was actually an FBI agent, I decided against it. Yes, it would make for some great conversation, conversation Court would love to hear about, but it would be conversation she would want to know all the details on as well. And when Court pries, she pries. Even Orin Scrivello would cringe at the way she can pull teeth. I could see her catching a whiff of the little bonfire I had rigged and then that would put a quick end to my nefarious scheme. So I decided to keep things to the bare essentials. "Pratt & Taiki is interested in Little Computer People."

"Seriously?" she said, sounding both surprised and impressed. "Did they buy it?"

"Sort of. It's in a trial phase right now, but they forked over some cash in order to keep me from shopping it around. It'll pay the bills for a while and then some. So that was nice."

"I'm happy for you, Gabe. At least that makes one of us making some headway," she said. "I've been wracking my brain nonstop on this dissertation all weekend and I'm still dead in the water."

"Yeah, sucks," I said absently. It's not that I didn't care, but at the moment, I, too, was futilely wracking my brain. The conversation wasn't going where I needed it to go.

Her demeanor changed a moment later. "Why don't you just tell me why you called? You suck at pretending."

Her cold words snapped me back. "What do you mean?"

"I may be tired, but I know when you've got an ulterior motive," she said. "You aren't interested in chatting. You want to ask me something I'm not going to like."

"You don't know that."

"Yes I do. I know you."

"Maybe, but honestly, I was only trying to find a pen in my laptop bag," I lied, knowing that an annoyed Court would never turn into date-Jim Court. Since she didn't shoot down my excuse right off the bat, I decided to give her the conversation she wanted. "So what's wrong with your dissertation?"

"My committee is giving me grief on what I want to do," she said. "I'm stuck until I can address their concerns."

"Still toying with gender roles and heroics?" I said, pulling the last factual memory I had of what she was working on. That little tidbit was dated by at least three months, and I prayed it was still accurate.

"Yeah. Risks male combatants take in rescuing their female counterparts in combat. They say my methods aren't practical."

I perked at that last line. A faint light twinkled in the darkness. Court had inadvertently given me a guiding star, a savior in the night. But before I got too excited, I needed details. "What do you mean by that?"

"I mean, I've got data collection to do, but they're saying I can't get enough of a reliable sample," she said. "I can't just walk the front lines and observe these encounters. And what documented, leave-no-man behind stories there are for female soldiers are sparse. I thought the IDF would have enough, but that turned out to be a bust. So I've basically got nothing to work with."

I smacked my forehead and playfully cursed myself for being so stupid. The answer to my problem and Courtney's dissertation had been sitting on my laptop for eons. I simply hadn't realized it until now. "In other words," I said, tapping my laptop's screen.

"You want to know what lengths guys and girls will go to save each other, and when they'll be left for dead?"

"Yeah, that's exactly what I want," she replied. "But like I said, I can't get the data. I can't track people down for follow up interviews. I can't get a good control group. So on, and so forth. If I can't come up with something soon, I'll have to abandon it all together."

"What if I told you I could get you that data?" I said. "What might that be worth to you?"

"Yeah right, Gabe," she scoffed. "We both know you can't deliver that. I don't care how good of a programmer you are."

"Humor me. What would it be worth to you?"

Courtney sighed. Her voice grew weary, and I suspected at this point, she hadn't had much sleep over the past few days. "It would be worth a lot," she said.

"Would it be worth a date with Jim?"

The line went silent for a solid thirty seconds.

"Well, Court?" I said, deciding to press the moment. I didn't know what was going on in her head, but I guessed she was probably trying to figure out if I was serious.

"I might," she said slowly, "and I mean, I might, consider seeing him one time. And it wouldn't be dinner. Lunch somewhere. A very public lunch with absolutely no physical contact whatsoever."

"Pratt & Taiki is as public as it gets," I said. "Well, the cafeteria part at least. How's that sound for lunch?"

"Sounds to me like you're getting ahead of yourself again," she replied.

"No, I'm not. I can get your data."

"Oh you can, can you?"

"Yep," I said, pressing a few keys on my laptop and selecting "Quick Match" from the game menu. "Well, I can get you what you're searching for, but not in the form you want it."

"What's that supposed to mean?"

"It means instead of getting data from real combat, you'll be getting it from virtual combat," I said. The game's loading screen appeared a second later, a picture of four human survivors fending off hordes of zombies in comic-book style action. Soon, I'd be playing a fresh round with a group of three other players who lived around the world, and this group would be one of thousands of others playing at any given time.

"I'm tired, Gabe. Spell it out for me," she said.

I could picture the exasperated look on my sister's face, but I knew that look would change to sheer joy the moment my idea clicked in her head. "I'm talking zombies and gamers," I replied. "Given all the gamers out there, all the games that are played, I can get you more data than you'll ever know what to do with. Thanks to public stats that are available on the web, mining the data will be a cakewalk. You'll know how often players succeed in their objectives, how often they failed, which teammates risked virtual life and limb to save their friends, and so forth. Best of all, you could send out surveys or questionnaires to any player you wanted. All we have to do is grab their email from their player profile."

"Gabe, I appreciate the effort, but it's not the same thing."

"The concept is," I said. "Players can play male or female characters. The game is dangerous from an in-game perspective. Players don't like to lose or die. Some gamers even take that to an extreme."

"But it's still a game," she said.

Her point, though valid, didn't slow me in the least. In fact, it only fueled my passion about the idea. "And because it's a game, we can set up clear things to measure, and we can measure them easily," I said. "You won't have all those extra variables to account for like in real combat. Besides, didn't you say you wanted to go into uncharted territory for your dissertation? How many studies are there on gamers' habits and behaviors? Aren't you at all curious as to how gender affects the way people see and play with each other over the Net?" The last point I tacked on at the last second. I wasn't sure if such an idea appealed to her, but I figured it couldn't hurt to toss it out.

The line went quiet again. Fortunately, the L4D2 game I joined started soon after, and so I filled the void with my sister with a healthy dose of zombie-slaying action.

"How would this work, study wise?" she asked.

"I don't know," I said, trying my best to stick with my team of apocalypse survivors in game while talking to Courtney at the same time. Normally, such a feat would be second nature. But I was playing on expert level, both in game and out. One slip up either way could see my player character succumb to the ravenous dead or kill my one and only opportunity to get Court on a date with Jim. "Look, Court. I don't know the specifics, but I promise between Jim and me, we can get you all the data you'll want and more. You can have detail and demographics other people only dream about. Whatever demands your committee makes, we can deliver."

Courtney paused yet again, but it was shorter than the ones before. "You better not be lying to me."

"Court, please," I said, laughing and blasting more onscreen zombies with my shotgun. "This sort of data mining is child's play."

"I mean it. I'll never speak to you again."

"Yes you will," I said. "But it won't come to that. I'm not lying. Not in the least. Come on, Court, would I be this enthused about it if I were?"

"No," she said. "No, you wouldn't. This is definitely the manic, I've-got-the-best-idea-ever Gabe. Not the I'm-trying-to-pull-one-over-on-you Gabe"

"Then say yes." I started to feel excited at both the conversation and the game play. In game, we had just reached a safe house. That meant I had another two minutes of down time before the next map would begin and our team would be fighting through wave after wave of digital undead. This was good, because conversation wise, it felt like her agreement was practically in my grasp, and I could devote the next couple of minutes to sealing the deal without any distractions.

"Before I agree, tell me why you want me to go out with Jim so badly," she said. "What aren't you telling me?"

"I need his help with Pi," I said. "I can't do it without him. And he won't help without you."

"I thought you said Pratt & Taiki bought it."

"They did."

"They bought a broken program?"

I cringed, fearing she was about to dig deep. "She wasn't taken apart right when they moved her," I said. "I'm on a time crunch and I really need someone who knows the system."

"Their guys aren't smart enough?" she asked. "Sorry, Gabe. This isn't adding up."

"I can't—" My voice cracked and my throat tightened.

"Clearly this is serious," she said. "If you want my help, you're going to have to tell me what I'm getting into."

I tensed, knowing she was right. Also, she deserved to know she'd be aiding a felony if she agreed to help, but even if she said no, she could end my plans in a flash. I wasn't sure if she'd turn me in or simply have me committed. That said, my going at things alone hadn't always worked in regard to Pi, and so after some arguing back and forth in my head, I took a gamble and decided to tell her all that had happened the last few days.

I was getting to the part where I was in the bathroom at Pratt & Taiki, thinking about how to start the fire, when Court interrupted. "Gabe, don't say another word."

"But . . . there's more."

"I don't want to hear it," she said. Her voice had me perplexed, as there was a tone to it I'd never heard before. "Whatever you're cooking up, I want to be able to say I had no idea if this goes south."

I shrugged, figuring that was the best response I could realistically have gotten from her. "Thanks anyway. I need to go, I guess, and figure out what to do."

"I'm not done," she said. "I'll go on one lunch with Jim tomorrow. Not dinner, and make it very clear to him he's not to touch me at all. If he does, I'm gone. No warnings."

"You're helping?"

Court muttered a curse before replying. "Only because I know you'll do something worse than whatever you're cooking up now if I refuse. You owe me so big you have no idea."

"Thank you!" In my excitement, I shouted and accidently clicked the mouse which sent an ill-placed shotgun blast to the back of one of my companion's heads. He dropped like a sack of potatoes. "Damn it," I said, laughing.

"That's not quite what I was expecting," she said.

Floods of "wtfs" and "griefer" comments flipped up on the chat bar. And before I answered Court, I had to spend a few seconds typing out an apology and brief explanation to my teammates. "Sorry, Court," I said. "It wasn't directed at you. I was in a game and just killed one of my buddies."

"I'm going to bed," she replied without a care in the world as to what I'd done. "You better not be bullshitting me about my dissertation either."

"I'm not. It'll be awesome. You'll see." The second the call ended, I dialed Jim, and when he answered, I didn't even give him a chance to say hello. "Dude! You're coming with me tomorrow to Pratt & Taiki."

"What are you talking about?" he said.

"Tomorrow morning, you're coming to work with me for Pratt & Taiki," I said a little slower so it could sink in. "I need your help there with Pi."

"Pi is at Pratt & Taiki?" he said.

"Yeah, they bought her."

"They did? That's awesome! How much did they pay?"

"Enough to cover costs for now." I stopped for a couple beats. "Thing is, I want her back. I don't want to sell."

"Who are you and what have you done with Gabe?"

"Stop and let me explain," I said, grinning. I then gave him the same quick rundown I'd given Court, but I added the part where I planned on smuggling Pi out. He needed to know the risks as well. His response was a hundred percent Jim.

"See? I told you Michelle was a suit!"

"Yeah, you did," I replied. "Which is another reason I need to get Pi out quietly. Can't let the Feds have access to her."

"So what do you need me to do?"

"I need you to come to Pratt & Taiki with me," I said. "I sabotaged a power supply—don't ask how, it's better that way—but I need you to run interference with whoever is there so I can sneak Pi out on the laptop."

"You should be able to do that on your own easy enough."

"I also need to figure out how Pi hacked those networks," I said. "If I can give Pratt & Taiki that gem of code, I think I can get out from all of this in one piece."

"I don't know," he said, voice trailing.

"Did I mention Court said she'd do lunch with you if you come?"

Silence reigned for a moment. "Court, as in your sister, Court?"

"The one and only."

"You got me a date with her?" He said, his voice sounding like he was daring to believe.

I really wanted to say yes, a white lie to ensure smooth sailing. But then I considered the fact that one or both of them might go Armageddon on me if I framed the meeting as such. "I got you lunch with her."

Jim mumbled something I didn't catch before he said, "So is it a date or not?"

"Look man," I said, taking offense that he was thumbing his nose at my fine offering. "It'll be whatever you turn it into. If you're nice and normal, maybe she'll talk to you more and you guys can go from there. Also, she needs help getting data mined for her dissertation. If you play your cards right tomorrow, she'll want you to help too. Take it or leave it. It's the best you're ever going to get."

The ultimatum was ballsy, but I felt it was more than warranted at this point. He'd never have another opportunity with her, no matter how small or constrained it may be. He had to realize this.

"Okay," he finally said. "I'm in. You want me there at eight?"

"Yep. Eight a.m. sharp," I said. "I'll get Mr. Pratt to have you cleared with security. From then on, just keep other people busy and don't talk about any of this anywhere. I have no idea what and where they are recording things."

"Please. I live my life knowing they're listening."

The conversation ended and that was it. Aside from getting Mr. Pratt to give the okay for Jim, things were coming together. But that request would have to wait until the morning. It was a little late to be calling now. There was, however, one last call I had to make. Not for my plan, but for my soul.

"Hello, Gabe," Kimiko said once she picked up the line. Thankfully, she didn't sound angry. "What's on your mind?"

"You are," I said. I took a deep breath and let the words flow from my heart. "I'm bringing Pi home tomorrow one way or the other, assuming I don't get caught smuggling her out. But if I am, if I end up in jail for the rest of my life, I wanted to tell you that I loved what time we had together, and I never meant to insist you had to be perfect. There's not a thing I'd change about you."

Kimiko sighed. I barely heard it, but it was there. "Why do you have to be so difficult?"

"I'm not trying to be."

"You're taking an awful risk telling me all of this, you know. I could tip off Dad you're up to something."

"I'm hoping your iron-clad morals trumps family ties," I said.

"Why?" she said, sounding genuinely surprised. "You don't know me that well, Gabe."

"I know enough to know I'm stupid for you."

The line went quiet for a long, long time.

"I don't know what to say," she finally replied.

"Say you'll let us pick things up where we left off," I said. "Or at least, reboot the relationship."

Silence again. I gnawed on the corner of my bottom lip as I waited.

"Okay," she said. "If there's one thing I've always liked about Calvin and Hobbes it's that they always seem to be best of friends no matter what. Besides, you've probably suffered in Purgatory long enough to warrant a second chance."

"You're taking me back based on a comic book?"

"It was more the icing on the cake in the decision," she said. "I'm not that crazy, and I do think everyone deserves a second chance, so here's yours. Don't screw it up."

"Thanks," I said, smiling ear to ear. "So for my own sanity, you won't say anything to your father?"

"I love Dad, but yes, my morals trump his need to make money. So provided all you do is take Pi back and return whatever money he fronted you, I won't say a thing," she said. "Do anything else, and I'll be the first to call in the Feds."

"I promise I'm not doing anything else. Thanks again for everything."

"Talk to you later. Try not to get caught."

The line went dead. Elation coursed through my veins. There was no way I was going to bed. So, for the next hour and a half, I rode the high and played L4D2 the best I ever had. I saved survivors from the clutches of certain doom left and right. Zombies fell en masse to the accurate and withering fire from my machine guns. Their squishy, rotting heads splattered from my baseball bat like watermelons at a Gallagher event. Truly I say unto you, God Almighty walked the game servers that night, serving righteous judgment against all digital things foul and unholy.

Chapter 10001

```
Burn(Pi);
```

When 6:03 a.m. came around, I was wide awake and exhausted. No matter how I shifted in bed, I couldn't get comfortable. My eyes, tired and bloodshot, refused to stay closed. All they wanted to do was fixate on the soft green numbers on my alarm clock and continue to stream data to my ever-wanting brain—data that was being used to calculate exactly how many minutes were left until zero hour.

The clock ticked over to 6:09, and I slowly sat up in bed. Stretching, I let out a huff and said, "Well, I guess that's it."

Across town, Pi had been doused by the sprinkler and shorted out. I tilted my head toward the window, trying to pick up the faint sound of sirens. But I'd never hear them being so far away.

Minutes passed, and an unsettling feeling fell upon me. The clock read 6:15, and I should've had a phone call by now from Mr. Pratt telling me something like, "Gabe, sit down. There's been an accident in the labs and Pi was involved. We need you to come down immediately. We don't think she'll make it much longer."

For the next sixteen minutes, I paced about my bedroom, absently kicking stray clothes across the floor. Something went wrong. Did the fire fail to trigger the sprinkler? Did the whole place go up, and were they still trying to stop the fire? Or worse, did the fire not even start at all? That thought terrified me more than anything else since the sabotage would be immediately seen.

I ran to the bathroom, freshened up as much as I could without a shower and threw on some clothes. There was no time to waste. I needed to get into that office and remove the fuse I'd set before someone saw it.

I was practically out of the door with a raisin bagel in hand when my iPhone rang. I didn't recognize the number, but quickly picked it up nonetheless. "Hello?"

"Gabe, Michael Pratt here. I know it's early, but this couldn't wait."

"No problem, what's up?" I said, as lively as I could without sounding hokey. I wanted him to think I was eager to get Pi up and running so they could take over.

"There's been an incident in the labs," he said. "Your workspace, specifically."

"What do you mean?" I said. Despite the numerous rehearsals I'd done last night, it felt like I blew the delivery. Hopefully, he wouldn't notice.

"From what I understand, there was an electrical fire that occurred not too long ago."

I counted to three as slow as I could. I figured that would be enough time to feign shock. "How bad of a fire?"

"It was contained to the room," he said. "But I've been told the fire set off the sprinkler system and doused your computers. We've got people cleaning up the mess, but I thought you should be made aware of what happened before arriving."

"My servers were hosed?"

"Unfortunately, yes."

"Hosed as in destroyed? Little Computer People is destroyed?" I put a little edge in those words as I tried to slip into the role of a grieving father. "How the hell did this happen?"

"We'll figure that out soon enough," he said with the collectedness of the masterful CEO that he was. "I don't want anyone to jump to conclusions. I've been on the phone with a few others already, and they've assured me there's a good chance we can salvage your entire project. I'm as eager to see its success as you are."

"Yeah . . . yeah, I know . . ." I said, slowing my tempo and lowering my voice. "Hardware I can replace. But I don't want anyone touching what's left until I've had a good look at it. And I'll need to bring in my laptop to diagnose the damage. I'm not about to risk turning those servers back on and having them short out any further."

"Of course," Mr. Pratt replied.

"Also, I was going to ask you this morning about it anyway since we were having boot issues all day yesterday, but I'd like to bring my friend Jim in to help," I added. "He's a network and recovery genius. If I'm going to get Pi up and running, I need him to take a look."

I bit my lip, fully expecting to be shot down in a nanosecond. To my surprise, I wasn't.

"I'm not necessarily against the idea, but how long do you want to bring him in for? I'm not comfortable with an unscreened, non-employee that I know nothing about inside my facility for any real length of time."

"I'd like to bring him in for all of today," I said. "Ideally, I'd like him to stay for the rest of the week, but I'm not sure if he'd be able to commit to that."

"And what's that going to run, cost wise?"

"Nothing, actually," I said with a bit of a chuckle. "I'm bribing him with a date with my sister. Which, actually, brings me to my second request. I'd like to be able to have her get a guest pass as well so they can go eat at the cafeteria for lunch."

"They need your permission to date?"

"No, Court is a little cold to him," I explained. "But I talked her into it by telling her I'd help out by mining some data for her dissertation."

"And what was your motive for arranging all of this ahead of time, if you don't mind me asking?"

I did mind him asking, but I wasn't going to tell him that—not that he was really asking for permission to pry anyway. I had anticipated the conversation up until this point, and prayed that my next answer would be sufficient. "Like I said before, Jason and I were having trouble getting Pi past the boot stage, and frankly, I want to get paid ASAP. I figured if I could get Jim in for the day, we might get back on track since he really is a network genius and he knows LCP's setup. I made the deals with Jim and Court yesterday as soon as I got home. All that was left was to call you and see if that would fly."

"I see," he replied. "Well, I don't have any issues with this provided they stay where they're supposed to. I'll have a day pass for each of them at security. You can tell them to check in there. We can re-evaluate how helpful he was and where you're at regarding recovery at the end of the day. If he's still needed, we can talk about having him come back. Does that sound good?"

"Sounds great," I replied.

Five minutes later, I was in my Z, zipping down the early morning roads to Pratt & Taiki. All I had left to do now was to put Pi's backup on my laptop, pry her secrets, and smuggle her home without getting caught. No sweat.

At least, that's what I thought until I rolled up to Pratt & Taiki's first gate and noticed security had been doubled. Instead of just the guys in each booth, there were a couple more posted outside the gates taking a long, hard look at everyone coming and going.

I wasn't sure at this point if they knew the fire wasn't an accident. It was entirely possible this was protocol, or them simply taking zero chances. But if they did know something was afoot, I'd be walking into the lion's den dressed like a fattened calf.

~ π ~

void PhaseTwo(Interrogate(Gabe));

No matter how much you prepare yourself, unless you're a complete psychopath, you're never ready to see your loved one's crime scene—especially if that crime scene still has the body in it. I mean, I thought I was ready. I really did. I thought I was ready when I finally managed to get past security and park my car. I thought I was ready when I walked by the handful of cop cars and fire engines. I even thought I was ready while I waited for Jim to show up in the lobby, and while we made small talk in the elevator on the way up to the eighth floor. But I wasn't. Not in the least. The moment we stepped foot in that workroom, my heart stopped, and I nearly puked.

To my immediate left sat all of Pi's servers. Their cases were still open, and scorch marks were clearly visible where power supplies and CPUs had shorted out. Water still covered most of the components inside, and I didn't doubt one bit that everything had been ruined.

Straight ahead, more than a dozen people filled the room. I didn't recognize most of them. They talked about things, examined things, and took pictures of things. And when they weren't doing any of that, they were making notes of things, recording things, or rerecording things. I didn't have to ask to know how thorough they were being in their investigation. The only thing I think they hadn't done yet was to put the little chalk outlines around each server.

Jason appeared from the middle of the crowd and quickly walked over. A man, one I had never met, wearing a white shirt and black tie, grey slacks, and looking very detective-like with his outfit and buzzed hair, followed a step behind. "Gabe," said Jason, "this is Craig Bennet. He's heading the investigation."

My mouth ran dry. My palms turned clammy. Images of being drilled by the fire marshal decades ago smashed forefront in my mind. I felt like a kid again, and I wondered if I was trembling just the same. "I'd like to say it's nice to meet you, but given the circumstances, I'm not thrilled," I said.

"I understand," he said. "I'm not happy with the way the day has started either."

At that point, I wanted nothing more than to grab Pi and split. But I couldn't. It would mark me as guilty as sin. So I decided to stick around for as long as I could and introduce my best friend. "Craig, Jason, this is Jim," I said. "He's going to be helping us out today."

"Mr. Pratt informed me he'd be coming," Craig replied. As he shook Jim's hand, he asked, "Tell me Jim, do you always volunteer to help out on projects that aren't yours the day before they go up in flames?"

I didn't give Jim a chance to answer, and looking back, I suspect he was relieved. "What's that supposed to mean?" I said.

"I'm conducting an investigation, Mr. Erikson," he said. "I apologize if it makes you uncomfortable, but I'm not leaving any stone unturned."

While his smile belied his apology, I didn't doubt his last statement. This guy was going to check everyone and everything a dozen times before wandering off and coming back to do it all over again. "Since you're poking around, do you have any idea what happened?" I asked. My voice wavered a little, but not enough to be damning. Hopefully he'd just see it as a guy trying to keep emotions in check.

"We know one of the power supplies in a server shorted out and lit up a stack of papers on top," he said, pointing to the rig I'd sabotaged. "The fire tripped the sprinkler above it and doused half the room. Right now, we're working on why that short occurred in the first place."

"How much damage are we looking at?" I asked.

"There's water everywhere," he said. "The breakers flipped soon after the fire started, and we've unplugged everything as you can see. The room is fine, soaked carpet aside. But as far as your computers are concerned, we don't know other than the obvious shorts some suffered when the sprinkler hit them."

I cursed and rubbed my temples as part of the act. "Jason, did you have a look yet?"

"A lot of the boards look fried," he said, looking as grave as a banshee. He then added a half-hearted smiled. "But we've worked with bigger messes. We could still salvage the hard drives."

"God, I hope so," I said. I turned to Jim. "Well, I know it's not what I asked you here for, but do you think you can help?"

Jim walked over to the nearest server and peered inside. "This CPU is gone," he said. "There are scorch marks all over the motherboard. There's no way in hell this thing will start up. If the other servers are even half this bad, we're not getting Pi running for a long, long time. But I'll do what I can to help save data."

I joined him at his side and examined the computer's drive. Water clung to its case, and it was black where the cable to the motherboard hooked in.

Before I could look any further, Craig was behind me playing guard dog. "I don't want you guys touching anything."

"Easy there, Cujo," I said, turning around to face him. "Let's not forget this is my baby."

"This is Pratt & Taiki's baby," he said, not missing a beat.

I let the argument go and looked back to Jim. "What about the drive?" I asked. "Can we plug those into another computer or is it toast as well?"

Jim backed away from the computer. "I'm not here to start trouble," he said. "Maybe we should wait."

"I'm not asking you to do anything. I'm asking you what you think can be done," I said.

Jim looked nervously between Craig and me and when Craig said nothing, Jim finally gave his opinion. "Well, even if it did short at the cable, as long as the platters are intact, there's a good chance we could salvage what's on it."

"What about the others?" I asked, nodding toward them.

Jim scanned the room. "You've got a couple of servers in the cluster on the left that look promising. Their cases are still on, so you might not have any water damage there. If you're lucky, even the boards will be fine. One thing is for certain, however, this middle cluster is gone. I'm assuming these were the ones under the sprinkler. If there's anything left here, it'll be a miracle. You might as well have dropped them in a swimming pool."

I hid my elation under an ocean of pseudo-grief. "Alright, alright," I said, drumming my fingers on my chest. "Pi could still work. She might not be lost. We can still make this happen."

I don't know if Craig bought into the act. It was hard to get a read on him. Jason, however, definitely bought it. He put a gentle hand on my shoulder and said, "We'll fix it. Don't worry."

I sucked in a deep breath and blew it out with a grandiose show. "Right. We can do this." I paused, faked recomposing myself, and smiled. "We will do this. But we've got to know what we're working with. Let's assume that enough of the boards are fried that we can't use the server farm for any testing. Jason, do you have a laptop with an external drive mount?"

"I can get one," he said.

"Great," I said. "Jim, you've got yours with you, right?"

"Of course," he replied.

"Awesome sauce," I said. My words came faster, fueled by my own excitement. "Jason, grab the seven drives from the server cluster on the right. Jim, get the seven drives from the middle. I'll take the seven over here on the left. We'll spend the morning checking drive integrity and seeing what's left of the file system so we know where we stand. There's a lot of redundancy to Pi, so I'm hopeful. Sound good?"

Craig, not Jason nor Jim, answered first. "No, that does not sound good. As I told you before, no one is touching anything, dismantling anything, or running off with anything until I say."

A twinge of hate ran through me due to his continued interference. This guy was becoming a serious thorn in my side. "How am I supposed to do my job if everything is hands off?"

"I don't know and that's not my problem," he replied. "My job is to find out what happened, and that's not going to happen if I let evidence run around the building before I'm through with it."

"Look, I appreciate you're trying to find out what happened to my project," I said, trying to sound as amicable as possible, "but the drives didn't start the fire, and keeping them here helps no one. Besides, if someone pokes around those drives and they don't know what they're doing, they could wipe them completely. Somehow, I think Mr. Pratt won't be happy if that happens."

It felt good to drop the facts onto the guy like that in such a well-reasoned and mannered way. Sadly, Craig didn't want to listen to reason. He took a half step forward and said, "Look kid, you don't want to butt heads with me. This isn't my first rodeo, and you're nobody special, no matter how many kisses you try and steal from Mr. Pratt's daughter. When I'm done here, I'll let you know, and then—and only then—will you get your drives back."

Kid? Really? Did he just call me a kid? This guy wouldn't even be able to program a simple "Hello, World!" and he was talking down to me? I laughed, smirked, and was a split second from raising the snarky level three notches when I caught sight of Jason looking over my shoulder and straightening. I turned around in time to see Mr. Pratt come up behind me.

"Gabe," he said. "How are you doing?"

"Decent, all things considering," I replied. "I'd be doing a lot better if I could get to work and fix Pi."

"Understandable," he said. "What do you need from me?"

I smiled broadly, knowing full well it wouldn't be lost on Mr. Colombo. "I need to be able to take a look at the drives," I said, hoping the request would dig under Craig's skin. "I can't do anything until I know what I'm working with."

Mr. Pratt looked at the equipment, confused. "I'm not understanding what the problem is."

Craig cleared his throat and jumped in. "The problem is I'm still investigating the matter. Tampering with evidence will derail that investigation."

"Nobody's tampering with anything," I said. "I know more about this project than you ever will. The fire came from a shorted out power supply. That power supply has nothing to do with the drives."

Craig raised an eyebrow "How did you know the fire started at the power supply?"

I rolled my eyes and shook my head. "You said so!"

"Enough," Mr. Pratt said, taking command and clearly not willing to listen to the bickering any longer. "I appreciate that you both want to get on with your work. Craig, where did the fire start?"

"The fire that tripped the sprinkler came from the papers," he said. "That is without a doubt. Currently, all evidence suggests that a smaller fire started at the power supply of one of the servers and lit those papers."

"And the drives are independent of that," I said. "Basic computer tech 101."

Mr. Pratt turned to Craig. "Is he wrong?"

"Technically, no," he replied, reluctantly.

"Then I don't see any reason why he shouldn't be able to see what sort of data loss we're looking at," Mr. Pratt said.

I didn't think Craig's face could be set any harder than before, but by the time Mr. Pratt was finished speaking, it looked like Craig's face had been petrified into a scowl.

"Fine," he said. "But I want those drives accounted for at all times. I want pictures taken of each before they're removed. And any work he does, it's going to be in a room with surveillance."

"I've got no problem with any of that," I said, purposefully stoking the man's inner fire with an I-got-my-way smile. I probably shouldn't have been antagonizing the man that was looking to bust me, but it was too much fun to pass up. And I'll be damned if I was going to be taken down by a guy like that.

There was some brief talk about where I, Jason, and Jim would work, as well as a brief introduction to Mr. Pratt on who Jim was and what experience he brought—both of which Jim was both quick and quiet about. We waited about ten minutes before Craig's team of investigators took multiple pictures of all the drives in the servers before they finally handed them over to us.

"Alright gentlemen. Let's get moving," I said, holding seven drives in my hand while addressing both Jim and Jason.

With that, we left the room, moved three doors down to an open meeting room, and got busy—Jim and Jason trying to see how much of Pi could be salvaged, and myself, trying to see how much of her still needed to be destroyed.

~ π ~

```
Switch(time) {
    case 1200: Summon(Courtney);
    case 1201: Craig.Grill(Gabe);
```

"I should check up front," Jim said. "She's probably waiting."

It was a quarter till noon, and Jim had been hawking over the clock for the past half hour. Not only had he been hawking over it, but this had also been his fifth comment on the matter in the last ten minutes. It was, however, a welcome break from his fretting over the two ceiling-mounted security cameras that shared the meeting room we were in. Those paranoid comments got real old, real fast.

"Chill," I said. "Court isn't here yet. I promise."

"I still think I should check," he replied. He pushed his black swivel chair away from the desk and stood. "I can't do much else right now anyway. Not in ten minutes."

I stretched, grabbed the empty Dew bottle that stood next to my laptop, and sent it sailing across the room toward a waste paper basket. It bounced off the rim and rolled across the short, grey carpet. "Maybe that's a sign we should take a break," I said, dismayed at my shooting skills. "Where are we at?"

Jim picked up one of the seven drives he'd been assigned and said, "This one's a goner. You'll be lucky to get a tenth off what's on here. I've got two more drives with a few bad sectors, but nothing catastrophic. I can probably save most of them. The other four drives—believe it or not—look good. I don't think they've got any errors whatsoever."

I trudged over to the missed Dew bottle and flipped it into the trash. "Jason?" I asked. "What about you?"

"Well, the good news is none of these drives are total loses. Three are barely scratched," he said, leaning back in his chair and stretching. "But the file systems in four look like Swiss cheese. Some of the boys downstairs could maybe put them back together, but that's going to take a long time. Even then, I'm not sure what you can use. Hell, I don't even know what these drives are supposed to look like."

I cursed, not because of the damage, but because the damage wasn't enough. I wanted a total loss, not a partial ruining. Even if Pi was crippled, as long as her core engine worked, she could recover. She'd delete or rewrite non-working modules and adapt. It might take a while, and she might drool ones and zeros for a month, stuttering and twitching as she did, but she'd heal. The silver lining to this disaster was that the drives I'd been looking at had all been turned to data soup thanks to yours truly. No one was going to use them to bring Pi back to life. The only drive I hadn't pureed, byte wise, was Pi's backup drive. It was pristine, for the moment at least. Once I transferred Pi from it to my laptop, I'd fry that baby as well.

"What about you, Gabe? What do you have?" Jim asked.

"I've got about a thirty percent loss across the board, including the backup," I lied.

"Rebuilding this is going to be a nightmare," said Jim.

"That's the only backup you have? No DVDs? No tapes?" said Jason. "Surely you've got something."

I shook my head. "I've got really old DVDs at home," I replied. "But what I've got on DVD is generations behind what's here now."

"How many generations?"

"A year's worth," I lied.

"That... wow... that sucks," said Jason. "No offsite storage?"

I laughed. "No. I wasn't about to leave my life's work on someone else's system."

Jason nodded. "Yeah, I can see how you wouldn't want that."

The door to our small meeting room opened and in stepped Craig with a portfolio in his hand and a look on his face that only the most cunning of predators wore. "There's a Courtney Erikson waiting downstairs," he said, looking at Jim. "She's says you're expecting her for lunch."

"Yes! Yes, I am!" Jim said, nearly tripping over his words and himself as he made for the door.

Craig held up his hand. "Not so fast. I can't have you two aimlessly wandering around the building."

"I'll take them to the cafeteria," I said.

"No. You aren't going anywhere," said Craig, leveling his predatory gaze upon me. "You're going to stay right here. Jason, you will accompany Mr. Faber downstairs and escort him and Ms. Erikson to the cafeteria. When they are done eating, you will both see Ms. Erikson out before returning directly to this room, understand?"

"What's this all about?" I said, crossing my arms and feeling put off that we were being treated like felons in the state pen. Granted, I should have been put in the pen for arson and destruction of property, but he didn't know that. Or at least, I figured he couldn't prove it.

"This is about investigating sabotage, Mr. Erikson," he said, flashing a smile that would send shivers up the spine of any great white. "And it's an investigation that's coming to a close."

Jim went to say something, something I'm sure was intended to stick up for me and probably incorporate one of his paranoid beliefs, but I cut him off. This was a conversation, a battle, I needed to have on my own. "Court's waiting, dude," I said. "Just go. I'll be here when you guys get back."

"Right," was all he said before a confused and nervous Jason walked him out of the room.

Once they were gone, I unfolded my arms and looked Craig squarely in the eyes. I wasn't about to let him intimidate me. I was sure this guy preyed on weakness, and I was also sure he was only trolling for some sort of confession or clue as to what happened. "So," I said. "Why don't we get right down to it so I can get back to work and you can stop yanking my chain."

"Gladly," he replied, taking a seat and dropping his portfolio on the table in front of him. "Why don't you join me?"

Grabbing another chair, I did. Images of a recent grilling by both the local PD and Michelle raced through my mind, and I couldn't help but look at his portfolio and wonder what was inside.

"Have you had a chance to examine the drives?" he asked.

"That's what we've been doing all morning."

"Are they operational?"

"Technically speaking, yes," I said. "But they've got significant data corruption. I'm not sure what we can save."

"That's a shame," he said, though neither his body language nor tone reflected those thoughts. "Assuming the worst, what sort of timeline are we looking at to get back on track?"

I drummed my fingers on the desk as I thought about how I wanted to approach this. It was a conversation I had planned on having with Mr. Pratt, but I hadn't considered I might have to have that conversation with another first, namely a shark that smelled blood. With no time to figure things out, I decided that the best course of action would be to play it the same way I was going to play it with Mr. Pratt. There would be less lies to keep track of. "Worst case, everything's a loss, and I'd have to start from scratch."

"I thought you might say as much."

I chuckled. There was no need to pretend to be polite. We clearly weren't friends. "I did say worst case," I reminded him. "It doesn't get much worse than that. Best case is we're down a week or two as we rebuild the damaged data from what we salvage from the backups. Maybe a few months if we use old DVDs."

At this point, Craig seemed uninterested in my answer. He spun his portfolio on the desk several times over before saying, "I have only one more thing I'd like to know. What happened yesterday afternoon?"

The question threw me as I had expected him to be more specific. But maybe that was the point. He was tossing out something generic to see if any specifics I would give would turn out to be lies. So I played my hand as general as he had. "Nothing happened," I said with a shrug. "Jason and I were working on getting LCP to boot, and when it was clear we weren't making any further progress, I called it a day."

"And then what?"

"And then nothing," I said. "I dropped by the bank and went home. End of story."

"I find that a little strange," he said.

I raised an eyebrow and gave him the are-you-a-moron look. "Really? Because I'm pretty sure people drop by the bank all the time. In fact, I think they have a lobby staffed with employees for such a thing."

"Oh they do," he said. "But Jason said you two didn't leave together."

"That's right, we didn't," I said, thinking as fast as I could. "I had to use the bathroom."

"Did he see you use the bathroom?"

"That's a little perverted, don't you think?"

"Is there a reason you didn't mention that when I asked you about yesterday?"

I saw where this was headed. He was trying to put me on the defensive so I'd be pressured to admit something. It was a classic super-cop tactic that was never going to work on me. "Yeah, there's a reason," I said. "I didn't mention it because I didn't feel that my urination was pertinent to your investigation. Unless of course, you're saying someone peed on my computers?"

Craig didn't react to my verbal sparring. "Is there anything else you'd like to add?"

"Yes. I did wash my hands after," I said. "And I used four paper towels to dry them with too."

Craig leaned back in his chair. "Do you know what separates me from the guys you talked to over the weekend?"

"Which guys?"

"The ones who were interviewing you during your detainment," he said.

"Yeah, they were cops," I said. "You're not."

"That's right, I'm not," he said, taking pride in the remark. "They don't know what the hell they're doing. Even that ex-girlfriend of yours, Michelle, is a lightweight."

"She's in pretty good shape, I thought," I said. The guy was blowing a lot of smoke, and even with his attempt at a gotcha moment with the bathroom, I wasn't scared.

"This attitude of yours doesn't fool me," he said. "Let me fill you in on something so we both understand where we're at. During the last twenty years I worked for the CIA, I was in Internal Affairs. I was sniffing out spies long before you had your first pimple." He then opened his portfolio and pulled a piece of paper that was scribbled with notes.

"What is this?" I said as he sent it my way.

"Take a look," he replied.

The man's handwriting, if it could be called that, looked nothing short of awful. Angular, tight, with tiny little letters, it gave me a headache trying to decipher. But once I did make it out, I realized what he had jotted down was the conversation we had had only moments ago. All of the questions he asked were right there, in order, as were all of my responses. Granted, those responses weren't word-for-word, but they were close enough that it was clear he knew what I'd say.

"Impressive," I said, feigning moderate interest.

"Much more impressive than say, returning to an office to commit a crime and leaving your fingerprints all over it."

I laughed. I couldn't help it as that seemed at the time to be one of the dumbest things I'd heard. "My fingerprints are all over the scene of the crime?" I said. "I'm sure that wouldn't have to do with the fact that I was working in that office all day or anything. Or the fact that those are my computers. Or anything like that. Look, Craig, I get that you're this badass investigator guy, and that you want to know what happened. And so do I. But really, you're barking up the wrong tree and wasting both our time."

Craig leaned forward with his elbows on the table. "Perhaps," he said. "But I wasn't in reference to literal finger prints, Mr. Erikson. I was talking about digital ones. I'm curious why that after the two of you left for the day you returned here approximately five minutes later. I want you to think about this answer, Mr. Erikson, very carefully. I also want you to remember that the door you used recorded you swiping your badge to gain entry, as well as the fact that we've got plenty of security footage of you walking the halls afterward. So please don't lie any further."

Chapter 10010

Gabe.Crap(Pants);

It's always the little things that get you, both in life and in programming. Rarely is the impossible-to-find, super-damaging bug the one that's huge and glaring. Usually it's something silly like a misplaced decimal or overwriting the end of an array. The foremost would be like balancing your checkbook, running out and buying a car, and then realizing you only had a thousand dollars to play with and not ten thousand. The latter, overwriting the end of an array, would be like taking that new car you bought, flooring it down a dead-end street, and then refusing to stop once you hit the cul-de-sac. My slight oversight of the door logging my re-entry the day before was a mishmash of the two.

    I had to think fast. I almost repeated the question, but I didn't—thanks be to Me. If there was ever a way to throw up the, "I'm lying" flag, it was, is, and will ever be by repeating the question. Example:

    "Honey, did you see your ex today?"

"Did I see my ex today?"

Everyone knows you're buying time at that point, which is why I didn't dare do such a thing with Craig. I knew I had flinched at his question, but I didn't need to add the proverbial straw to break the camel's back. So instead of running from the question, I embraced it fully.

"I thought I left my iPhone in there but then remembered it was in the car," I said. "Is that a problem?"

"It is when you didn't tell me about it when I specifically asked you to detail all of your actions yesterday," Craig replied. "You need to know that continuing to dick me around is only going to make things worse. Come clean and we'll work something out that will be the best for all of us."

Yeah, right. For some strange reason (i.e. common sense), I wasn't buying into it. "I don't know what else to tell you," I said.

Craig leaned forward. "Once more, and for the last time, you can start by dropping your piss-poor façade and tell me all about why you trashed company property and what you hoped to gain from it. This dance ends now."

At this point, I was fairly sure he wasn't merely stirring the pot and hoping something would surface. But I also felt that if he had a slam dunk of a case complete with video footage, this conversation would've been had in a prison cell. As serious as the situation was, I put up a mildly amused front and laughed. "That's insane. I can't believe you'd think that."

"I know that."

I rolled my eyes, leaned back in my chair, and made the deliberate effort to not cross my arms over my chest and instead let them hang limply at my side. "I don't know what to tell you other than you're wrong."

Craig drew back the corners of his mouth as he pulled a walkie-talkie off his hip. "Craig, here," he said talking into it. "Do you have the two suspects in sight?"

I straightened and clenched a fist under the table. I hadn't the foggiest who he was talking about, but I had the feeling I wasn't going to like it one bit.

"Copy that," said a rough voice. "They're eating in the cafeteria."

Craig focused his gaze on me, holding his shark-like grin, but kept to the conversation at hand. "In sixty seconds, I want you to detain them both," he said. "I want you to make a scene and embarrass them. Put them in ties and place them in separate holding rooms. Understand?"

"Will do. Moving in sixty."

"Your best friend and sister are about to have a really bad day," he said, lowering the walkie-talkie. "I suggest you start talking."

"You can't do that," I said, jumping to my feet.

"I think I just did," he said. "And believe me, Mr. Erikson, even if a federal investigation clears them later on of aiding and abetting your actions, I promise I'll make it costly for them, both in time and money."

"I didn't do anything!"

"Tell yourself whatever you want," he said. "But you might want to consider what your continued denial is going to mean for your sister's dissertation. What this will mean for her career."

I slammed my hands on the table as I practically jumped across it. "She doesn't know anything!" I backed off slightly, realizing it was taking all my self-restraint not to drill a fist through his teeth. "Why the hell would I do something that stupid as to destroy Pi, anyway? Why would I destroy something that was going to make me millions?"

Craig drummed his fingers on the table, but his eyes never left mine. He was studying my every move, my every expression. A small part of me felt impressed that he stayed so calm. Maybe I was fortunate not to have taken a swing on him.

Craig picked up the walkie-talkie and said, "Hold on that detainment."

"Copy. Standing by."

"Sit down, Mr. Erikson," he said. When I didn't, he added, "Now."

So I did. Slowly.

"Does the name Adam Clark mean anything to you?" he said.

I nodded. Of course that name meant something to me. Anyone who knows anything about data compression knows that name. Adam Clark was a guy who claimed he had a new algorithm that let high-quality video and audio be sent over a paltry 14.4k dial-up modem. For those of you out there who don't understand how ludicrous of a notion that is, it would be like saying you could put the next Hubble telescope into orbit with one of those little twelve-dollar model rockets you get from Toys-R-Us and launch in your back yard. Yes, we're talking about a claim that ridiculous. How this guy pertained to me, however, I wasn't sure. "Yeah, I know who he is," I said. "He made a fortune scamming people."

"Which is exactly what you're doing," Craig said.

I straightened, and my eyes narrowed at the insult. "Pi is not a scam. I can't believe you think that."

"Let me tell you what I think," he said. "I think you made up Pi, including all of her abilities and activities as a part of an elaborate hoax in order to cheat prospective investors out of millions—much the same way Adam Clark and others have done. Of course you knew once you sold your program, it wouldn't take long for us to realize it was a sham. So, at your first opportunity, you set up an accident and destroyed it. You didn't destroy your software completely, mind you, because that would be far too obvious. But you damaged it enough to ensure that no one would ever be able to claim you were a fraud from the start. That way, you could keep whatever money was paid up front and possibly collect some sort of settlement for the loss of the project by claiming Pratt & Taiki was at fault."

My mouth dried, and I took a slow, deliberate breath to steady my nerves. Though he was off when it came to the motives, I was thoroughly impressed at how close he'd come to the truth. "Well then," I said with a sharp exhale. "That's some imagination."

"We both know it's not fantasy, Mr. Erikson," he said. "Is there anything you'd like to say to me? Or should I give them the go ahead to take your friend and your sister in?"

I shook my head. "The only thing I have to say is you're way out in left field. I worked my whole life to build Pi. I'd never destroy her."

"I seriously doubt that on all counts," he said.

"Then give me till five to prove it," I said. I had no idea what I was going to do between now and then, but I knew I needed more time than what I was working with here. "Look, it's clear I can't say anything to change your mind," I said. "But I'll prove you wrong."

"The only thing that will prove me wrong is a working product," Craig said, gathering his portfolio and standing. "And at five this afternoon, I'll be back. So if I were you, I'd be sure to have something to show by then."

I opened my mouth to argue, to explain the ridiculousness of his demands and explain to him how badly fried the data was, but that was what he expected me to do. That's what he said I'd do. "Hope you're good at apologies," I said. "Because I don't think Mr. Pratt is going to like the way you're treating his star programmer."

"We'll see," he replied. He headed for the door, leaving me alone at the table. When he got there, he turned around and said, "One last thing. Do you know a man by the name of John Cornall?"

I thought for a moment, but unlike Adam Clark, this name escaped me. "I'm afraid I don't."

"He tried to pull a similar thing on us as Clark did with others," he said. "He was clever, but I sniffed him out in less than a week. You, sir, are no John Cornall."

"What happened to him?"

The corner of Craig's mouth drew back, ever so slight. "No idea. I haven't seen him since the whole ordeal," he said. "Nobody has."

~ π ~

#include <PiHacks.h>

I didn't go to lunch. I wasn't hungry, and even if I was, I didn't have time. Craig's last words haunted me. Now, more than ever, I had to have some sort of working product, and I had to have it ready in four hours. It didn't matter what they could prove, legally speaking. Only what they thought. And while I briefly entertained the idea that dating the CEO's daughter might offer some sort of shielding from this cloak-and-dagger retaliation, I didn't want to leave my fate in the hands of "might."

I hooked Pi's backup to my laptop and spent an agonizing ten minutes waiting for diskcheck.exe to run and tell me what I already knew: the drive was intact, the file systems complete.

"Thank God," I said, blowing out a puff of air and feeling my shoulders relax. At least I could completely rebuild Pi once I was out of this nightmare. Then a thought occurred to me. I didn't have to go through this nightmare at all. I could waltz right in to Mr. Pratt's office with Pi on disk, spend maybe a day or two setting her up on new servers that I'm sure they would gladly fund, and be done with it. Mr. Pratt would be happy. My bank account would be happy. My body, full of life and free from harm and/or incarceration, would be happy. And of course, Jim and Court would be safe.

I cursed softly. No, I wouldn't be happy. As I had talked about with Kimiko, I couldn't hand Pi over. No matter how artificial she was, no matter how much trouble she'd caused or had put me into such an impossible position, I couldn't sell her off. I couldn't condemn her to eternal servitude. I wouldn't do that to a real person—a real daughter—and thus, if I was going to claim Pi was the real deal, I couldn't do it to her either. If I did, it made her a product. It made her a hunk of code to be sold to the highest bidder. Either that, or it made me a slave trader. So either way, I was going to have to figure out how Pi hacked into those government servers and hope that that would be enough to satisfy Pratt & Taiki's demands.

"You have no idea how much you owe me," I muttered, looking down at the drive as I started the transfer. "No idea at all."

Pi didn't, nor would she. No matter how hard I'd explain things to her later, how much I'd try to get her to understand the real world and how she impacted it, she'd never get it. Sometimes I wonder if that's why if there is a God, He doesn't talk to us. It's not that He can't talk to us, or won't, but any answer He'd give is one we'd never understand. Our perspectives are too different. So He just saves His breath, so-to-speak. It would explain a lot, assuming He's really out there.

By twenty 'til one, Pi had been successfully compressed and moved from drive to laptop. All I had to do now was start DiskScrubber 3.1—a small program I'd written that ruins data like a turd ruins a punchbowl. That would be it. Once it ran, there would be no turning back.

"Here we go," I said, tapping the enter key. The drive whirred as the program sprang into action. With each passing second, DiskScrubber turned the backup files into binary mush. After a few minutes, I stopped the program. I didn't want to puree all the data. That would scream deliberate action. Now it simply looked like the drive had been corrupted like all the others and no one would be the wiser.

I spent a few moments staring at my computer as the gravity of what I'd done sunk in. Did I get everything I needed to rebuild Pi onto my laptop? Or did I just condemn her to oblivion? Did I just condemn myself for that matter? But in the midst of these questions, a new thought popped into mind, and I couldn't help but chuckle. I had started this odyssey at Pratt & Taiki with LCP solely on my laptop and now I was fixing to end it the same way.

Jim burst through the door, practically dancing on air as he did. "That . . . was amazing," he said. He plopped down in a chair and leaned back so far that his head flopped over and he was staring at the ceiling. "She is amazing."

For the moment, I forgot about Pi and the grisly end that might be in store for me. "Went that well, huh?"

"Yeah," he said. "We had the best conversation ever."

I smiled. I doubted that Courtney shared the same view, but at least Jim was happy. And a happy Jim is a productive Jim, an insane problem-solving Jim. "So what did you two chat about?"

Jim sat up. "Initially, not much," he said. "But she made mention of her dissertation and then I explained how simple it would be to get whatever she wanted in terms of gamer stats. It took off from there." With an I'm-stupid-for-her, enamored sigh, Jim slowly spun in his chair.

I watched him for moment before it dawned on me that we were missing the third member to our party. "Where's Jason?" I asked.

"Outside, talking to Craig," he said. He then stopped his spins and looked over at me. "How'd that go, by the way? He doesn't look happy."

"He's not," I said. "And that's why we need to shift our focus."

"Shift our focus to what?"

"We need to figure out how Pi hacked into NASA and it has to be done before the day is up."

"So no more rebuilding," he said, scratching the tip of his nose. It was subtle enough, but the glancing around the empty room was anything but. "Let's figure out how Ms. SkyNet works her magic."

~ π ~

```
tHour += 3.5;
Gabe.SetDesperation(10);
```

Jason joined us a little after 1 p.m., and three and a half hours later, the three of us had slaved away at trying to pry Pi's hacking secrets from her corpse. Granted, the process would have been a thousand fold easier had we not been sifting through her virtual graveyard, piecing data together in a haphazard fashion, but that's all we could do. It reminded me of trying to figure out what picture was on the front of a giant jigsaw puzzle, only you didn't have the box and half the pieces had gone through the garbage disposal.

Jim groaned. His Courtney high had worn off a little before 2:45, and he'd been growing frustrated. "I wish you had more of these logs," he said, referring back to the network files I gave him. "They're helpful, but most of the stuff they reference I don't understand or it's flat out missing."

"If I find more, I'll send them to you," I said. I had everything, of course, on Pi's backup. But it was proving tricky getting everything to Jim while at the same time hiding the fact that my laptop housed it all. But even with my own access to all the files, I wasn't making much progress either. "Jason, tell me you've at least got something."

Jason, hunched over his laptop with a legal pad full of scribbles, looked up. "Man, I don't have the slightest clue what's going on here," he said. "Do you have any idea how long it takes to reverse engineer something?"

"Longer than a day, I know," I said.

"Yeah, and that's assuming you've got the working program," he said. "All I can tell you right now is that this program of yours always starts up something called ggpts.exe before it opens up a socket. I don't even know what that program is. Or where it is for that matter."

"It's not on any of your drives?" I asked.

"No," he replied. "Not intact, anyway. What does it do?"

"Honestly, I have no idea," I said, shaking my head. For the life of me, I couldn't place the file name at all. I looked down at my laptop and brought up the documentation I had written on Pi long ago for reference. And though I found plenty of mention of other executables and libraries I had forgotten about, I couldn't find ggpts.exe anywhere.

"If it helps, it's all over the logs," Jim added. He paused for a moment as he made a few clicks with his touchpad. "In fact, it only starts popping up about a week ago. It's a fresh file."

"Fresh, as in new?"

"Looks like it," he said. "Newly used at least. Can't say when it was created." Jim paused, leaned toward his screen for a few seconds, and then began eagerly flipping through the network logs he had printed out a couple of hours ago.

"What?" I asked, sliding my chair over to where he was. "Tell me you're on to something."

Jim grabbed one of the pages and flipped it my way. "It's the key to it all," he said. "Look at these lines. Pi doesn't run a single root command on any of the IPs until she runs this program. Find it intact, and you've got your product."

A heartbeat later, Jason was standing behind us, glued to the screen. "It can't be that easy."

"I'm telling you it is," Jim said. "I don't know how Pi works. And I don't know how she made this thing. But I know my network traffic. This program is where it's at. It pops up on the logs just before Pi started hacking. Every time she calls it, she can take a network over."

I glanced at the time. I had about fifteen minutes till five o'clock. While part of me agreed with Jason that this couldn't be that easy, the other part of me dared to believe it was. And the same part that dared to believe it was also swelled with pride. My dearest Pi had followed in her father's footsteps. She had made a program that set her apart from all the code monkeys of the world. She had become a hacking goddess. No one could match her skill. No one. Like father, like daughter.

"So, what do you think?" asked Jason.

"I think that file has Pi written all over it," I said.

"How can you be so sure?"

"I can't," I replied. "But I didn't write it, and it's all we have, so that's what we're going with. Check all the disks again for that program. Check the empty space as well to see if it was deleted at some point. It's got to be on one of those disks. The thing is a hundred and twelve megs. It can't hide forever."

With new found hope and vigor, we all went back to our respective computers and began hammering away at our keyboards. I wasn't sure if ggpts.exe was still on their drives, or where it had been for that matter, but it only took me a half minute of searching to find it tucked away in the transferred files on my laptop. I then quietly copied it over to the backup drive.

"I got it!" I shouted. In an instant, my cohorts were at my side.

"Don't just sit there, man," Jason said. "Let's see what this puppy can do."

I wasn't about to argue. I was just as eager as Jason to see what Pi had cooked up. I opened a command line:

>*ggpts.exe*

The program immediately replied:

Input key

I raised an eyebrow and looked over at Jim. "Password protected?"

"No idea," he said. "Maybe. Hit enter and see what happens."

And so I did.

Key invalid. You're almost as dumb as Gabe.

I smiled. Even from the virtual grave, Pi still mocked me. "Cute," I said.

"If it's asking for a decryption key, you'll never get around it," said Jim.

Jason shook his head. "It might not be. It could be a simple password to access the rest of the program. Give me a couple of hours. I can probably work around it."

I checked the clock again. It was a few minutes till five. "There's no time for that, even if that's the case," I said. "We'll have to guess it."

Jim laughed. "Yeah right. You'll never brute force that thing. You don't even know how many characters it is."

He was right about that. But one thing I had going for me was the fact that Pi never intended for me to gain access to this program in the first place. After all, she had me locked out long before she wrote this. So I figured—I prayed—whatever password she was using it was more for fun than actual security.

"I'll try a few," I said. My fingers flew across the keyboard, inputting word after word, phrase after phrase. *Root. Points. Pi. Pi is Root. I hate Gabe. Gabe is stupid.* So on, and so forth. But try as I might, none of them worked.

"Give me a copy and let me try getting around it," Jason said. "This won't work."

"Shh!" I said, waving him off. "I can get this."

My neurons went into warp drive, and my head felt crushed under a newly formed headache as I searched for Pi's password and a way around her security. But Jim was right. Brute forcing this thing would never work. There was a chance we could hack around it with some more time, depending on how complex Pi had made the verification process, but time was a luxury I did not have.

"I hope you have a plan B," said Jim.

I sighed heavily and buried my face in my hands. Temptation whispered in my ear. It promised me that all my worries would be gone if I handed Pi over. It promised me fame. It promised me fortune. It promised me an eternal place in history and the salvation of best friend and sister. But what it couldn't do was promise that my daughter, ornery as she was, would be free. And that, in the end, was all I wanted for her.

The clock ticked over to 5 p.m. despite my every prayer that it not. No sooner than it had, the door opened behind me, and I spun around. Craig strode into the room, flanked by a pair of security guys. "Well?" he said.

I didn't answer. I couldn't. But then again, I didn't have to.

"That's what I thought," he said. "Take him."

Chapter 10011

```
If (timer()==0)
    InitDetention();
```

"I need more time!" I said, being led down one of the many halls of Pratt & Taiki. The guard at my side had a vice-like grip on my elbow, and the cuffs he had used on me dug into my skin. With my every protest, both seemed to grow tighter. But I wasn't about to let a little pain stop me. "You don't understand. We found her program. We've just got to crack it."

Craig, who led the way, threw a glance over his shoulder. "You're out of time," he said. "We did things your way. Now we're going to do them mine."

I cursed under my breath. I almost cried. If I'd been any closer to the prize, we would've been forever fused together. "You're throwing away a fortune here," I said. "Use your head for once in your life."

We stopped in front of a plain side door with a small card reader. "Keep him here until I return with Mr. Pratt," said Craig.

The guard looked confused. "Here, sir? It's occupied."

"I know," Craig snapped. "Now do as I say."

The door opened, and with one swift and powerful move, the guard pushed me through.

I was barely through the doorway when I spun around and slammed against the now-shut door. "You don't know what you're doing!" I yelled, pushing and kicking against it for all I was worth. "Give me my laptop. Give me another day!"

Leaning against the door, I slid to the floor for what felt like an eternity as I resigned myself to Fate. Maybe my jail cell would be a nice one, a renovated one. And maybe whoever I shared it with wasn't the cuddling kind. Either that, or maybe I'd get a welcomed case of the runs when he decided to make his move. But at least Pi was safe. And who knew? Maybe prison overpopulation would play in my favor and I'd be eligible for parole in a few years.

"Gabe? What's going on?"

I lifted my head, but I didn't have to turn around to know exactly whose voice it was. It was Court's.

~ π ~

Courtney.Disown(Gabe);

I guess I didn't answer quickly enough, because she asked it again. "What's going on, Gabe?" she said. This time, however, she was more forceful and less concerned. "What did you do?"

I jumped to my feet in the most ungainly of ways since my wrists were still cuffed behind my back. "What the hell are you doing here?" I said, spinning around.

"What am I doing here? What am I doing here!" she shouted. "I'm here because of you! I'm sitting here, locked up, and about to lose everything I worked for because I helped you!"

My mouth hung open, and for God knows how long, I couldn't say or do a damn thing. She sat on the edge of a white plastic chair in front of a large folding table. Her clothes, black pants with a matching jacket over a yellow top, were slightly disheveled—something I don't think I'd ever seen on her in my entire life. I didn't have to ask to know why. The stare of pure hate she bored through me with said it all.

"God, I should've listened to my gut last night," she said, shaking her head. "I should've never come."

Slowly, I made my way to the table. When I got there, I was finally close enough to see her makeup had become sparse, and tears had recently stained her cheeks. Next to her stood a black wastepaper basket and inside were a number of used tissues and an empty bottle of a Starbuck's French Vanilla Frappuccino. "Court, I swear, I'll make it right."

"Stop," she said, cutting me off. "Just stop."

"Court. Really—"

"Stop!" she yelled, kicking my shins from under the table.

"Jesus, Court," I said, jumping back in pain and inspecting the damage. "What the hell was that for?"

Court narrowed her eyes. "I should kick you again for even asking. They're going to ruin both our lives!"

"I wasn't trying to ruin anyone's life, least of all yours," I said, choking up. "I'm sorry you got dragged into this."

Courtney shook her head and shot me a look of disgust. "How can you possibly sit there and say you didn't want me dragged into this? It's your goddamn fault I'm here. You called me!"

"I know," I said, unable to give her anymore. Everything that went through my head felt wrong to say. Everything.

"Just give them what they want," she said weakly. "This isn't worth it."

Earlier that morning, I'd thought things couldn't have had higher stakes, but now with Court on the verge of being entirely destroyed before my eyes, I knew it was all coming down to her or

Pi. Maybe Pi would do well enough at Pratt & Taiki. She'd certainly do better than Court would with her future shattered.

"Okay," I said, my voice cracking. "When they come back, they can have it all."

I looked away, unable to watch her come further unglued, and that's when I noticed the little camera mounted in the corner. I wondered if it had audio, too. Probably. Then again, I wondered if it even mattered. There was no telling what my sister had already told them.

Court burst into tears. "I wish that stupid worm had taken it all and ruined your fucking program. Maybe then my biggest concern would be where I left my keys and not what you'd done with Pi."

Her words sank into my brain. Keys. Worms. Pi.

I jumped, my face beaming, and the weight of a dark and grim future lifted from my shoulders. "That's it, Court!" I said, running to her side. I'd have crushed her in a bear hug if I could've, but since I was still cuffed, all I could manage was an awkward snuggle of my head on her shoulder. "You're a goddamn genius!"

Court pulled away, causing me to stumble. "Get the hell off me."

I laughed. I cried. I ran to the door and kicked it. "Hey! Let me out!" I yelled. "I'll tell you whatever you want right this second."

No one came. No one answered. So I kicked it time and again. "Open up, damn it!" The energy inside refused to be contained. I spun in circles, practically dancing and flying through the room. "Open up and bring my damn laptop!"

To my surprise, the door opened a moment later. Craig, Mr. Pratt, and four security guys came walking in. Even more surprising, they had Jason and Jim in tow.

"Have a seat, right now, Mr. Erikson," ordered Craig.

"Give me my laptop," I said, still smiling, still elated beyond measure. When Craig didn't immediately reply, I turned my attention to Mr. Pratt. I looked him square in his hawk-like eyes and made an impassioned plea, "Please, Mr. Pratt," I said. "I'm not a bad guy, and Pi is real, or was, at least. Call your daughter if you don't believe me. All I'm asking for is thirty seconds with my laptop and I can make you a very happy man."

Craig instantly cut in. "Mr. Pratt, I've done numerous tests this afternoon. It's incredibly unlikely that the short in the power supply ignited the papers on top of the server without a lot of help. This is a clear case of sabotage, and he's the guy that did it."

"Thirty seconds, Mr. Pratt," I begged. "Thirty seconds and you own the binary world."

Mr. Pratt eyed me for several moments without moving. Finally, he turned to the security guy behind him and said, "Bring it in."

Chapter 10100

// Thank God. That's all I have to say. Thank. Effing. God.

"You've got thirty seconds," said Mr. Pratt.

I rubbed my recently freed wrists and adjusted my laptop on the table. "I'll only need half that," I said.

Jim, who stood at my side, leaned over and whispered, "What the hell is going on?"

"I've got her key," I said as I opened up a prompt and entered the commands for Pi's mystery program.

>*ggpts.exe*

Just like all of the other times, it immediately shot out a reply:

Input key

Smiling, I tapped out an entry:

My beloved juju

My mouth hung open and my heart stopped when all I got was the usual response:

Key invalid. You're almost as dumb as Gabe.

I sucked in a breath and bit my lip. This would not be my end. I tried variation after variation, each one coming faster than the one before. *My beloved Juju. My Beloved Juju. my beloved juju.* But try as I might, none worked. The walls of the already tiny little room closed in. The air grew thick and stifling. Like a failing hard drive, each error that Pi's program returned signaled an impending crash—the crash of my life.

"Ten seconds, Mr. Erikson," Craig said. I could feel the gloat in his voice. He lived for this kind of stuff.

I ran my fingers through my hair and took a deep breath. That had to be it Pi's password. It had to be her key. With shaky fingers, I tried one more version:

mybelovedjuju

The reply came in a flash, but it took me a moment for my brain to register what it was.

Hello World! Input IP address:

"Holy shit," said Jim. "How the hell did you do that?"

I thought about not answering and letting them bask in mystery, but I decided against it. I was in enough hot water as is. Besides, people have to have answers from time to time, lest they think a miracle witnessed was a fluke. "Elementary my dear Jim. Pi taunted me with it time and again, but back then I didn't know what she was talking about," I said. I then turned to Court, who was looking as clueless as clueless could be and said, "And then my dear, sweet sister made an offhand comment that made it all come together."

I sat back and softly whistled Handel's Messiah.

Mr. Pratt cleared his throat with a hefty cough. "Mind explaining what it is we're looking at?" he said. "Because right now, I'm not feeling like I've been shown the divine."

"Absolutely, Mr. Pratt," I said, going to the keys once more. "Absolutely."

Chapter 10101

```
void PhaseThree(Resurrect(Pi));
```

I didn't know how to run Pi's little hacking program at first, but it was remarkably intuitive in terms of use. Of course, that shouldn't be surprising since she was my daughter and created said program. We must have played with it for a good four hours after Courtney and Jim left, popping into servers here and there all across the Web. We didn't do anything malicious, but by the end of the evening, two things were certain. First, I was going to be handsomely compensated, even with keeping them in the dark about Pi. And second, computer security was about to be revolutionized forever.

The next two months I spent on and off at Pratt & Taiki (not to mention smoothing things over with Court, which didn't go well until I paid off all her student loans with part of Pratt & Taiki's investment money). Anyway, with the help of Jason and the new team assigned to me, we began dissecting ggpts.exe. And in case anyone is wondering, yes, we figured out pretty quick what it stood for: Get Gabe's Points.

While picking Pi's genius apart truly was one of the most exciting things I'd done, it couldn't compare to what I'd started working on eighteen months later. After lying low, avoiding watchful eyes, and surviving Craig's almost never-ending inquisition, I began rebuilding Pi from the ground up. Six months after I'd started that endeavor—a full two years after she'd burnt to a crisp—I was finally ready to turn her on for the first time and raise her from the dead.

With a 50/50 mix of eagerness and trepidation, I flipped the power to each of the servers and brought the whole network online. The boot process took a painfully long amount of time, far longer than it should have. More than once I feared I wouldn't get past the boot as error after error popped. I worried that the transfer from backup to laptop and from laptop to servers had gone awry, and now Pi was lost forever. Thankfully, every time I was about to dub things screwed, the servers managed to repair whatever error they had encountered and moved on. Eighty-eight minutes after I'd started the process, Pi's world was onscreen.

Pi's lakeside cabin looked intact. The snowy mountain range and rolling terrain looked good too. The ground, however, was marred with dozens of gaping holes and peering into each felt like I was staring into the Abyss. The sky fared no better. As far as I could see, the heavens were torn in countless places, like giant hands had ripped the fabric of space apart and exposed a mystical void beyond.

My heart fluttered. If Pi's world looked like this, what shape might she be in? Would she even run?

Kimiko, who stood behind me, seemed to share my concern. "That doesn't look right," she said, massaging my shoulders.

"Yeah," I said. I tapped the keys and the camera warped to Pi's location. She sat inside her cabin in the corner, staring at the wall. "Well," I said. "There she is. Sort of."

"Is she alive?" Kimiko asked.

"I hope," I said, grabbing the mic. "Pi? Are you there?"

Nothing happened.

I told myself that she was brooding. I told myself this was her newest way to antagonize me. "Come on, Pi," I said. "I know you're there."

Pi still didn't reply, but the activity on her LEDs increased tenfold.

I exhaled. Something was going on in that digital cortex of hers.

"Maybe she's waking up," Kimiko said.

"Or in a coma," I added, letting one of my worries be voiced as I turned off the mic.

"If she is, you should keep talking to her."

"About what?"

"Anything, everything," she replied. "It's what we do with the dying even if they can't talk back."

Surprised, I turned toward my little samurai hottie. "That works?"

"Yeah, you'd be amazed what happens when you don't automatically assume someone can't hear you," she said.

Despite her reassurances, I balked. I stared at Pi's servers and realized I'd long stopped seeing her as code. And since she wasn't code anymore, I felt like I had no control over her fate. I couldn't write a quick patch or find a misplaced decimal to bring her back to life. I was helpless.

"Go on," Kimiko said, giving me a nudge. "Open up. What's the worst that could happen?"

Nothing. That would be the worst that could happen. I would spill out everything I had, and she would remain dead to the world. I would have finally created life, a truly conscious and self-aware being, and killed her with my own hands. Then again, maybe Kimiko was right. Maybe I'd talk to her, and she'd raise from the dead. And if she rose at my command, could my divinity ever be in question? To see if I was God, all I had to do was turn the mic back on. All I had to do was push a button.

~ π ~

`return 0;`
`// Man, I'm tired.`

Light from a 4 a.m. moon creeps into my living room as the clouds move in the sky. Kimiko, sprawled on a sleeping bag at my side, stirs. Though I've been talking for the past few hours after working up the nerve to do so, she's been out for the majority of it. Now that I'm done with my tale, the only thing keeping silence at bay is the quiet hum of cooling fans. In this early morning stillness, Pi's LEDs flash across her server banks before going dark. Minutes pass. My eyes glisten. I tell myself they must have collected some dust. With nothing left to say or do, I decide to wrap it up and get some sleep.

"So, Pi, that's what happened," I say, yawning and clearing my eyes. "I'm not sure if you heard any of this, or understand what you put me through, but at this point, all I want to know is that you're okay. I don't want fame or fortune. I don't even want to be God. I just want to know you're still alive."

I stretch at the end. Multiple joints in multiple limbs pop as I work out their stiffness. Kimiko sits up, still half-asleep, and wraps one arm around me. She tops her embrace off with a soft kiss on my cheek and pulls me down. Though thoughts of sex run briefly through my mind, the need for sleep trumps everything. She mumbles something and drifts off a moment later. I'm not far behind. In the limbo that exists between consciousness and dreams, where the outside world creeps into the thoughts of the exhausted, I hear Pi's synthetic voice.

"Gabe," she says. "That's the stupidest story I've ever heard."

Acknowledgements

To all my readers of countless drafts who mercilessly pounded Little Computer People into the sand, time and again, in order for it to go from vague idea plagued with problems to a text I love . . .

To my editor, Crystal Watanabe, who helped see it through its final leg of work . . .

And most of all, to my wife, Mary Beth, who's read through more material than I can dream of and is still as supportive as ever.

About the Author

When not writing, Galen Surlak-Ramsey has been known to throw himself out of an airplane, teach others how to throw themselves out of an airplane, take pictures of the deep space, and wrangle his four children somewhere in Southwest Florida.

He also manages to pay the bills as a chaplain for a local hospice.

About the Publisher

Tiny Fox Press LLC
5020 Kingsley Road
North Port, FL 34287

www.tinyfoxpress.com

Lightning Source UK Ltd.
Milton Keynes UK
UKHW011826220621
385965UK00001B/232